**Praise for Jack Stein,
Psychic Investigator**

Metal Sky

"The blend of science fiction with mystery offers satisfying elements of both."   —*Midwest Book Review*

"[Caselberg's] storytelling is brisk and accessible; it never loses your interest."   —*SF Reviews*

"Nicely written."   —*SFRevu*

Wyrmhole

"A fun, fast-paced SF mystery."   —*Booklist*

"Fascinating and well-imagined . . . a terrific read, combining all the elements of great science fiction: originality, speculation, and consequence."
          —Julie E. Czerneda, author of *Regeneration*

Turn the page for more rave reviews. . . .

Jay Caselberg is an Australian currently based in Germany. He writes novels, short fiction, and poetry; he has seen publication in multiple venues around the world and online, both as Jay Caselberg and as James A. Hartley. While growing up, he lived in different countries, including Turkey and England, and that continued during his working life. He currently works as an independent IT consultant when not writing, performing large multicountry implementations. He can be found online at www.jaycaselberg.com.

Jay Caselberg

WALL OF MIRRORS

A ROC BOOK

ROC
Published by New American Library, a division of
Penguin Group (USA) Inc., 375 Hudson Street,
New York, New York 10014, USA
Penguin Group (Canada), 90 Eglinton Avenue East, Suite 700, Toronto,
Ontario M4P 2Y3, Canada (a division of Pearson Penguin Canada Inc.)
Penguin Books Ltd., 80 Strand, London WC2R 0RL, England
Penguin Ireland, 25 St. Stephen's Green, Dublin 2,
Ireland (a division of Penguin Books Ltd.)
Penguin Group (Australia), 250 Camberwell Road, Camberwell, Victoria 3124,
Australia (a division of Pearson Australia Group Pty. Ltd.)
Penguin Books India Pvt. Ltd., 11 Community Centre, Panchsheel Park,
New Delhi - 110 017, India
Penguin Group (NZ), cnr Airborne and Rosedale Roads, Albany,
Auckland 1310, New Zealand (a division of Pearson New Zealand Ltd.)
Penguin Books (South Africa) (Pty.) Ltd., 24 Sturdee Avenue,
Rosebank, Johannesburg 2196, South Africa

Penguin Books Ltd., Registered Offices:
80 Strand, London WC2R 0RL, England

First published by Roc, an imprint of New American Library,
a division of Penguin Group (USA) Inc.

First Printing, December 2006
10 9 8 7 6 5 4 3 2 1

For Laura Anne

Acknowledgments

My thanks as always to my editor, Liz Scheier, who has done much to make this a better book. Also thanks are due to my agent, Rich Henshaw. Often neglected, I would also like to thank my copy editor. A keen eye can save a few red faces.

As this book rounds out the series with Jack, I must also thank Jennifer Heddle, who made this possible with the acquisition of the first two novels.

As always, thanks for the support and encouragement of friends and family. Let's see where we go now.

One

Jack Stein was fuming. The anger welled up inside him, making him totally aware of his powerlessness complete with the knowledge that there was absolutely nothing he could do. Once again, Outreach had managed to make him a pawn in their own game. At least he assumed it was Outreach. He knew he couldn't say anything that would help. Not to the impassive face across from him watching from the opposite bunk, nor to anyone else. His new friend wouldn't have listened anyway. All spiky hair and stubble, the guy was nothing more than a hired thug. He shifted on the edge of the bunk, his expression unchanging, his pale eyes devoid of emotion. Jack ground his teeth together, narrowed his eyes, and looked away.

Why was it that Outreach Industries couldn't leave him alone?

He knew the answer: They thought he had something they wanted, or at least the key to unlocking the knowledge they wanted. They could be right; Jack wasn't exactly sure.

Back behind him, far, far away now, lay Utrecht and Balance City, teetering impossibly on its rock spire, all metal and glass, and somewhere within that urban construction was Billie. A changed Billie, but still Billie. Maybe by now she had found Dog McCreedy and discovered what had happened to Jack. At the thought of McCreedy, Jack's fingers tensed on the bunk edge and the anger welled up in him anew. He had trusted McCreedy. They had a history. That would teach him.

Never again. History counted for nothing.

He turned back to the man across from him and broke the silence.

"Do you have to sit there watching me? I'm not going anywhere."

His companion grunted.

Jack sighed. "Okay, be like that. Not much of a conversationalist, are you?"

The slight narrowing of the man's eyes was the only acknowledgment that Jack had said anything. Great company.

And Jack wasn't going anywhere. Not anytime soon. They were on one of Outreach's ships, heading back to a past he didn't want to relive. At least they'd already been through the gut-wrenching sensation that was the jump. He didn't think they'd be going through another one. He hoped not, anyway. He'd been through a few now, but he wasn't going to get used to the feeling, the way every cell in his body turned inside out. Damned jump space.

There was nothing he could do, nothing he could say. He glanced across at the cabin's other occupant, but knew he was unlikely to get any further information. They'd be at their destination in a few hours anyway, and there Jack would find out precisely what Outreach wanted from him.

Somewhere else on the ship, probably in his own personal cabin, sat Thorpe, his impeccable slick smugness locked away out of Jack's reach. Right at this moment, Jack would have liked to stretch out and ruffle that presence just a little. Thorpe was Outreach through and through. If nothing else, Thorpe had told him they were headed for the Locality, but that was scant information to work with.

Jack growled inwardly at the thought. Back to the Locality, back to his roots. Jack Stein had moved on from everything the Locality represented. The self-contained, programmed urban structure had been the breeding ground for many ills, and if he thought about it, wryly, Jack knew that he fell into that category too. Four years. It had been four years since he'd been anywhere near the place. And yet, here he was, heading back to the hive, back to everything dirty and corrupt that he'd left behind. Would it have changed? He doubted it. Well, perhaps physically, but that was natural; as it crawled across the landscape, its programmed buildings grew afresh at its tip, right up at the far end of New, and then they decayed and fell apart, to be consumed by the whole down at the end of Old. Inside, its populace mirrored that decay, whether they knew it or not. Jack wasn't looking forward to returning to those roots at all.

He glanced back at his guard and sighed. The guy hadn't shifted. Reconciled to the wait, Jack leaned back on the bunk, swung his feet up, and linked his fingers behind his neck. If that was the way it was going to be, he could at least try to get some rest in the meantime, hired muscle be damned. He closed his eyes, still intimately aware of the other presence in the cabin, feeling the vague energy of another person almost as background noise in his extended senses, and knowing full well that any attempt at sleep would be little more than pretense.

Two

Billie stood in the doorway to Dog McCreedy's sparse living room, staring at him incredulously, her fists planted on her hips.

"What do you mean, he's gone?" she said.

"I don't know," said Dog, shrugging helplessly.

"Gone where?"

"I told you I don't know."

"Well, what happened?" Billie stepped into the room, her fists still on her hips, her expression turning hostile. "What *happened*, Dog?"

"Some suits came and took him. What can I tell you?" Dog McCreedy flicked a stray strand of dark hair out of his eyes and moved to the couch. "Jesus, Billie. There was nothing I could do. I suppose you wanted me to get shot. And yes, they had guns, all right? I think I look better without gaping holes in me."

She let her gaze wander from head to toe and back again, leaving him in no doubt about what she thought of his last statement. He sighed and sat heavily.

"Nuh-uh. Not good enough, Dog."

She'd been away from Jack and Dog for only a few hours, having left them to pick up a few things at the university. It didn't make sense. She glanced around. There was no sign of any sort of struggle. The empty order of the apartment looked like just that . . . empty order. She chewed at the side of one finger, thinking, as Dog watched her. What would Jack do in her place?

Dog reached down beside him and lifted a glass with a few sips of what looked like scotch in it, and took a swallow, grimacing as the burn hit his palate. Another glass sat on a side table next to one of the armchairs. Jack's glass, she presumed. That much tied in with Dog's story, not that she had any reason to doubt him. She was just naturally suspicious, she guessed. Her life up to now had taught her that much.

"So tell me again what happened."

Dog leaned forward, cradling his glass between his hands and staring down into what remained of the contents.

"Jack and I were sitting here having a drink, talking. Someone came to the door. I answered. They forced their way in. Three of them—one suit, two others. Somehow, they knew Jack was here. One of the guys pulled a gun when I made a move. The one in the suit said that Jack was going with them. He said something about the Locality or something like that, about knowing him from there."

He lifted his face to look at her. "And that's it."

She crossed to the vacant chair and sat, pulling her legs up in front of her, keeping her gaze fixed on Dog's face. "That's it?"

"Yeah."

"Uh-huh." Think, Billie. What did they want? What could they want with Jack? And the Locality. Despite herself, a chill went through her. There were too many things about the Locality that she just didn't want to remember. She had spent too long with the Family in Old, in shadows between crumbling walls, servicing the clients who came to find them with one sole purpose in mind. That was until Pinpin Dan had found her and taken her to a better life. She pushed the thought away.

"How long ago did they leave?" she asked.

"I dunno, maybe three hours, maybe more."

"They didn't hurt him?"

Dog shook his head.

She lowered her feet and sat forward. "We have to stop them."

Dog sighed. "And how are we supposed to do that, Billie? Huh? They're long gone. We have no idea who they are or where they went."

"Have you got a system here?" She glanced around at the walls, looking for the telltale signs of a wallscreen.

"Sorry," said Dog with a shrug. "I'm not here much. And when I am, I have better things to do." He gave her a sly little grin.

"Yeah, yeah, Dog. You're great. Where can I get access to one?"

There was the university, but as with most of the places on Utrecht, it seemed technologically backward. She shouldn't have been surprised that Dog had no system of his own.

Dog ran his fingers through his hair, frowning. "Um . . ."

"Your ship," she said.

"What about it?"

"Well, you've got a system there. I can use it to get access. If they've taken him offworld, there has to be some transport record. If they've even left yet."

"But we'd have to get up there, Billie. That will take time. I'm not even sure my ship will give you access to what you need."

"Uh-huh," said Billie, determination creeping into her voice. "You let me worry about that. Well?"

"Well, what, Billie?"

"What are you waiting for?" She stood, crossed her arms, and glared at him, the challenge clear in her tone.

Dog returned her look with one of resignation, put down his now-empty glass, and got slowly to his feet.

Dog's old, beat-up shuttle was berthed in Balance City's docks, not too far from his apartment in Algol. Billie pushed him out the door and told him to lead the way.

Algol was okay, she guessed, for one of the less reputable parts of Balance City. She had seen far worse. In fact, even the worst areas of Balance City were a far sight better than much of what Billie had known in her seventeen years. But it was weird now, with this whole time thing. Meeting Jack had been a shock. It looked like he had lost about ten years. Inside, he was still the same Jack, but on the outside, he was definitely younger. She kind of liked the old Jack.

The temporal backlash had taken Billie the opposite way. She knew she looked about twenty-seven now, maybe more. For some reason, the temporal buildup had affected her and Antille dissimilarly. Jack was younger; Billie was older. It looked more like they belonged together now. If things had been different . . .

No, she couldn't even think like that. She owed a lot to Jack, but their relationship wasn't like that, *couldn't* be like that.

Now. Dog, on the other hand . . .

She watched him appreciatively as he walked along in front of her, his shoulders slightly hunched, the resentment evident in his carriage.

She sniffed the sleeve of the jacket she was wearing. Yeah, there were traces of its owner impregnated in the black pseudo-leather. It was only a little too large for her. Dog and Billie were roughly the same size . . . now. He had lent her some of his clothes on board the *Amaranth* after he and Jack had effected their rescue. A pity the clothes weren't programmable too, because she kind of liked the jacket. But it would just have to do as it was. Same as the black pseudo-leather trousers. Spacer's gear. Like Dog. Still, she wished she'd had time to get some new clothes. Nothing she had back at the university fitted her anymore. She hadn't had time to do anything really, except have a shower and rummage through her things. She'd found the white oversized T-shirt that she was wearing now, but it wasn't that oversized anymore. She hadn't grown much with the transition, but she'd grown enough, in ways she might not have expected or thought about.

Everything else would have to wait. Sorting out the Jack problem was more important for now. Dog's mention of the Locality made her think of Outreach. Anything to do with the Locality had to do with Outreach in one way or another. It always had, and she'd gotten into Outreach—or at least the edges of it—before. If she could get some decent access from Dog's ship, then she could get into the data mines she needed, maybe Outreach itself. Then they could identify the people who had taken Jack. And if she couldn't do that from out here, at least she could find out if there were any recent or planned ship movements back toward the homeworld.

"Dog, have you got any contacts?"

There was a slight offbeat in his step, but he answered back over his shoulder with nothing apparent in his voice.

"Yeah, some. What do you need?"

"I don't know yet. I'll think about it."

He stopped in midstride and turned to face her. "Jesus, Billie. Ask a question. Don't half ask it. You want me to help you? Then tell me what you want."

She narrowed her eyes. "I don't know yet. It depends what I can get with your system."

He shook his head, causing his long, dark hair to fall across his face. He flicked it back out of the way before answering. "I don't like your chances. This is Utrecht. It's not exactly the most advanced planet."

"Every place has a network you can tap into," she said. "If I can get into one network, I can get into others. Information's like that. There are bridges and pathways. Otherwise the whole network couldn't work. And where there's a bridge, there's a way in."

He looked doubtful and shrugged.

She pursed her lips and gave his arm a little shove. "Come on. Time to go."

They walked into Balance City's dock area, with all the sleek ships arrayed in even lines, and Dog led her reluctantly toward his own excuse for a shuttle. Dirty, banged up, it looked out of place among all the other well-maintained vehicles parked nearby. He stood, staring at the ship, as if waiting for something. She was just about to ask him again what he was waiting for when he spoke.

"Look, Billie, are you sure? I don't know what you think you're going to achieve."

"Let me worry about that, Dog." She studied him, trying to work out what was forcing his reluctance. There shouldn't be any reason for him not to help her. It was almost as if he was delaying. "What's the problem?" she said.

He shrugged. "No. No problem. I just wanted to make sure you knew what you were doing."

"Uh-huh. Well, you can be sure," she said.

Dog keyed the sequence and the door slid open. He let her clamber in first, then took his own place at the controls, reaching up to toggle equipment and hit switches. She

watched all of his moves carefully, trying to remember the
patterns. The last time they'd been in this craft, she'd been
too absorbed with talking to Jack and Hervé Antille to pay
real attention. The shuttle thrummed into life and lurched
backward as the docking mechanism kicked into action. She
nodded to herself. She thought she had a pretty good idea
what she needed to do to get the shuttle moving. Along with
the stuff Dog had shown her on the *Amaranth*, if worse came
to worst, she would be able to fly this thing . . . maybe. She
continued watching, imprinting, as he touched more controls and eased the shuttle out of its berth and into the
hangar, letting the parking controls draw them to the lip that
led to open airspace and the yawning gap over the chasm
above which Balance City rested.

He spoke to the port controllers, seeking clearance. There
was a brief back-and-forth, and then Dog sat back.

He gave her one last look. "Sure you're sure?"

"Shut up, Dog. Fly."

He slapped the panel and the engines roared, launching
them out into the void and up, away from Balance City into
the Utrecht skies.

Three

Jack spent some time on the voyage testing his memory, looking for places where there might be holes. Somehow, what had happened to him didn't make any sense. Things had been too much of a whirl since he and Dog had rescued Billie. It was only now that the full implications were really beginning to sink in. Though he seemed to have lost about ten years chronologically, his memories seemed pretty much intact. How would he know? If you lost a chunk of your existence, what would tell you it was gone? But then, he didn't really understand how the brain worked anyway. What was it about Jack Stein's neural pathways that gave him his special abilities? Maybe everyone had them, but some were just more aware of them than others. What had happened to him in the jump space was better than the other way around, he guessed. Imagine being years older with nothing having happened in the missing interval. It would be like having a vast hole in your memories, a blankness with nothing to fill it. Or perhaps there were, in some alternative plane of existence, in some other universe, the things that were meant to fill that hole. He wondered briefly how Billie felt about that. Maybe it was okay for her. Really, she could have no proper idea of what she'd missed by going through the experience. She was still too young to miss the absence. And anyway, sometimes not having the memories was better than having them hanging around to haunt you. He sometimes wished that some of the memories he carried around with him weren't there.

Back to the homeworld. Back to the Locality. Unlike in the outreaches of Utrecht and Balance City, there was no shuttle down, no orbital platform. As they neared, his stubbled shadow escorted him to the ship's seating area, guided him to a padded chair sculpted to match the body's contours. He indicated that Jack should strap himself in. The man took another seat facing Jack and reached for his own harness. Thorpe was already there, two seats down, safely secured. He didn't even turn his head as Jack and the bodyguard entered the landing lounge.

"Well, Mr. Stein," he said finally, turning to face Jack. "How do you feel?"

Jack snorted. "What's it to you, Thorpe?"

"Now, Jack. That's hardly the attitude."

Jack shook his head and bit back his reply. Thorpe was a corporate functionary, doing what he was told. Jack's issue was with whoever called the shots, and he had a pretty good idea who that might be. He knew how Outreach operated.

"I would think," Thorpe continued, "that you might be feeling something. Nostalgia? After all, it's been a while since you were back in the Locality. Back home, as it were."

Jack gave him a narrow-eyed glance. "And how do you know where the hell I've been?"

"Oh, we have a good idea of your movements over the last couple of years, Jack. We have been keeping an eye on you."

"Yeah, I bet you have," Jack shot back, venom in his voice.

Thorpe didn't react.

Jack set his jaw and looked away. He could feel the ship realigning and moments later, the deep-throated growl of the conventional drives kicked in, stirring his chair with vibrations. They were on their way down.

Jack spent the time avoiding the eyes of both Thorpe and the hired muscle, though the blank ship walls gave little distraction. He could feel the weight of their descent in the pit of his stomach. The drives increased to a muted roar, and then, a few minutes later, there was a clear jolt as the ship met ground. It settled, rocking once, twice, and the drives cut out, leaving the aftermath beating in his ears.

"It appears we are here," said Thorpe, unnecessarily.

Jack wondered how far they were from the Locality. Though the port itself was a fixed complex, the inch-by-inch crawl of the Locality across the landscape might leave them farther or closer than when he and Billie had left. There was no way of knowing which way the Locality might have moved; its programming saw to that, seeking out the materials for its ongoing growth and renewal, dictating the direction it traveled in next. He tried to do a quick calculation in his head, but it was beyond him. He no longer even had his handipad to assist. His captors had removed it as soon as they had reached the ship, removed anything that might be of possible use.

Thorpe unstrapped himself and indicated that Jack should do the same.

"Well, in a short time, we will be at your new quarters, Jack, and there I will be leaving you."

Jack took his time over his harness, thinking, testing the options. If he could find a means to slip away from this pair, maybe he could disappear. They were hardly likely to try to harm him if they thought he was so valuable to them. At least he hoped that was a fair assumption. They had to be at the port now. He would have three opportunities: here at the port; on the way to the Locality; the Locality itself. Outreach would likely have put on a flier to get them from docks. He couldn't imagine them bothering with ground transport. That was going to limit his options severely.

"How are we getting there?" he asked. "And who am I going to meet? I suppose I'm going to meet someone," he added to throw attention away from the first part of the question.

"All will become clear soon," said Thorpe, watching him appraisingly.

Jack stood slowly. "So . . . ?"

Thorpe gestured to the room's other occupant, and the gray-suited gorilla stepped across and gripped Jack's upper arm. Jack tried to shake his arm free, but the man's meaty paw was firmly in place.

"This way," said Thorpe, leading them from the cabin and out into the corridor.

As they emerged from the ship, Jack looked around at the familiar spaceport. It brought back memories with the wash of fuel and ship scents, and the flat expanse of stained apron. He hesitated at the top of the steps, trying to get his bearings, looking for any opportunities. Four or five other ships stood in place, and off to one side, not far from their own parking position, sat an unmarked flier. No one in sight. He'd been right. The port buildings were a long way off. Too far. In the other direction lay open fields. Reluctantly, he succumbed to the pressure on his arm and stepped down to be led across to the waiting flier. It looked like he was going to have one chance, and that would be when they arrived at the Locality. In the Locality's own port, there should be people, witnesses, perhaps the chance for a distraction. Wait and see, Jack. Let fate play the numbers on this one.

The flier rose, and shot forward, and as they reached the height of their ascent Jack craned to one side, trying to get a decent glimpse of that crawling iridescent beast that was the

Locality itself. Seen from this distance, the roof panels, programmable from the inside to reveal displays designed to keep the masses inside entertained, reflected the light, moving with waves of rainbow highlights. Here and there, blank panels overlooking parks and green spaces revealed the Locality's murky depths. He felt his stomach lurch, and the cold emptiness grow within him. There were too many associations here. Too many failures. Too much darkness, and here he was winging his way back into the heart of it. He wondered if any of the old contacts still survived. If not, there'd be others like them, scrabbling away an existence against the crumbling walls of morality that lived in the belly of the beast. He swallowed back a sour taste and looked away.

Originally a corporate innovation, the Locality functioned as a self-contained city environment to give those with links to Outreach a secure, serviced existence as the world around it had deteriorated. It was removed, guarded, and screened; nothing outside could touch them. Early in its history, there had been trouble, rioters attempting to pull down the shielded walls, but the Locality's defenses had proved more than equal to the challenge. Over time, it became more than a community, more than a town, and it had grown quickly to city status as it attracted more people to the shelter and certainty it provided. But like any hive, it also grew inside, guarding its own corruption, concealed from the outside world and able to creep throughout, controlled only by those who owned whatever happened within those walls. Billie had come out of that, in some ways so had Jack. Despite himself, he leaned over to take another look. The taste in his mouth was not pleasant and he tried to swallow back what he was feeling as his lip curled in response.

*   *   *

The flier swung lower, banking into an approach. Jack
watched the Locality suspiciously as it grew larger, domi-
nating his view. No good could come of this. No good at all.
He took several deep breaths, trying to steady himself. He
had to be ready to act as soon as the opportunity presented
itself. He glanced at his companion, but he was sitting staring fixedly ahead and balling and unballing his fists. He
couldn't see what Thorpe was doing. He was up front with
the pilot, separated by a screen. Jack turned his attention
back to their approach.

At the front of the Locality, the port area was clearly defined. Large curved transparent panels marked the section,
retractable as necessary and then closing again after incom-
ing ships. Probably unnecessary, but they gave the air of
completeness to the Locality's domain, securely self-contained
and protected from the rest of the world. Having the port located at the leading end also added to the initial impression
for visitors. At the extreme front, the buildings, the districts,
were newly grown, slick, and fashionable, a far cry from the
crumbling hulks at the far end of Old. To Jack, it just rein-
forced the artificiality of it all. It was a gloss, a patina of polished cleanness that could be wiped away in an instant if you
looked hard enough.

Jack could feel their descent in his belly and he leaned
sidewise to catch a forward glimpse of the ceiling panels re-
tracting into their invisible slots. He couldn't make out much
detail yet, but it looked as if there was only limited activity
down in the port. He grimaced. No crowds, no throngs of people he could slip through. He had to hope for an opening between the ships and buildings. The port layout was kept
reasonably constant within the changing structures. Sure, it
had been more than four years, but he thought he remembered
enough. Then, if he managed to slip away, he could . . .

He could what? He hadn't thought that far yet. If any of his old contacts still remained, he wasn't sure he could trust them. Not against Outreach. If he could get down to Old . . . but then there was a matter of survival. No handipad. No clothes. Nothing. Even though he often forgot to eat, he could still get hungry. He growled to himself, prompting an immediate reaction from his guard, who turned to look at him, eyes mere slits.

"Nothing, friend," said Jack. "I just don't like this place."

And he didn't. He didn't like it one bit.

They swept down and the flier settled to a stop. Jack's captor unstrapped himself and stood. The front panel that concealed the passenger area from the forward section of the flier eased back and Thorpe looked aft and nodded. The panel slid shut, and the besuited gorilla gestured with one hand that Jack should get up too, and at the same time reached inside his coat meaningfully. Jack sighed, released his own harness, and stood as well, waiting for the side door to open. As it did, his shadow stepped up close behind, pressing something hard into Jack's back.

"I guess you want me to get out," said Jack.

The other guy said nothing. Jack was tempted to turn and look at him, but a shove in the small of his back quickly took all thought of doing so away. He stepped out of the flier and down to the ground. Thorpe was standing at the bottom of the stairs waiting for him.

"So now what?" said Jack. He could sense the presence of the other man close behind.

"We go to your quarters."

Jack took a deep breath. "Give me a minute, will you? It's been a while." He made a show of looking up, checking out the ceiling panels, then scanned the port facilities. Nothing immediately presented itself. Thorpe strode off to talk to a port official, flipping out a handipad and rocking back and forth while the man in the uniform checked over whatever was on the screen. It took only a moment for the man to snap upright, clearly in deference to Thorpe, hand back the device, and take a pace back. Yep, always the same. Outreach moved and shook within the Locality.

Thorpe nodded and walked briskly back to join them.

"Our transport will be here in a few moments," he said.

Meanwhile, Jack was still scanning, taking in everything around them, trying not to be too obvious about it, looking for that small spark in his gut that would alert him to opportunity. He still didn't know what he might do if he did manage to get away, but for now, the important thing was to make the first move.

A square white vehicle pulled up at the edge of the landing apron.

"Ah, here we are," said Thorpe, stepping back and holding out one hand to his side in invitation. "Mr. Stein?"

"Yeah, yeah," said Jack. "You can drop the polite formality, Thorpe. This whole thing's enough of a charade as it is." He made a move toward the waiting vehicle.

Behind him, Thorpe gave a pained sigh.

Walking as slowly as he could, still alert to anything he could use, Jack reached down inside himself again, seeking any spark from his inner senses, but there was nothing there either. It appeared that Jack Stein was on his own. Even his extended senses had deserted him.

He resisted glancing back over his shoulder at Thorpe or the other man. He had to make it look like he was playing along right until the last possible moment. As he neared the white vehicle, he strained to see inside, but tinted windows obscured his view. So for now, there was Thorpe, the muscle, and one, maybe two, inside. Fifty yards or so separated him from the transport; Thorpe and the other guy were close behind. Jack quickened his pace. A cluster of buildings, non-descript, probably administrative offices, lay off to the right. They presented the only opportunity he could see.

Now or never, Stein.

Jack broke into a run, peeling off to the right in the direction of the buildings.

"Hey!" yelled Thorpe. "Get him."

There was the sound of pounding feet. He risked a glimpse back over his shoulder. The gray-suited guy had drawn his weapon and was heading after him. He had the gun leveled, out in front of him.

"No!" yelled Thorpe again. "Don't damage him. Take out his leg."

Shit, thought Jack, breaking into a sprint and zigzagging at the same time. A shot burned into the ground nearby. Jack swore and zagged.

Another glance showed that he was drawing away from his pursuer, but the white vehicle's doors had opened, and two others had joined the chase. They had picked his destination and were charging toward the small cluster of buildings too.

Jack put on another burst of speed as another shot sizzled past uncomfortably close. There was something to be said for the missing ten years he had regained. His new body was holding up well. He had just about reached the first building when another shot zipped past him. Dammit. Close. Too close.

He ducked between the buildings, not risking another look yet. Directly in front of him stood the astonished official who had checked Thorpe's documents. His jaw dropped open, and he thrust out his arms in some sort of futile effort to block Jack's progress. Jack barreled into him and they both went down.

"Fuck it," said Jack, scrambling to his feet, pushing off from the ground and catching the official with his back step. Served him right for interfering. The yelp of pain gave Jack only a moment's satisfaction. He cut quickly right between two of the buildings, then left, then right again.

"That way," he heard a voice behind him. Great.

He pressed up against a wall, breathing heavily. The sound of running feet had subsided. They were stalking him now. Jack looked quickly each way, but there were just the narrow passages. He ducked down, but there was no space beneath the buildings. Of course not. Everything in the Locality was grown from the ground up. Looking up at the nearest gap between structures, he could see wall. His gaze drifted up, tracing the wall right up to the ceiling panels. Up . . . yes, but he'd have to be quick. Sometimes the old training came in handy. If you wanted to hide from someone, you went up. People just didn't naturally look above them unless they had a reason to do so.

"Over this way," said a voice, close.

"Shit," whispered Jack. He turned to face the wall, searching for something that would give him purchase. There was a window, and it had a slight frame. He ducked his face around the edge of the frame and back quickly. The glance had shown him the inside appeared to be unoccupied. Maybe they'd gone out to join the search.

With one hand, Jack gripped the edge of the frame, lifting one leg to get some sort of support. It was awkward, but with an effort, he was able to boost himself up and catch the upper lip with the fingers of his other hand. He almost lost his grasp, ripping the skin of one of his fingers. He winced against the pain, precariously clutching against the wall and reaching up with one hand for the edge of the roof. His face was flat against the top of the window, turned sideways. He couldn't look. He found the edge, sliding his fingers flat at full stretch, and then, straining, slowly reached up with his other hand. He had a grip, but it was only with the edge of his fingers. Repositioning, he pushed himself up to the very ends of his toes, sliding his hands farther onto the roof surface.

Jack heaved himself up, getting his elbows onto the edge, then wriggling his hips up and over, and finally his legs.

Just in time. Gray Suit ducked around the corner, his weapon still drawn, looked both ways, then disappeared from sight again.

Staying perfectly quiet, Jack inched back on the flat roof, and then allowed himself the luxury of a long exhalation, the cool roof surface pressing against his cheek.

Now all he had to do was wait.

Four

They spent the journey up to the orbital in silence, Dog making the occasional adjustment to the controls and Billie watching, filing information away. Ships, systems, they were easy. Easier than people, anyway. She could read people well enough, figure out how they worked too, but mostly, she didn't really like what she discovered when she did. There were one or two exceptions: Jack, Antille, Pinpin Dan when he'd been around and before what happened between him and Jack. There were the members of her Family down in Old too, but that seemed a long, long time ago now.

As they neared the orbital, she watched its looming presence grow. Mere hours had passed since they'd been here, with the vast rotating cylinder and the winged arrays stretching out from it in the blackness, ships lined up in their docking bays like awkward projections from the extended wings. She couldn't remember how many ships had been parked here when they'd left, but she could make out the *Amaranth* clearly as they swept up toward the landing dock. The large bulge toward the nose containing the drives announced quite simply what sort of ship it was. She did a quick scan, searching for anything else that looked like it might have jump capability, but there was nothing. If the people she was looking for had been here, they weren't here anymore. She suppressed a sigh and clenched her teeth together tightly, barely stopping herself from shooting Dog a narrow-eyed look of accusation. It wasn't his fault. It wasn't her fault either, but she was starting to feel as if it were.

Their shuttle nestled into its docking bay, and again, Dog seemed to hesitate.

"What is it now?" she said.

He turned to look at her, obviously working on what he was going to say next. After a couple of moments, he spoke.

"What is it with you and Jack, Billie?"

She took a deep breath and held it before letting it out slowly as a sigh.

"Nothing."

"Oh, come on," he said, peering at her through strands of dark hair that had fallen over his face. "Why this huge concern? Jack's a big boy. He can look after himself. It's what he does, isn't it?"

Billie thought about that for a second. "Nuh-uh. Well, sort of."

"Come on," he said again. "It's more than that. Anybody'd think you were . . . you know . . ."

She screwed up her face and gave her head a little shake, as if she were trying to throw his words back away from her.

"No," she said.

Dog sat watching her. The silence between them grew uncomfortably. He opened his mouth to say something, but she cut him off with a wave of her hand.

"Don't say anything," she said to him. "Not a word."

Not looking at him, she fumbled with her harness.

"Can we go?"

"Sure," he said after a moment. She heard him releasing

his own harness. She gave him a quick sidelong glance, but he was concentrating on the controls. That was good. She didn't want to meet his eyes. What he'd suggested was uncomfortable, not because of the thought of it, but more because of her history. But there was no way he could know that, and he didn't need to know either.

The seal was in place around the doorway, and she palmed the control to open the hatch. Not even looking to see if Dog was following, she stepped into the walkway that would take them into the orbital proper, and reached for the steadying handholds.

Dog caught up with her a few moments later, stopping her with a hand on her shoulder.

"Wait," he said. "Where are you going?"

"The ship, of course."

"Well, you need me to get into it, don't you?"

"Yeah," she said, taking another deep breath. "Come on, then."

She shrugged off his hand, and headed up the passageway.

It took them only a few minutes to get to where the *Amaranth* was berthed, through the shops and offices and living quarters contained within the rotating cylinder that made up the orbital's bulk. A couple of times, Dog had tried to slow them down, acting like he wanted to talk, even suggesting at one point that they stop for a coffee or something, but Billie hurried him along. She stood tapping her fingers on the side of her thighs impatiently as Dog opened the *Amaranth*'s hatch and stepped aside to let her on board.

Dog's ship was a complete contrast to the small shuttle he ran back and forth to Utrecht's surface. In some ways, it was even a contrast to his own slightly disheveled appearance. Take one look at Dog McCreedy and you'd hardly believe he maintained a ship, let alone a ship in such an ordered condition. She guessed the shuttle was more in keeping with his Balance City persona. Billie had had to be good with people, had to know how to react to them and play them. Somehow, though, Dog was full of contradictions that she hadn't worked out yet. He seemed to be good at what he did. He was a good pilot. And what she needed was a pilot—and a ship. Getting up to the orbital to use the *Amaranth*'s systems was merely an excuse; when it came down to it, Billie was going to the Locality and the only way she was going to do that was with Dog's assistance. Not that he knew that yet. All that she needed to set her plan in motion was the proof that she needed to go there.

She headed straight for the bridge, though she could have used the ship's systems anywhere, Dog close on her heels.

"So, what do you need?"

"Give me access, full access," she said.

He was standing behind one of the seats, his hand resting on the back, chewing at his bottom lip.

"What, Dog?" she said. "Afraid I'm going to find something?"

He frowned and shook his head. "I'm just not sure—"

"Let me worry about that," she said. "I know what I'm doing."

She slid into a seat, scanning the bridge for the best access point. "Can you put the display anywhere here?"

He pointed at a blank section of wall off to the right and she nodded, swiveling the seat to face that direction.

Dog reached across to the front panel and placed his palm flat on a polished area in the middle of where the displays appeared when the ship was in flight. "Full access, new voice," he said.

Billie gave a quick gesture of affirmation. "Links," she said. The blank section of wall was no longer blank. An array of links filled a rectangular illuminated area and she stood, stepped closer to the screen, and started reading. Dog was well connected. She nodded to herself.

"Scroll," she said, letting the list drift slowly down. "Faster."

Getting impatient with the system's speed, she placed a finger on the display and moved the list to where she wanted it. Patterns of interconnected nodes ran back and forth in nested clusters.

She had what she wanted in less than five seconds. There was a gateway to the orbital's systems there. Probably secured, but that wouldn't stop her for long. A couple of seconds more, and she was in.

From there, she had a network of links that stretched far beyond what the *Amaranth* offered. She plotted the pathways in her head, and checked, confirming that they would lead her where she needed. But before she did that, she wanted to take a brief detour into the orbital's own systems.

Dog gave an audible sigh behind her. "Can I do anything?"

"No. Just be quiet," she said, waving a hand behind her. She barely noticed the sound of him taking a seat, the slight hiss as the seat realigned and conformed to his weight. Billie was in working mode now. Not much disturbed her when she was.

Satisfied that she was where she needed to be, Billie moved back to her own chair, pulled her legs up in front of her, and scanned the record display. This was the orbital's own log of ships coming and going over the last day. There was nothing there.

"Shit," she said.

"What?" said Dog.

"They couldn't have had a surface ship, could they?" she said, spinning her chair slowly to face him.

He shook his head. "Unlikely. Not on Utrecht. The regulations would kill you. Or you'd have to pay someone enough. . . ."

She narrowed her eyes. That was the sort of thing Outreach might do.

"Nah," said Dog, clearly seeing where her thoughts were going.

She agreed. If they were going to snatch someone, they'd want to do it with as little fuss as possible, and landing a ship where no ships normally landed, that was fuss.

"Okaaay," she said. "They got to the records. It only shows eight coming or going over the last day. None of them are going back home. Unless they lied."

"Uh-huh."

"Wait a second," she said, turning back to the screen. She tried pulling up the crew and passenger manifests, but couldn't access them.

"Damn." She rubbed her fingers in her hair, frowning.

"What now?" said Dog.

"They're encrypted. If I was home, I could pull the algorithms. It would take too long now."

"So what do you want to do?"

"I've got something else," she said, and then gave a short growl under her breath. "That's going to take too much time too." She slapped the seat arm. "Dammit!"

"Um, Billie . . ." Dog had risen and crossed to stand behind her chair. She looked up at him as he placed his hand on her shoulder. "Maybe I can do something."

"Like what?" she said.

"Don't worry about that. You keep doing whatever it is you're doing. I need to go and see someone."

Billie looked at his eyes. He obviously picked up the unspoken question.

"It doesn't matter," he said quietly. "There are things that you do, and things that I do. Just trust the old Dog."

"Hmmm," she said.

"I'll be back in a while."

She watched him leave the bridge and head down the corridor, the question still clear in her mind. At least he trusted her enough to leave her alone with the *Amaranth*'s systems.

Just for a second, when she was sure he had gone, she thought about taking the ship herself. It was a nice idea, but no, she hadn't learned enough yet. She wasn't sure she could handle the *Amaranth*, let alone get it to where she needed to go. For now, she was reliant upon Dog McCreedy, whether she liked it or not, and Billie didn't much like being reliant upon anybody.

By the time Dog returned, Billie was bored and frustrated with her searches. Dog stood in the doorway, looking at her a slight grin teasing at the corners of his mouth.

"So?" said Billie.

"Yeah," said Dog. "I don't know if this is going to be any help."

With a flourish, he pulled a sheet of laminate from behind his back and gave a short bow.

Billie was out of her seat in an instant, grabbing at it.

Dog made a little play of keeping it out of her reach, and then at last handed it over. It was a picture of a guy in a suit. She peered at it, then shook it beside her.

"Who's this?"

"That's the guy," said Dog.

"But how . . . ?"

"Never mind. That's the guy."

"No name? The ship?"

Dog shook his head.

"Great," said Billie. She held the picture at arm's length as if looking at it a different way might mysteriously reveal the man's identity, and then she grimaced.

She crossed to the screen part of the wall and spoke a command as Dog looked on interestedly. "Accept image," she said, and placed the laminate flat against the display area.

"Search. Cross-reference Outreach Industries."

"Now what?" asked Dog.

"Wait," said Billie, and moved back to her seat to do just that, studying the picture. She wasn't sure how good the search engines would be with this set of remote links, but it was her only option. She frowned at the picture. There was something vaguely familiar about the face. It was a while ago . . . and yet . . .

She had it. Back in Yorkstone with Jack. Some guy had called about the artifact when they'd finished with that case. He'd been from Outreach. Jack had put him in his place. She remembered thinking how impressed she'd been with Jack at the time. Yes, this could easily be that man.

What was his name? She'd only been half paying attention at the time.

"Add parameter," she said. "Soundalike 'Thaw' or 'Thorne.'"

Dog had moved to his seat and was watching intently, a slight frown on his face. "Why that?" he said.

"I recognize him," she said. "His name was something like that."

"Recognize him? From where?"

Billie shrugged. "Back in Yorkstone. It was something to do with a case we were working on."

"A case?"

"Uh-huh. Someone had stolen an alien artifact from one of the sites. Only they hadn't. But they thought they had. It was complicated."

"Yeah, it sounds it."

The screen flashed, showing a hit. Billie turned her attention to what it contained. There was a small news article and a blurry picture. It looked like the same man. She stood to move closer and read the text.

"Andrew Thorpe, of Outreach Industries said today . . ."

She looked down at her feet, thinking. "Clear," she said. She had the name. She knew who he worked for, but she'd already known that. This was just confirmation.

Thorpe's mention of the Locality was enough. Or at least Dog's saying that he'd mentioned it. If they wanted Jack, it had to have something to do with the aliens, and the only place they'd want to deal with him was somewhere close, at the heart of their operations.

Maybe.

It was always maybe.

Maybe they'd taken him off to some remote world to do experiments on him.

Maybe.

It didn't matter. Outreach was the Locality and the Locality was Outreach. That's where they were going.

She turned slowly to face Dog, looking at him through her hair.

"You'd better get ready," she said.

"What?"

"You'd better get ready, whatever you have to do. We're going back home."

Five

Despite her insistence, despite the knowledge that she had to go back to the Locality, Billie wasn't really sure how she felt about winding up back there. There were memories there—and people. In Yorkstone with Jack, and then on Utrecht with Hervé, it had been okay, different. She could be whoever she wanted to be and not have to worry about it. Now she was sort of someone else anyway, so maybe it didn't matter. She wouldn't know until she was back there. Being there with Dog would be all right, she thought. She looked over at him surreptitiously, and then quickly glanced away. She hadn't convinced him yet, not quite; she could tell.

Thinking about Hervé reminded her. She'd better let him know what she was doing. He might get worried.

"Dog?"

"Yeah," he said unenthusiastically.

"Can I make a call?"

"Who to?"

"If you must know, I want to let Hervé know what I'm doing."

"And what are you doing?"

She narrowed her eyes at him. "You, Mr. McCreedy," she said, standing and crossing behind his chair, "are taking me to the Locality." She leaned over so her face was close to his.

"Am I, now?" he said, looking into her eyes trying to maintain a stern expression, but he grinned despite himself. "Yeah, I guess I am," he said.

"Thanks," she said, reaching over and touching his face. "And so, I have to call Hervé."

"Well, you've got full access to the systems. Just call."

She was conscious of him watching her as she walked back to her own seat. People used to look at her like that. Pinpin Dan used to look at her like that. Others. Jack never had. Having Dog do it made her slightly uncomfortable. Thinking about the Locality brought it all back.

She put in the call, but Hervé didn't answer, so she left him a message. After cutting the connection, she turned back to look at Dog, folding her hands in her lap.

"So . . . ," she said.

Dog's grin had faded. "What? You don't expect us just to go, do you?"

"Uh-huh."

"Jesus, Billie. There are things to do. I can't just take off. What about a bit of preparation?"

"Why can't you? We've wasted enough time already."

Dog sighed. "If they've jumped, and there's a very good chance they have, they'll be there already. An hour here or there isn't going to make a difference. And what are you going to do when you get there? Have you thought about that?"

No, she hadn't. And Dog was right, of course. It was her turn to sigh. "I just want to be doing something."

Dog was looking thoughtful now. A slight frown marked his brow.

"Okay," he said reluctantly, almost as a whisper, and turned to his controls.

While he was calling up charts and numbers on the display

in front of him, touching panels and buttons, highlighting readings and dragging them off to one side, she walked over to stand at his back, watching over his shoulder.

"How much do you know about this place, the Locality?" he said, not looking up.

"A lot. We used to live there."

"Hmmm," he said. "But not for a while, right? Things could have changed."

She leaned over to look at a particularly tricky piece of calculation, taking a second to answer. "Nuh-uh. I don't think so. The buildings might have changed, but not the people. Not really. Haven't you ever been there?"

"It's been a long time since I've been back to Earth," he said distractedly. "No. I've never been."

"But you knew Jack before, right?"

"Yeah, but that was before then."

"Um . . ."

"Billie? Can you go and sit down for a couple of minutes? You're distracting me." His hand was paused in mid-action, hovering over the displays.

"But I want to watch," she said.

"Just do it, Billie," he said. Then, almost as an afterthought, "Please?"

She gave a little pout and moved back to sit, pulling her legs up in front of her, her arms crossed in front of her knees. She couldn't see as much from that position, but if it got them to where they were going more quickly, she guessed it was okay. She wasn't sure she particularly liked Dog's tone, though.

Finally, Dog leaned back. "She'll take a couple of minutes to plot the trajectories, and then we can get going."

"So, why did you leave?" asked Billie.

Dog chewed at his bottom lip, then grimaced. "That again. Let's just say I had my reasons." He shook his head.

Okay. She knew better than to push where she wasn't wanted. She would have answered just the same.

"Do you need anything before we leave?" Dog asked.

"Nuh-uh." Billie shook her head. "We're only going to be a few hours. I can get whatever I need down there."

Dog set his jaw in a firm line, breathed out heavily through his nose, and then nodded once. "Okay."

He opened a channel to the orbital, sought clearance, and mimed to Billie that she should strap herself in. "Coordinates on their way, Orbital Control," he said.

He glanced once at her questioningly, almost as if he was expecting her to change her mind, but she nodded again and gave him a little frown.

"Okay, here we go."

The seals around the *Amaranth* withdrew, and the ship eased slowly back. Checking some figures, Dog touched the controls and the conventional drives throbbed into life, pushing them out and away from the bristling array that was the orbital itself. Dog was busy checking things, so Billie occupied herself watching the retreating station and Utrecht's globe beneath them. Don't worry, Jack, she thought. I'm coming. We're both coming.

The drives increased in intensity—she could feel the vibration through her seat—and the ship shot out and away, into the blackness. Behind them, Utrecht glowed in the void.

With a last touch of the controls, Dog seemed satisfied and he settled back. He glanced once at Billie, then out at the surrounding space, seemingly lost in his own thoughts.

Already, Billie was bored. The region around Utrecht was relatively empty, and now, for a while, she couldn't access any of the world-based systems to continue her searches.

That would all have to wait for the Locality. At least there, she'd be on familiar territory.

"Dog?" she said.

"Yeah." He didn't look at her.

"Jack said some things about when you two worked together. I thought you'd saved his life a couple of times."

He linked his fingers behind his neck and looked up, then closed his eyes. "That was a long time ago, Billie. Things get colored by time. It wasn't anything special. We were serving together. It's just the sort of stuff that happens."

"Jack made it sound a lot more than that."

"Yeah, well. You know, when you're on missions, things happen. People get into difficult situations. You help each other out. That's the way it is. Like I said, nothing special." He lowered his face and opened his eyes. "We've got about an hour until we reach the jump point. I think I might go to my cabin for a while. You can either stay up here or go down to the second cabin along. You know the one."

"Uh-huh," said Billie, giving him a little frown. She watched him release his harness and head out of the bridge, the characteristic slouch of his shoulders made even more pronounced by his hands tucked firmly into his armpits.

"See you in a while," she said.

If Dog responded, she didn't hear him.

She turned back to look out at the stars, thinking about the worlds that lay out there still undiscovered, and the alien homeworld, and wondering whether she'd ever get a chance to really go there. She and Hervé's last attempt had been a disaster.

Jack had seen the aliens. Dog had seen them.

Maybe they'd get the chance again.

Maybe.

It was always maybe.

*   *   *

Dog was wearing a sour expression as he looked out at the cloud-swirled blue world ahead of them.

"I need a parking orbit," he said. "Why can't they put up an orbital like anywhere else?"

"There used to be one," said Billie.

"Yeah, and what happened to that? What happened to half the population of the place?"

He got through to ground-side control and eventually received clearance. No banter this time; it was all rigid formality.

"I remember some of the reasons now why I got off this stupid planet," he muttered. "Okay, Billie. Let's go. When we get down there, I'm not sure how long I'm going to stick around."

She gave him another little frown, but didn't pursue it. There'd be time for that later.

Together they moved to *Amaranth*'s onboard shuttle, a far sight cleaner and better maintained than the one they'd left back at the orbital. Dog was still muttering under his breath. Billie shook her head. It was almost as bad as hanging around with Jack. She stifled a grin.

Once they were strapped in, Dog reached up and toggled controls, for the moment absorbed in the needs of piloting rather than his own misery. The flier eased out of its bay and below the *Amaranth* and slowly accelerated toward the watery world in front of them.

"You're sure you know the way?"

"Yes, I know the way," he snapped.

Billie reached across and touched his thigh. "Dog?"

He turned, sudden hostility on his face that faded in an instant. "Sorry. Just old memories, Billie. Not you."

He patted her hand. She watched the motion, and then

turned her own hand over, gripping his fingers gently in her own.

"I need your help, Dog. I need you to be clear."

He looked down at her hand and gave her fingers a little squeeze. "I know."

He was looking at her face now, something in his eyes.

Not now, Dog. Not now.

She gently pulled her hand away, holding the look for just a second. Then turning to the front screens, she pointed at the steadily growing continent. Mountains, forests—all lay obscured by clouds in some parts but clearly recognizable.

"See, there," she said.

He tore his gaze away from her and looked up at the screens. He tapped his finger on the continental mass that projected south from the place where she was pointing.

"And see there? That's where I first met Jack."

At that moment, a flash of light, some trick of reflection, drew her attention back to where the Locality performed its slow crawl across the continental surface. She could just make out its shape now. A hollow sensation crept through her chest. Over the other side of the continent lay Yorkstone, but there was nothing for her in that place, no memories, nothing. There, below, lay her real memories, the start of her life with Jack. She pressed her hand gently against her abdomen, trying to still the feelings that were threatening to well up inside her. She had to start thinking about what they were going to do when they got there.

They'd have to get a hotel when they got down and that wouldn't be cheap. There was no one she could stay with. She glanced at Dog, but quickly pushed that thought away. She reached into her pocket and pulled out her handipad. She thumbed it on, but apparently they were still too far out.

With a tut, she switched it off again and slipped it back into her pocket.

"So what do we do when we get there?" Dog was watching her again.

Billie shrugged. "Find somewhere to stay, a hotel or something. From there I can get into the local systems and start looking around. I need to see what the Locality looks like now. Things could have changed a bit since we left. Outreach has got buildings, but I think they've got other facilities too."

"And how are we supposed to pay for that?" asked Dog.

"Haven't you got money?" she asked.

"Jesus, Billie. If you think . . ."

She grinned and tapped the place where she had slipped the handipad. "It's okay."

"Shit," said Dog, and returned her grin.

He shook his head and looked away again, focus now back on the controls. "Shit, Billie," he said under his breath, but he still had the traces of a grin on his face.

By the time the small flier touched down, it was already dark. Dog had sent through all the required identity codes and they'd been cleared for entry. As they stepped from the shuttle amid a shadowed landscape, individual ships picked out with directed lights, Billie scanned them one by one. Not a single one of them had the telltale jump bulge, and she felt her heart sink. If only she could be sure.

As if reading her thoughts, Dog tried to reassure her. "Look, they could have landed, taken off again. They might have parked in orbit. You never know."

Billie just nodded.

She flipped out her handipad and started checking Locality hotels.

"So, are we just going to stand out here?" said Dog. "Where to?"

Billie waved in the direction of the port buildings. "The shuttle to the Locality is through that way."

He took her upper arm and started steering her toward the open hangar. "Come on, then."

She followed without protest, still concentrating on the hotel availability. She was tired now. Tired and hungry. It had been a very long day, and now that they were on the ground, suddenly she was starting to feel it.

Six

Something was moving beneath his cheek, and Jack pulled away in revulsion. There was a new scent wafting around his face too, reminiscent of crushed insects. What was this? The Locality didn't have bugs. It took him a couple of moments to work out what was going on. Then the realization hit him; the roof was trying to reject him, or absorb him—one or the other. Its programming had recognized him as something foreign, something that shouldn't be there. He slipped sideways, farther toward the roof's center, hoping that would forestall the programming for a little. He turned his face the other way, rubbing vigorously at his cheek with one palm. Urgh. It had felt like tiny little suckers being applied to his skin.

Below, the noise of the search continued. Thorpe and his boys were checking each of the buildings in the small cluster now.

"No sign over here," called a voice from farther away.

"Well, he's got to be here somewhere." Thorpe's voice.

"Nothing in here," came another voice from almost directly below.

Jack held his breath, finally hearing footsteps heading away from his hiding spot. The roof was starting up again, and he grimaced against the sensation. Damned if he knew what it was doing to his skin, but he couldn't move yet. His heart pounded as he expected that at any moment there would come a shout announcing his discovery. The seconds dragged into minutes, and then, finally, Thorpe's voice came from somewhere close by.

"All right, Mr. Stein. Have your little bit of fun. We *will* find you. Where can you go?"

Good question, Thorpe.

A few seconds of silence followed, broken only by the sound of a flier taking off. Jack tilted his face slightly, straining to track the craft as it rose to the ceiling panels far above. He couldn't tell whether it was the flier they'd come in on or not. He just hoped to hell they didn't spot him. The clear ceiling panels retracted; the flier accelerated upward and then shot out of sight. Slowly, slowly, the panels slid back into place.

Jack waited for a few minutes more, listening hard. The sensation against his skin was really starting to annoy him, and if anything, the smell had intensified, becoming more acrid. He wormed his way to the edge of the roof and risked a glance over. There appeared to be no one around. He turned his attention to where the vehicle had been parked, but there was no sign of it either. It seemed that Thorpe and the others were truly gone, for now. Thorpe might have left someone behind to keep an eye out for him, but there was no trace of anyone as far as he could see. He took the opportunity to get his bearings and map out the area around the small cluster of buildings. It looked like if he kept close to the outer walls, he could circle around to where the shuttle stop was, and then get into the Locality proper, hopefully without being spotted. He edged back across the creepily alive surface to the rear of the building, slid his legs over, and dropped to the ground.

Looking in both directions, he determined the way was clear and made a quick dash to the next building, taking care to avoid the window as he went. Two more buildings and he had only open ground between him and the wall. He'd be exposed for about a hundred yards before reaching the side of the next building, one of the main port terminals. There was nothing for it. Steeling himself, his heart still racing, he stepped casually out from the building's shadow and into the open. He strolled unhurriedly across the expanse. Someone walking would draw less attention. The last thing he wanted to do was run.

As soon as he reached the side of the next building, Jack felt himself relax. He had made it without being spotted.

Jack walked along the side of the building, rounded the corner, and almost walked straight into Gray Suit. The flat-faced muscle looked as startled to see Jack as Jack was to see him. That instant was all Jack needed. As Gray Suit was reaching inside his jacket, Jack hit him, a hard uppercut to the chin, and followed that with a rapid blow to the now-exposed throat. His silent former captor staggered back, clutching at his throat, and Jack hit him again. This time he went down. Jack flexed his fist, ignoring the pain. There was something to be said for these new reflexes. In an instant, he was on the guy's huddled form, wresting his weapon from its place of concealment. The downed man made a grab for the gun, but Jack was too quick for him. Jack stepped back, checked that the weapon was on and the safety was off, and then leveled it.

"On your feet," Jack said quietly.

Gray Suit clambered slowly to his feet, one hand still clutching at his throat, coughing roughly, eyes full of icy fire.

"Turn around," Jack told him, and then, when the guy hesitated, "Just do it."

Slowly the man turned.

"Sorry about this, friend," said Jack.

Jack hit him at the base of the skull, hard. He went down again, still without any real sound. Jack leaned down to check him and, satisfied that he wasn't going to get up again any time soon, stood back up, flipped on the safety, and shoved the weapon into his waistband underneath his coat at his back. The guy would live, but he wasn't going to be very happy when he woke. Jack felt slightly guilty. All the man had ever done was sit there in silence. Still, it came with the territory, and Jack was less than inclined to feel any sympathy for him.

He looked around. There could be others, but now he had a weapon, not that he had the urge to use it, he needed to get out of there and quickly. With a brisk tread, he set out in the direction he'd been headed and then stopped as a thought hit him. He turned back to the crumpled form and rummaged through the guy's pockets. There, he felt the hard shape he was looking for. He pulled out the guy's handipad and slipped it into his own pocket, then walked quickly away from the unconscious body. A gun *and* a handipad. Jack was feeling a whole lot better. He picked up his pace, flexing his fingers. His hand was starting to throb now, but it was going to hurt a lot less than his friend on the ground back there.

When he reached the shuttle stop, and the wash of familiarity that came with it, all sorts of conflicting emotions ran through Jack's gut. That sense of comfort with the known, being back in the place where he used to live and breathe, it was strange. In some ways, despite the familiarity, it was almost as if he were here for the first time; he felt so removed from it all, cut off from it by some sort of perceptual barrier. With his new body—no, wait; that wasn't right—it was more like his old body. It just felt new. The way he looked now was probably not that much different from when he'd first arrived in the Locality all those years ago.

"Dammit, Stein. Keep your mind on the job," he muttered to himself. There was time enough for analysis later. For now, he had to get himself out of the area. There'd still be people looking for him and he didn't know how long it would be before his friend back on the ground was awake again. In the Locality proper, in Mid, or in Old, he could lose himself. Not in New. In New, he'd stand out too much. The problem was, if they came after him, they'd be likely to check his old haunts first. He could try to take a room somewhere in the Midside of Old, one of those seedy dives just starting to fall apart, but there was a problem. No funds. Until he got into the handipad and started messing around . . . he fingered the handipad in his pocket. When he got somewhere a little less hot, he could try to put a call in to Billie and let her know what had happened, at least warn her about McCreedy.

The shuttle whirred to a stop, the doors hissed open, and quickly checking in every direction, Jack slipped on board, ducking low and keeping his attention focused through the window. As soon as the shuttle was under way, still keeping low, he walked to the rear of the compartment and took a seat in the very back corner, partly shielded by the rear spar. He slid down in the seat. If memory served, this would take him to Mid-Central and then he'd have to either walk or change to an Old-bound shuttle.

Jack couldn't risk anything until he was out of the port area. He angled his head so he could watch the transition, see the way the city had changed in the few years that he'd been away. The first buildings swept up before him, slick, sharp at their edges, marked with subtle pastels. No advertising yet. That wouldn't appear until a few blocks farther down, where the buildings were fully occupied and their inhabitants or corporate leaseholders had moved in and customized the programming to their needs. Up at this end of the Locality, it was all corporate. No normal person could afford to live up here. If anything, the fashion appeared to have become more retro. The hard lines and industrial feel had been replaced by more of a cakelike sensibility, iced edges and sweeping curved moldings and pinks and yellows and blues.

The shuttle slowed, drawing into a stop. Nobody joined. Probably still too far up, and it was getting late. Jack risked pulling out the handipad and checking the time. It wasn't locked, so he was in luck, but it was still rare for anyone to lock their handipad by the looks of things. What time would it be back on Utrecht? He didn't know, couldn't work it out. Whatever it was, he had to call now and not bother about it. He could use this handipad only for a short time before they used it to trace him. That gave him another idea.

But in the meantime, he had to put in the call. He keyed up the commands and called the University of Balance City, Hervé Antille.

It took a while for Antille to answer, and when he did, he looked sleep rumpled, the eyes in his round, dark face bleary.

"Jack, where are you?"

"What time is it there?" asked Jack.

"Early, Jack. Early. Where are you?"

"No time to explain. Is Billie there?"

"No, Jack. She's gone. She's gone looking for you."

Jack ran his fingers through his hair and grimaced. "Shit. Well, tell her to get back. I'm back in the Locality."

"I can't do that."

"Why?"

Hervé sighed. "She's gone off with that Dog McCreedy. I received a message from their ship."

"Shit. Shit," said Jack.

"What is it?" asked Hervé, clearly puzzled. He had no reason to suspect McCreedy. After all, the young man had been instrumental in Antille and Billie's rescue.

"Listen," said Jack, leaning closer in to the screen. "McCreedy's in bed with Outreach. It was a setup. He's the reason I'm here. You've got to try and get a message through to Billie. I don't know. Say something, anything. McCreedy's not to be trusted. You're a smart guy. You can work something out."

"I see," said Hervé slowly. "I'll see what I can do, but I don't like my chances."

"Do what you can, Hervé."

"I will. And Jack?"

"Yeah?"

"Good luck."

Jack nodded and cut the connection. He closed the handipad and held it, one hand outstretched on the seat beside him. Shit. There was no one else he could call. He knew Hervé would do the best he could, but Jack also understood the truth of Antille's words. The chances weren't good. Even if Hervé could get through to the *Amaranth*, what could he say that wouldn't alert McCreedy?

Jack was starting to get hungry. It had been a long day already and he'd been burning energy. He needed something, and he needed a coffee too. That slight nagging headache was starting to rise in his temple, telling him he'd been far too long without one. It was funny. . . . He might have expected the transformation of his body to purge him of his dependency, but then, how long had he been drinking coffee? How long had he been drinking too much coffee? No, never mind.

The shuttle had taken him about halfway down New. Now was as good a time as any, and unless the general layout had changed much, there should be a convenience plaza somewhere in the vicinity. Normally, even this late, there'd be something open, places catering to the later office workers. He jumped off the shuttle at the next stop and stood, trying to get his bearings, as it whirred away. Something quick like Molly's would be good, but in this district, he was unlikely to find one. They catered more to the middle market. Glancing above, he noted that the ceiling panels were playing clear moonlit night. At least he wouldn't have to put up with rain.

He had to walk a full two blocks before he found the entranceway. Promotional lights crawled up the side of a building and it was the same on the building at the other corner. Looking around, but seeing no one, just a port-bound shuttle heading up his way, he ducked into the side street, onto wide, clay-colored tiles and a clear pedestrianized roadway. Benches and small shrubs were dotted along the length in front of stores. He'd not gone ten paces when an advertising drone hit him with lights and a burst of music. Jack flinched away automatically.

Dammit, he'd forgotten about these things. He drew his hand away from behind him and strode quickly out of the drone's range. Normally, the things weren't let anywhere near the quiet spaces. Maybe they'd relaxed the rules in the time he'd been gone.

Dead ahead was an open plaza, and he walked quickly toward it. Jack stopped at the entrance, scanning it. There was a café serving customers across the other side. A couple deep in conversation occupied one of the tables. A solitary man sat at another, reading something on his handipad. It would do. He stepped past the requisite flowing statue in the center and crossed to an empty table. He pulled out a chair, with a clear view of the square, his back to the other patrons, and keyed up the menu. A quick perusal, and he ordered a sandwich and a coffee, paid with the handipad, and waited for the order to arrive. He blanked the menu, and the table-top reverted to a black-and-white checkered tile pattern.

He nodded as the server brought his order. That was nice. Actual human service. And he had to give them credit; they were quick. He wolfed the sandwich, barely tasting it as it went down, and then sipped appreciatively at the coffee. It was good. It wasn't espresso, but it would do. He thought about his next steps as he sat there. Slowly, he was starting to come up with the germ of a plan. Some of it relied on luck, but then luck had always been Jack's stock-in-trade.

He finished the last of the coffee, draining the dregs, gratefully pocketed the handipad, and stood. The table, would clean itself. He headed out across the plaza and back to the shuttle stop. There was a Mid-bound shuttle with him in a couple of minutes. He hopped on and made his way to a cor-ner seat, avoiding eye contact with the four other passengers already on board, late workers by the looks of them. Hud-dling in the corner, he pressed his face up against the win-dow, watching the ceiling panels far above them, seeing the fake clouds scudding against the background of a fake moon. He merely glanced at the passing buildings, some fa-miliar, some not. A few had clearly been reprogrammed in his absence. Other passengers came and went on the way down to Mid-Central, but none gave Jack the briefest pause. He remained huddled in his corner, and barely anyone looked at him. He was the last one left when the shuttle pulled into the terminus at Mid-Central.

Jack left his shuttle and crossed over the platforms to Old-bound. Mid-Central was the place where shuttles from Old ended their journey, then sat for a period while they self-cleaned, removing the detritus and damage from the compartments, until ready to head back down into the battlefield of their abuse. The platforms were empty, and Jack leaned back against a wall, waiting for the next one to appear. He tried to fade into the background, because in the Locality, you never quite knew whom any city official or functionary worked for. He had to face it; the word had probably already gone out.

Before long, an Old-bound shuttle whirred into the platform and the doors hissed open. Jack stepped on board and rapidly made his way to the back of the compartment, pulled out the handipad, and shoved it under a seat, deep in the corner. He slipped out of the compartment and watched with satisfaction as the doors slid shut. Let them track him now.

Next stop, the library. Things might be coming together after all. He'd be on foot now, but that suited him too. People didn't walk anywhere in the Locality, well, not any real distance. Outreach would be unlikely to be looking for him on the street. It was quite a hike from Mid-Central, but there was no chance that Jack wouldn't be able to find it. The library was one of the few fixed structures in the Locality, along with some other limited facilities. The rest of the city slowly flowed around it in a slow migration to the decaying end of Old. The self-replicating, semiorganic structure was constantly renewed, maintaining the essential data sources and information links in one fixed location. It was easier to maintain that way, and ensured uninterrupted access, when the rest of the businesses and services were forced to relocate as their buildings shifted and decayed.

On the long walk down, Jack was alone with his thoughts and the echoes of his footsteps. He had a lot to think about, including the hint of guilt he now felt about the last time he had been at the library and the person who worked there. Jack had left without a word. There'd been something there, something, maybe, that could have been more, and he'd just left without saying anything. Typical Jack Stein. Of course, there had been Billie then, the whole Outreach thing, but still . . .

He reached the building and looked across at the stairs, at the huge doors, feeling torn. He had no other choice. None. Steeling himself for the inevitable, he crossed the street and strode up the stairs. Alice would help him. He knew she would.

He stepped up to the doors and . . . they were locked. Dammit, he should have thought. It was late. Alice didn't live at the library, did she? That was, if she even worked there anymore. Stupid Jack.

He banged his palm against the door and winced as the blow jolted through his bruised knuckles.

There wasn't even an echo.

He turned around, scanning nearby buildings, reconciled to holing up in a doorway for the night. It wouldn't be the first time.

Seven

The spatter of raindrops on empty streets brought him awake. The boys in programming had, for some reason, changed moonlit night to light drizzle. Sure, the Locality needed its dose of rainfall, but they really could have chosen a better moment.

Jack huddled tighter into his coat, looking around blearily. It was still too early, and his neck was stiff from the awkward position he'd been sitting in. He'd been dreaming, but he couldn't quite remember what. It had something to do with Billie; he knew that much. In his sleep-muddled state, that gave him an idea. If he could regain the dreamstate, he could try to send a projection to her. It had worked once before, so there was no reason it wouldn't work again. He'd had that strange dream on board the *Amaranth* where he'd seen Billie and Antille's ship, and her sitting there, off in some uncharted system. She'd been aware of his presence then. It was worth a try.

Briefly, he wondered how long he had, what time Alice arrived at the library. He shifted position, trying to find one that was more comfortable in the sheltered doorway, attempting to ease the pressure on his neck, closed his eyes, and willed himself to relax. For a few minutes, he couldn't help fidgeting, restless against the hard pseudo-stone walls.

The waves of sleep descended finally and he found himself drifting in a blank space, aware that he was dreaming, but blank. Jack concentrated, focused his will, and thought of Billie, knowing what he had to do. He pictured himself seeing her, standing in front of her. Clenching his energy, he tried to force the image into being, but the formless void remained just that.

"Dammit, Stein. You can do better than that," his dream self muttered.

Another directed burst of concentration, and there was a slight change in the empty dreamscape around him. Gathering up his will, he pushed again.

Vague shadows took form behind the gray sleep veil, almost there and yet not. Somewhere within that indistinct cloud of shapes was what he sought, and once more, he concentrated on thoughts of Billie. Then, suddenly, the clouds were gone, and there she was. There was one slight problem; it was Billie from before, the young Billie, before her change.

"No, no. This is the wrong one," he said, and tried to will her away.

She looked up at him, an inquiring expression on her young pale face, her blond hair uncharacteristically neat. It was that that told him there was something different, that this was not what he was expecting.

"What's wrong, Jack?" she said. "Aren't you pleased to see me? Why do you want to send me away?"

"I don't want you," said Jack. "I want the real Billie, the *now* Billie."

With those words, she started to change, her figure filling out, her face becoming older.

"No!" said Jack. "Stop. That's not what I meant."

The alteration halted.

"What do you want, Jack?"

For the first time, he noticed figures, in the background,

other, tall, silvery figures, and walls. He was back with the aliens.

There was no reason for him to be there. It could be just dream stuff, echoes of the places he'd been over the past few weeks being dragged from the dark places in his subconscious to populate the dream, but somehow, he didn't think that was what was happening. Testing it, he tried to will the aliens away too, but they remained where they were, standing like burnished coatracks in a dim and gloomy club.

He looked at Billie. He knew that she wasn't really Billie, that she was the image from his memories that the aliens used as a mouthpiece. But it was hard to keep that knowledge at the forefront of his thoughts.

"More to the point," said Jack, "what do you want?"

"I'm going to tell you something," said the fake Billie.

"Okay, I'm waiting," he said.

Several seconds passed, as if she was gathering her thoughts. Then she frowned.

Taking a step forward, she reached up, placed one small hand on his shoulder, and shook.

"Hey," she said. "Hey!"

He tried to move out of reach, out of her grip.

"Are you okay?" a voice said.

There was a hand on his shoulder and it was not Billie's. It shook him again and Jack opened his eyes.

An unfamiliar face was looking down at him.

"Are you okay?" said the voice again. It was coming from the face.

Jack shook his head, caught in that half transition from asleep to awake, and groaned. Pain shot through his neck and shoulder.

"Yeah, I'm fine," he said.

The owner of the voice straightened, looking down at

him with a worried expression. "Well, I suggest you find a better place to sleep it off than in a doorway," said the man. "People have lives to get on with without having to look at you."

"Yeah, thanks," said Jack, levering himself to his feet and brushing off his clothes. "Thanks a lot."

The man gave him one more disapproving look, shook his head, and was on his way, off down the street that Jack had come up the night before. He glanced once back over his shoulder before he disappeared from view. Great, that was all Jack needed—some community-minded citizen ready to report him for cluttering up the neighborhood. He probably presumed that Jack was some denizen of Old, up out of his stamping ground and sleeping off a drunk. It might be smart to vacate the immediate area for a while, just in case the man became a bit *too* community-minded and did report him.

Jack smoothed his coat and looked up and down the street, then across at the library doors, running his fingers through his hair in a half-futile attempt to make himself presentable. The library still looked like it was closed, so he had that much for which to thank the passerby. He glanced at the surrounding buildings, one by one, seeking another place he could stand and wait. He couldn't use the library stairs; they were just too exposed, and by this time, the Outreach boys would have had time enough to get the word out. He never knew when a city patrol might just cruise by.

He waited in the new doorway another thirty minutes, watching as one by one, the numbers of people heading off to their daily rituals increased. After all this time, he was starting to become despondent, and still there was no sign of the librarian. He sniffed at his armpits, but he was okay for now. His stomach gave a growl of protest, reminding him that he hadn't had coffee yet either. Usually that was enough to keep any pangs at bay. For now, he was completely reliant on his seemingly fast-fading luck. Perhaps it hadn't been such a good idea to get rid of that handipad.

He was about to give up all hope, when a half-familiar figure walked briskly up the steps and toward the library's front door. The hair was different, but then you'd expect that after a couple of years. He was pretty sure it was the woman he'd come to see. Checking that there were no city vehicles in sight, he dashed across the street and up the stairs behind her. She was reaching into her bag, pulling out a card of some sort, and he stretched and placed a hand on her shoulder.

"Alice?"

She jumped, and then turned slowly. "What do you . . . Jack? But I thought you—"

"Alice, it is you. I was worried for a minute."

She stood back from him. "After the last time . . . well . . . I thought . . ." And then her face took on a puzzled expression.

"What's happened to you? It is Jack, isn't it?"

"Yeah," he said. "Long story."

He glanced nervously over his shoulder. "Listen, can we get inside? I'll tell you about it there."

She was chewing on her bottom lip, checking him out from head to toe. "Yes, okay. We'd better get you inside." She slipped whatever it was she had been looking for into a pocket and pushed on the door, which swung open easily at her touch. She stepped in, and beckoned Jack to follow.

She was still the Alice he remembered, short, slim, with pale skin. She'd cut her long hair and it sat in a bob, no longer pulled back revealing her face. Slight lines had grown at the corners of her eyes, and there were a few strands of gray starting to creep in, but there was very little else to mark the passage of time since last he'd seen her. As soon as he was inside, she pushed the door shut after him and leaned back against it, her hands behind her, fixing him with a steady gaze.

"It's been a long time, Jack."

He ran his fingers through his hair, feeling sheepish. "Yeah, I know. I guess I should apologize for back then. There was a lot going on, and what with Billie and everything . . ."

"Hmmm."

"Yeah, I know. I know. No excuses."

She wasn't going to let him off that easily, and her expression became sterner.

"So, Jack Stein—you are still calling yourself that?—what brings you to darken my door again?"

"I'm in trouble, Alice."

She gave a short laugh and pushed herself off from her position by the door. "Now, there's a surprise. What is it this time?"

She walked past him into the library proper, not waiting for the explanation.

For the few seconds they'd been standing there talking, Jack had slowly become aware of an underlying hum cutting through the walls. He followed Alice through the large double doors that led into the library itself. The hum was louder here and there was the smell of . . . he couldn't quite put his finger on it. It was sort of like machinery, but different, with a sharp tang about it. Jack stood just inside, his mouth falling open despite himself. He'd forgotten what this place looked like. Not in essence, but certainly in impact. Ranks and ranks of colored walls disappeared into the background, but they weren't just colors; they were iridescent. Bright glowing blues, reds, oranges—all colors imaginable were stacked in tiny cubes, one on top of the other. They filled the vast room from floor to ceiling. Jack let his gaze rove, tracking the lines, seeking some pattern in the ranks of softly glowing color. He remembered standing here on his first visit, doing just that.

Alice had crossed to her desk. A comfortable-looking swivel chair sat behind a kidney-shaped desk with rows of flat screens arrayed before it. She was perched on the edge of the desk, watching him intently.

"What's happened to you, Jack? Or perhaps my memory is playing tricks on me. You seem . . . different."

He closed his mouth and crossed to join her. "Like I said, it's a long story. It's got to do with Outreach—"

"Ha. Our old friends."

"And some alien homeworld."

"Okay. That's new," she said, completely unfazed.

"There's this accumulation of temporal energy if you perform any series of long jumps and it has a certain, apparently random side effect." He swept his arm in a half bow. "And there you have it."

"I'm not sure I really understand, but you can explain it to me in more detail later. For now," she said, looking him over critically, "let me guess. You could do with coffee."

"I could do with more than that, but right now, yeah, that would be great."

"Come on." She got off the desk and headed toward a doorway Jack hadn't seen before. It led to a small kitchen and eating area. She dialed up a coffee and leaned back on a counter, waiting for it to brew, still watching him appraisingly. She had her hands shoved into the pockets of her white coat. He thought he liked the new hair. She seemed to have put on just a little weight too, and it suited her. Jack pulled out a chair and sat. After the night in the doorway and the hurried flight the evening before, he was starting to feel a bit rough. He probably looked it too. He propped his chin on his hands, returning her gaze while they waited for the coffee.

The silence between them was growing, along with Jack's discomfort. He cleared his throat.

"So, how *is* Billie?" asked Alice finally.

Jack wondered whether she was speaking just to fill the empty spaces. He cleared his throat again before answering.

"Yeah, fine. Though she's changed." He gave a wry little laugh. "More than you can imagine."

"Where is she?"

"Back on this world called Utrecht. She was working with this guy at the university there. Xenoarchaeology."

"Really?" she said, sounding interested. "That must be something. I remember, she was very excited by all that sort of thing."

"Mmmm. I don't really get it, myself."

Alice turned to deal with the coffee, and Jack watched her as she moved. She looked good, but then she'd looked good before. He wondered for a moment if the whole body thing had sparked some old urges. Of course they'd always been there, but just now they seemed to be stronger. She turned, holding a coffee mug, and caught him looking. There was the vaguest of smiles as she placed the mug in front of him.

"I hope you like it as is. I don't have anything here."

"Yeah, good," he said. He drank the smell in, savoring, before taking a tentative sip.

Still with that little smile, Alice took a seat opposite, lifting her mug with both hands.

"So, Jack. I think you'd better tell me what's going on."

As he started talking, explaining, the smile quickly slipped away. He told her about the aliens, about the temporal buildup, about Billie's rescue, and about McCreedy. All throughout, she listened attentively, taking the occasional sip from her mug. Finally, he went through the events leading up to his dash from Thorpe and his people.

"So, I don't know who's left in the Locality, Alice. Not anyone I can trust. I thought of you. I'm here without a handipad, without a change of clothes, and with no idea what I'm going to do. I need a place to hole up while I work out my next steps. I know it's a bit of an imposition, but I don't know where else to turn. I guess I'm lucky that you're still here."

She had placed her mug down and was tugging at her lower lip. "And you're sure it's Outreach?" she said.

"Oh yeah. I've had dealings with this Thorpe guy before."

"Hmmm."

She traced her fingers up and down the side of her mug. "You can stay at my place, Jack. I'm probably an idiot, but I don't see any option." She sighed. "And a couple of days later, you'll just wander off and disappear again."

He held up a hand. "No, Alice. It's not like that."

"Whatever you say, Jack. Listen, my place isn't very big, but we'll have to make do."

Jack had a sudden thought. "Is there someone in your life, Alice? Because if there—"

She gave a short laugh. "No, Jack. There's no one in my life, as you put it."

Involuntarily, he briefly narrowed his eyes.

"Oh, don't worry. There have been possibilities. Encounters. Nothing's ever gone very far, though. Currently, I am between . . . arrangements." She looked down into the remains of her coffee and tilted the mug back and forth in her hands.

He decided he'd pursue that one at a more convenient time. Alice was an attractive woman. Did she have some bizarre personality flaw that made things not work out? He stopped that thought right where it lay. Look at yourself, Stein. You should talk.

Alice's apartment was in a reasonably quiet area of Mid, close to the borders of New. It was small, but functional, situated on the seventh floor at a corner of the building. The view from the windows was New-bound. She had decorated the flat in pale blues and whites. She gave him the quick tour, seeming slightly embarrassed. He looked for traces of things that made the space uniquely hers, and reached out with his senses despite himself and despite the exhaustion he felt, but the place was strangely devoid of the hints of energy that spoke of long-term occupancy. Maybe it was just that he was tired.

"How long have you been here?" he asked.

"Oh, only about a year. I moved up when the last place started getting too close to the Old end of the district. It was a pity, I liked the place, but property moves on, you know. Districts change."

He moved across to the window and looked up the broad avenue heading up the Locality's leading edge.

"Nice view."

"It's nice enough," she said, and then she was suddenly all business. "But we need to think about getting you sorted out, Jack. Enough about me. You're going to need some clothes. Perhaps a handipad, but I think we'll need you for that."

He turned from the window and held up his hands. "Hey. All I asked was for a place to stay while I worked out what I was going to do."

"Look at you, Jack," she said. "You're in no state to do anything. Give me your sizes. I'll go out and get a few things. Meanwhile, you get in there and take a shower and then get some sleep. A couple of hours at least."

He frowned, but was in no state to argue. He told her his fitting sizes and she noted them down. "You're sure?" he said.

"Do as you're told, Jack Stein."

He bit his lip.

"When you're cleaned up and you've had some rest, we can get you something to eat and then and only then, you can use my system. I think you need to be thinking clearly."

"Fine," he said. It was no different from being bullied by Billie, but in Alice's case, he was prepared to allow it. "I'll set myself up on the couch."

"You will not. You will sleep in the bed. *In* the bed, Jack. Not on it. Now, the shower's in there. Get going, mister."

"Yes, ma'am," he said with a little grin.

"Good boy," she said, patting him gently on the cheek.

As he headed for the bathroom, she was already checking her handipad and disappearing through the front door, leaving him to do what she'd instructed.

Somehow, all he felt was gratitude, and a growing appreciation. Right at this moment, he was more than lucky.

Eight

As they left the port area, heading for the shuttle stop right at the Locality's tip, Billie watched Dog with interest. He was all wide-eyed and touristy, brushing his hair out of his face, craning his head back to get a good view of the ceiling panels, and scanning all of the buildings they passed.

"And you're telling me this thing's alive?" he asked again.

"Uh-huh. Sort of. They're like little organic machines or something."

Dog shook his head. "Hard to believe."

She grabbed his arm and started dragging him toward the port terminus. He grinned in response and took the opportunity to slip his arm through hers. Billie thought about it for less than a second before deciding she didn't mind. She wasn't going to think about what might happen later, nor the idea that what she was doing was in some way a betrayal of Jack. She glanced at Dog's face, and then looked away again before he had a chance to catch her looking.

All the way across the port, she felt herself seeking some sign that Jack had been there, but how could she tell? She wasn't going to find him just by looking. It was stupid.

Dog gave her arm a little squeeze, but thinking about Jack had taken her back inside herself, and she didn't respond.

Dog was still looking around like a kid at a theme park.

"Haven't you ever been in one of these places?" she asked.

Dog shook his head. "Never had any reason to. It's impressive, but I think I'd feel trapped in a couple of days. People like living this way?"

Billie frowned. "Sure. Why not?"

Dog shrugged. "I don't know. I guess I like the feeling that I can get away. I always want to know where the door is."

They had reached the shuttle stop and she extracted her arm from Dog's grip, pulled out her handipad, and found a nearby seat. Dog watched what she was doing, but stood where he was, turning to take in the surrounds, hands clasped behind his back. It didn't matter that he was so much older than she was—really; he was still a kid, just like Jack was in a lot of ways. It was a guy thing. Had to be.

She turned her attention back to her handipad. The hotel was about halfway down Mid. They'd be there in about fifteen minutes once the shuttle arrived. It wasn't far from the place where she had once shared an apartment with Pinpin Dan, so many years ago now, it seemed. That was a lifetime away, in more ways than one. She thought it was going to be weird being in the old neighborhood. It was going to be even weirder being down in Old proper. She wondered briefly if Daman was still there. Jack's conviction that Daman had been involved in some way with Outreach had given her an idea.

She thumbed off her handipad and slipped it away. The shuttle was entering the platform, so she stood and crossed to join Dog at the platform's edge. He was nodding at the shuttle as it slid to a stop in front of them. The doors hissed quietly open.

"Nice," he said. "And where's this take us?"

"We could go all the way down to Mid-Central if we wanted to," she responded. "But we get off before then."

"What's at Mid-Central?"

She grabbed a piece of his coat and pulled him inside and toward a corner seat.

"It's the interchange. You change there to go down to Old."

The doors hissed shut again and the shuttle whirred into action. It smelled clean and newly fitted just like the shuttles always did at this end of the Locality.

"So, what's in Old?" he asked. "And why 'Old' anyway?"

Billie sighed. "A lot of questions, Dog."

"Yeah, well. I like to know what I'm doing."

She spent a couple of minutes explaining how the Locality grew and decayed, about how Old was the place where things fell apart.

Dog sniffed, looking out at the passing buildings. "Seems to me that it's more than Old where things fall apart."

"What makes you say that?" she asked.

"Doesn't matter," he said. He breathed on the window and drew a pattern in the fog with his finger, crosshatched lines, and then rubbed them out with the heel of his palm.

She glanced out, and noted they were already about a third of the way down Mid. "We get off in a couple of stops," she said.

Dog merely nodded, seemingly wrapped up in his own thoughts. Apparently, the Locality had already lost its fascination.

She dragged him up as she felt the shuttle slowing, indicating they were nearing their stop. The shuttle pulled in and they alighted. Dog watched it as the doors closed and it headed away down toward Mid-Central. He scanned the surrounding buildings, casting a jaded glance at the advertising slogans climbing across lintels and doorways and along the building edges.

He was nodding to himself again. An advertising drone cruised by and, sensing a male presence, hit him with a burst of colored light and noise. He jumped, half crouching and reaching for a nonexistent weapon.

Billie laughed at him.

"Shit," he said, slowly standing upright and working his jaw. He narrowed his eyes at the drone. It had delivered its message and was wobbling off on its way. He turned back to look at Billie.

"Very funny. You might have warned me."

Billie simply laughed again. He narrowed his eyes still farther, and then finally broke into a slow grin. "Yeah, okay," he said. "Where now?"

When they got there, Dog scooting out of the way of an occasional drone en route, they checked into a hotel that was just that, a hotel. It was nothing special and they headed straight to the room, a double. Billie wasn't sure they'd be spending much time here, but it was a base, and it would give her access to the Locality's systems. It was already quite late, but she wanted to check a couple of things out before sleeping. She had options. She could try to track down a couple of Pinpin Dan's old contacts and put the word out, or she could go straight down to Old and see if she could put things in motion. First, she wanted to see if she could identify any likely place where Outreach might be holding Jack, though she thought that was going to be difficult in the Locality, with so much of it owned and controlled by them.

She pulled up a chair and accessed the system. Meanwhile, Dog was sitting on the edge of the bed, bouncing slightly. She could feel him watching her. She ground her teeth and turned to look at him.

"What?"

"Well, I thought you might be coming to bed. It's late."

She sighed. "You go to bed if you want. I've got stuff to do." She turned back to the wallscreen.

"Humph," he said at her back.

She waved her hand behind her. "I'm going to work."

"Fine," he said. "It's late."

"Dog . . ." There was a warning in her tone.

"Okay," he said. "I'm going to the bar. I guess this place has a bar."

She didn't even look as he left the room and closed the door behind him.

Billie was already in bed with the lights out by the time Dog stumbled back into the room. She pulled the covers higher, pretending to be asleep. He headed for the bathroom and the sudden glare from the lights made it through the covers. She heard him emptying his bladder and then struggling with his trousers. She peered through slit eyelids, watching as he removed most of his clothes. There wasn't any harm in looking, was there?

The next moment, the light was gone, and she slipped farther beneath the bedclothes. His weight slid in beside her, shifting her. She could smell the alcohol on him and the other marks of the day and she wrinkled her nose.

"Billie," he said quietly.

She didn't respond.

He grunted to himself and slid closer. One arm moved across her body.

Billie groaned, shifted, putting on the performance, and then lifted his arm away from her.

"Billie?"

"Go to sleep, Dog," she said.

Lying there, the half-naked McCreedy beside her, she was suddenly a little nervous. All she was wearing was a shirt. No. Nothing was going to happen. She'd been thinking about Jack and she had decided. Nothing was going to happen. Not yet, anyway.

He shuffled closer to her, but she moved nearer to the edge of the bed in response.

"Dog, go to sleep," she said again, trying to give him no argument.

He grumbled, but then turned over, his back toward her. Within minutes, he was snoring lightly. Billie stayed awake, listening, a sense of unease working in her abdomen until she too drifted into a troubled sleep.

The next morning, there were only shades of embarrassment between them, but she caught Dog looking at her more than once, and filed it away. Would it have been so bad? Billie berated herself. She shouldn't even be thinking about it. They both had too much to do without getting distracted.

As Dog pulled on his clothes she took the opportunity to look at him anyway.

Both of them looked disheveled and they smelled.

"We need to get some things," she said.

"Yeah," he said, running fingers through his hair. "Have you got any idea what we do then?"

Billie crossed her arms. "Not yet. There are just too many places Jack might be. I couldn't find anything that stood out."

Dog grimaced. "So . . . ?"

"So, I have some places I can look for information that might not be on the systems. I'm all right, but I know some people who are better."

"Okay. Whatever you say."

She could tell that he didn't think much of their chances.

"But now breakfast, okay?" he said. "And you're right, some clothes and other things. We could probably get.some of that right here in the hotel."

"Why?" said Billie. "We're going up there anyway. We may as well do everything there."

"Yeah, I suppose. And we're going to pay for this how?"

Billie pursed her lips and shook her head. "You think I haven't thought of that? As soon as we got in, I linked to the accounts. We've got credits."

"Okay," he said, holding up his hands. "Come on."

Downstairs, they breakfasted in silence. Billie was starting to think there might be problems. Dog was clearly used to getting his own way, but then again, so was she. It was going to be interesting. All the time, she was glancing around, looking at the other people, remembering what it was like to be in the Locality. She had breakfasted in places like this with Pinpin Dan. That wasn't so unusual. The hotel was almost empty, and there were only one or two other guests at the breakfast buffet. When they'd finished, Dog sat back, wiped his mouth, and then flexed his shoulders, as if he was uncomfortable.

"What's wrong?" she asked.

"Bed too soft, I guess. Not used to it. What now?"

"Now we shop."

Dog pushed back his chair, tossing his crumpled napkin down on the table.

"Come on then," he said, but then stopped dead just as he was about to stand, ducking his head slightly.

"Shit," he said under his breath.

"What is it?" Billie asked.

Dog glanced up, behind her shoulder. "That guy over—no, he's gone. I could have sworn . . ."

Billie looked back over her shoulder. "What?"

Dog shook his head. "I might have been imagining it, but I think I just saw someone I recognized."

"Here?" said Billie.

"Yeah." The word was almost a sigh, and he shook his head again.

Nine

Jack slept as if he hadn't slept for years. And maybe in some ways he hadn't. The thought was bizarre, but he didn't want to dwell on the paradox of his own transformation. He struggled awake in Alice's bed to the smell of coffee, taking a few moments to work out exactly where he was. A fresh change of clothes was laid out on a nearby chair. He pulled back the covers and crossed to the chair, holding up and examining the trousers, the shirt. Maybe not what he would have chosen, but they'd do. He dressed and wandered out of the bedroom, feeling better than he had for a while.

"Good morning, Jack," said Alice cheerily from the kitchen.

He walked over and leaned in the doorframe, watching her as she poured coffee and arranged food on plates. She glanced up at him and smiled.

"Yes, not too bad," she said. "I thought they'd suit you. You'll do, Jack Stein."

He looked down at his clothes and couldn't help returning the smile, half-shy beneath her scrutiny.

"So where did you sleep?" he asked.

"That's not important," said Alice. "You looked like you needed the rest."

"Yeah," he said, still wondering. Maybe she'd slept on the couch. If so, she'd already tidied away any sign.

"Come on," she said. "Grab the cups."

He followed her out to a small table and she set the plates down, pulled out a chair, and gestured for him to sit at the other. He placed the cups down, the smell of the coffee teasing his senses. It was real coffee, proper coffee.

As he tucked into the breakfast—strange, he never used to be able to face food in the morning—she watched him, her fork held with one elbow propped on the table.

As he reached for his coffee, she put the fork down. "What are we going to do with you, Jack?"

He paused, the coffee halfway to his lips. "I don't know. I ought to think about getting out of here, getting away. I don't know how the hell I'm going to do that, though. Outreach is everywhere in the damned place."

She reached for her own mug and looked at him thoughtfully over the rim.

"Maybe you don't have to," she said.

Jack shook his head. "How so?"

"Well, if you stay here for a while, keep out of sight, the heat might die down and then you can slip away."

"Yeah, but I'm worried about Billie too," he said. "Hopefully Antille will get through to her, but I can't be sure of that. She's wandering around with McCreedy, and who knows where the hell he's going to take her? Besides, I just can't dump myself on you. It's not fair to you."

She put down her mug and looked at him squarely. "Jack, I don't mind. Really. I'm happy to help."

"I'll pay you back as soon as I—" The narrowing of her eyes was enough to cut him off in midsentence.

"Just tell me what you need, Jack."

He shook his head and bit his lip. "I don't know. Maybe a handipad, but that's going to be hard. I've got to be careful about being seen. I'm sure they're monitoring the sys-

tems too, so I can't really use them either. Shit. A few years
ago and it wouldn't have been an issue. Some of the people
I used to know . . . new identity? No problem." He shook his
head again. "I don't know. I need to think."

"And what about Billie?" Alice asked. "What would
she do?"

"I don't —"

"Well, if you were Billie. Put yourself in her shoes.
What's she likely to do?"

"Come looking."

Alice nodded slowly. "Yes."

Jack ran his fingers back through his hair. "Yeah, fine in
principle, but she's with McCreedy. He's not going to bring
her here, is he? It doesn't make sense."

Alice pushed her chair back, stood, and moved around
behind him, putting her hands on his shoulders and working
her fingers, firmly but gently.

"Listen, Jack. I need to go to work soon. You can stay
here, help yourself to whatever you need. You should be able
to use the system if you're careful. I'll set you up with access before I go. Meanwhile, you can think about what you
need to do, and I'll do some thinking about it too. The library has pretty vast resources and accesses. We might be
able to do some things from there."

He hadn't thought about her having to go to work. She
was right, though; he needed to figure out what he was going
to do.

"You okay?" she said, ruffling the top of his hair with one
hand.

"Yeah," he said. "I'm okay. And, Alice . . . ?"

"Shhh," she said. "Come on. Let's get you set up on the
system."

Jack didn't quite know where this was going, but he wasn't

going to complain about the direction now, neither out-
wardly nor inside. There'd been possibilities between them
a few years back and it looked like that hadn't gone away.
Sometimes you just have that click with a person and it stays
there until it's satisfied or one or both of you realize that it
was some other part of you talking.

Alice walked him through her system. Things hadn't
changed much since he'd last used the Locality's facilities.
Some of the search routines seemed to be a little more intu-
itive, but apart from that . . .

"You're sure you're okay, Jack?"

He nodded.

She looked as if she was going to say something and then
stopped herself. "Okay, I'll see you this afternoon," she said
finally. "Help yourself to anything you want."

Saying nothing, Jack watched her as she picked up her
things and headed out the door. After she left he stared at the
closed door for a long time, thinking.

A while later, he wandered over to the window and
looked out, seeing people heading off to work or shopping
or whatever they did in the morning. What was it like to
have a seminormal life? Whatever it was, Jack Stein didn't
quite fit.

He wandered back into the kitchen and made himself another coffee, poking through cupboards and the freezer,
looking at the sparse little that Alice kept for herself. He felt
no guilt about prying. He wanted to know more about her.
Would Jack fit into her life? Maybe his impressions wouldn't
work if he was to use them for his own ends. He didn't
know; he'd never really done it before.

Halfway through his coffee, he settled back into the living area and called up the wallscreen. There had to be someone from the old life still here and functioning, though how

anybody would react to Jack Stein appearing out of the blue
after so long was another matter. He racked his brain for old
names, old faces. There were those from Locality official-
dom that he'd worked with, but he hardly wanted to alert
them to his presence. There was Francis Gleeson, and he
owed Jack something, but no, the little clerk from Outreach
was just too close to certain people. William Warburg, Anastasia Van der Stegen—other names ticked through his head.
None of them were any use. What he needed were old contacts. Pinpin Dan would have been a name, but there was no
Heironymous Dan anymore; Jack had personally seen to his
demise.

There was a guy who used to work out of the upper end
of Old called Sharkey. Phil Sharkey, that had been his name.
He specialized in getting into places. Jack thought for a moment, but couldn't remember any of his dealings with the
guy going sour, so that was a start. Everyone just called him
Sharkey, and Jack had learned his first name only by acci-
dent. Yeah, it was a possibility. He had a problem, though;
Sharkey did nothing for nothing. Jack would just have to
bluff his way through. He called up the directory function
and put in a call.

Sharkey's dark features swam into view.

"Sharkey," said Jack.

"Jack Stein, shit . . . it's been forever," said Sharkey.

Jack waved his hand and put his finger to his lips.

"Okay," said Sharkey. "Where you been?"

"Away for a while."

Sharkey nodded, knowing better than to ask, and then
rapidly scratched the mat of tight curls covering his head.
"You're looking pretty good." The frown came a moment
later, as if Sharkey suddenly realized that there was something not quite right with the image he was seeing. If he had

questions, he chose not to voice them, though. "So, what can I do for you?" he said after a pause.

"I need some help. I'm kind of out of touch with the network. Thought you might be able to put me on to a couple of people."

Sharkey's eyes narrowed in suspicion. "You working for someone?"

Jack shook his head. "Relax. Nothing like that. I just need to get out of here and need some help doing it. Thought you might know the right faces."

Sharkey tilted his head and looked off to the side, frowning as he ran what Jack was saying through his less-than-sharp gray matter.

"Yeah, okay," he said finally. "How can I help?"

"We've been on too long as it is," said Jack. "Can I come and see you?"

"Sure. Twelve Fifteen Main in Old. Not far from where the old place used to be. Look for a faded blue building. Apartment thirty-six. You called me—you've got the address."

"Yeah," said Jack. "It'll take me about an hour. That okay with you?"

"Sure. It's a bit early for me to be doing anything else. . . ." He grinned.

"Thanks, Sharkey," said Jack. "See you in a while." He cut the connection.

He leaned back and clasped his fingers behind his neck. It was a start. It was almost like being back in the old life. Almost.

That gave him a sudden thought, and he headed into the bedroom. He'd completely forgotten about the weapon he'd removed from Gray Suit back at the port and he couldn't remember what he'd done with it. Last thing he remembered, he'd had it shoved in the back of his waistband. He'd pulled it out and put it on the bedside cabinet when he'd gone to take the shower, and then it had slipped from his memory along with all other thoughts as he'd succumbed to sleep.

It wasn't on the cabinet, and a quick search of his coat gave no joy either. Jack scratched the back of his head and grimaced. Alice must have found it and put it somewhere. He opened the bedside cabinet, but it wasn't there either. Where would he put a gun if he were Alice? The truth was, he had no idea.

He made a perfunctory search of the apartment, but then decided, only half reluctantly, that he didn't really need the thing anyway. If he could get away without using a weapon, then that suited Jack just fine. He doubted he'd need it with Sharkey. It would be a sure way to get Sharkey to close up tighter than a trap.

Finding Sharkey's place was no problem at all. As he'd said, it was almost where he used to live, the same geographic location, just a different building. The pale blue was easy to spot.

Coat pulled tight around him, Jack stood across the road watching for a few minutes, trying to feel for any threat with his inner senses. Nothing tugged at him, so he did a quick stride across the street and approached the building's entrance. A few wide steps led up to a battered set of double doors. Looking either way, he climbed the steps quickly and slipped in through the half-open door. Inside, the smell of old buildings and the sharp ammoniacal taste of derelict humanity washed into his face, causing him to wrinkle his nose. Yeah, very little had changed about where Sharkey lived. If he didn't know better, he could almost think that it was the very same building.

The resident display was patchy, and Jack ran his finger

up the list, avoiding actually touching the wall. Number thirty-six had no name listed. Jack nodded to himself.

Something was touching him at the back of his neck, a prickling, and he stood, looking around. An empty feeling opened up in the base of his stomach. He glanced around, seeking the source of unease. He knew better than to ignore the sensation. He ducked his head around the corner, looking up the hallway where the elevator lay, but the place was empty, just an unidentifiable lump of something about halfway along against the poisonous green walls. A thick door lay at the other end, faded deep red with a small dirty window set high. He looked out to the road, but there was no movement, no traffic. Jack frowned, trying to shake the feeling away. What the hell was going on? Maybe his senses were just kicking in, flexing from lack of use. Not good, Jack. He needed to be able to rely on himself at least.

Grumbling to himself about his quiescent abilities, Jack headed for the elevator. Some sort of psychic detective he was turning out to be. It was almost as if his interaction with the aliens had drained half of his capacity. He was starting to miss the spontaneous prompts, which was funny; he'd always seen them as a sort of semicurse. Halfway along the hallway, a staircase led up. An alluvial fan of dust spread out from the bottom step, a mark of the building's growing deterioration. There were things you forgot when you'd been away from a place for a while.

A noise from the steps stopped him in his tracks and he looked up slowly.

A figure stood on the stairs, weapon leveled.

"Hello, Stein," said the gray-suited muscle from the docks. "We've got some unfinished business."

Jack didn't like the implications of the grin on the guy's

face. He was decked out in a dark brown suit this time. He took one slow step, then another.

Jack glanced sidelong at the other end of the hallway, assessing his options. The door was too far away. The door at the opposite end looked like it was locked tight. Apart from that, there was only the elevator. Jack backed against the wall, cursing himself for not having bothered with the weapon back at Alice's place. Jack looked quickly again toward the front doors. A vehicle had pulled up outside, and two men in suits emerged, striding quickly up the front steps.

The other guy had seen them too and he covered the last few steps quickly, crossing the hall and standing right in front of Jack, a sneer on his face now marking his agenda.

"Sorry about this, *friend*," he said, smashing the butt of his weapon up into Jack's chin. Jack's head smacked back against the wall, filling his skull with light. Through screwed-up eyes he saw the gun being drawn back for another blow.

"Madsen, that's *enough*!" shouted Thorpe.

But by then, Jack didn't really care. His head was ringing, pain lancing from his jaw. He barely registered the tightly curled hair and dark features peering down at him from the corner of the staircase above—Sharkey; thanks, Phil. The man who had struck him grabbed his arm and hustled him toward the door.

Ten

Billie knew there was no real option, no matter how un-comfortable it made her feel. She wasn't going to find what she needed without venturing down to Old. There were too many memories down there, stuff she didn't really want to remember, stuff that she'd put away in little boxes inside her head, wrapped up tightly and out of sight. She didn't know either how Dog would take to Old and how Old would take to him. Nor was she certain that she wanted to risk some of the things Dog might find out about her in Old. All that stuff was a lifetime away, several lifetimes.

So why was she taking Dog?

She knew the reasons. She needed him there, not only for what he could do, but for a feeling of security, which made no sense in itself, but it made her feel better.

He was watching her, but she knew that there was no way he could read the tumble of thoughts and emotions that was going on inside her head. Billie was good at masking what she was thinking. She'd learned that particular skill a long time ago.

As they headed for the shuttle stop, Dog was no longer caught up in his wide-eyed-visitor mode; he seemed wary and watchful, tense. There was something going on with him, but she didn't have the space to think about it now. There were more important things to worry about. She thought about going back to the hotel and tapping into the system to try to track down Daman, Pablo, the others she used to know down there. Pablo in particular was careful, however, and he knew how to hide their traces. It was only those that needed to know who ended up finding them, and those who needed to know were an essential part of the way the Locality worked. She decided it was just as quick to get on the shuttle and find them herself.

Dog tore his attention from the ceiling panels and scanned the surrounding people.

"You think they're happy?" he said.

"What?"

"Do you think they're happy? I just couldn't see myself living like this. It's pretty artificial."

She stared at him for a couple of seconds. "I don't know. Isn't everywhere?"

He ran his fingers through his hair and then tugged at his bottom lip before answering. "Yeah, I guess you're right in a way. Okay, let me ask it like this. Were you happy here?"

Billie shrugged. "Kinda."

Thankfully, their shuttle was approaching, and she indicated it with a thrust of her chin, cutting off the line of questioning. Let Dog McCreedy work that stuff out for himself. Something had snagged his attention anyway. He was staring down the street, his eyes slightly narrowed.

The shuttle pulled into the stop and they climbed aboard, Dog leaning against the edge of the frame, watching as the doors slid shut. It was only a short hop down to Mid-Central, so she didn't even bother looking for a seat. As the shuttle eased out, Dog pressed his face up against the door. He spent the short journey leaning on a handrail, bent down to watch the passing streets, buildings, and people. Billie watched him thoughtfully. Whatever was troubling him right

now, he was becoming just a little too curious. Well, maybe
their visit to Old would do something to satisfy that curiosity.

At Mid-Central, they boarded an Old-bound shuttle and
Billie led him to a seat at the back of the compartment.
There wasn't much to distinguish this shuttle from the one
they'd just ridden from the New end of town, but by the time
it made the return journey, it would collect its burden of Old
detritus, marks and leavings. It was almost as if Old tried to
infect New with its decay, using the shuttles as carriers, but
the Locality's automated cleaning routines never let it, acting as a virtual prophylactic to the realities that lay below.

As they whirred along toward the district where Billie
thought they might find what they were looking for, the
decay started to become apparent on building walls and
the streets themselves. The sharp lines became smudged, the
gloss became tarnished, and the streets started to be specked
with the marks of those that had passed upon them. As the
Locality's substance crept toward the far end of Old, the
city's builders and maintenance routines lost the capacity to
keep up, to repair and to clean. Right at the far end, it was
all swept away and reprocessed, fed up toward the regrowth
at the front, but the builders had only a certain life span. Arterial routes ran from that far end up to the tip, carrying anything that could be reused and recycled, consuming
whatever there was to be consumed.

"So where are we going?" asked Dog, finally interested
in something other than watching what was outside or surreptitiously watching her.

"I used to know some people down here," she said.

"And?"

"That's all. If they're still here, then maybe they can
help us."

Dog's eyes questioned. "Why would they do that?"

Billie sighed. "Because they would."

"Hmmm," said Dog doubtfully, turning his attention to the window again.

Billie knew the sort of life Dog led, the expectations of the people he dealt with. Nobody did anything for nothing. That was Dog's philosophy. She had known people like that before. She glanced at him for a second. So what was he doing here? She thought she knew, but there was no way of really knowing if she was right. Not yet, anyway.

She turned her own attention to the passing streets. If Daman and the crew were down here anywhere, they wouldn't be too far down. Pablo liked to play, and the programming would be harder the farther down Old you got. Somewhere in the middle of Old would be the most likely, and here was as good a place as any to start. She gave Dog's sleeve a tug and stood as the shuttle started to slow.

They stood outside together, the shuttle's sound receding down the street as Billie got her bearings. The slight hum and whirr was replaced by the low creaks of buildings in a steady state of decline. A line of lights flickered up the side of one tall building on the opposite side of the street, sputtering with shapes that had once spelled out words but were now unreadable.

"Nice . . . ," said Dog.

Farther down, even the street lighting would become intermittent, strobing across the random urban landscape that the Locality had become.

Billie surveyed the surrounding streets, looking for any movement, any sign of a local presence, but the area was pretty dead.

"Come on," she said. "This way."

A block farther on, and a shape moved in a doorway. She peered into the shadows, but whatever it had been had

disappeared from view. She set her lips in a tight line and
shook her head. It had been either a person or an animal.
This far down, the Locality had its own wildlife, and only
half of it wasn't people. She moved closer to Dog and
started to walk more slowly, scanning every shadowed en-
tryway and side street as they walked. Dog seemed to notice
her tension and it was reflected in his movements. She could
almost feel a coiling within him, a tightening of his awareness, ready to spring into action if he needed it at a moment's notice. It reminded her of the way he'd reacted up in
New when he'd been surprised by the advertising drone. It
said a lot more about him than he did himself, and in a funny
way, it gave her a sense of comfortable security.

They kept walking, Billie keeping her eyes and ears open
for anything that would give away the presence of those she
sought. Glimmers of light, hints of movement, came from
some of the surrounding buildings, but she knew they marked
the presence of those alone or destitute, drawn away in the
warm comfort of solitary darkness. They were not the ones
she was seeking. Wherever Daman had set up operations, it
was going to be on the main strip, accessible, yet not overt.

Dog cleared his throat. "Do we know what we're looking for?"

Billie shushed him with one hand. They were being
watched; she could feel it. As far as she was concerned, that
was a good thing.

"Somewhere around here," she said quietly. She could
see the vague impression of light issuing from a doorway
farther down the block. "This way," she said.

She led Dog down to the doorway in question and
stepped inside boldly, searching the gloom of what had once
been a grand lobby. There were still traces of shiny marbled
surfaces, though mottled and powdery now. There was still

furniture—couches, large chairs—and it made the place look like a vague pencil sketch of what it should have looked like. As her eyes adjusted, she became aware of a figure sitting in one of the chairs, watching them silently, a youth of about fifteen, sixteen. It was hard to tell. As her vision became clearer, she could tell the furniture was new, programmed into place, rather than a legacy of the building's past incarnation.

The boy in the chair said nothing, big dark eyes just watching, the thin sallow face devoid of expression, strands of dark hair flopping around his ears. He wore a shapeless colorless top and pants, almost fading into the grayness of the background.

"Hey," she said. Behind her, she reached back with one hand, patting Dog on the arm, signaling for him to leave this to her.

The boy lowered his face and then looked up again, taking a couple of moments before answering. Billie was starting to sense the presence of others off from the lobby.

"What do you want?" he said. His voice was high, soft.

Billie looked around the lobby, making a show of taking in the details. "This is different from the old place," she said. "I want to see Pablo."

Another figure stepped from the shadows behind the chair. He was older by a couple of years, and he held himself with confidence.

"Who is Pablo, and who are you?" said the new boy.

"You know who Pablo is," said Billie.

"Nuh-uh," he said. "Who are you? What do you want here?" He remained hanging back in the shadows, half-defined in the darkness. The boy in the chair kept watching them with those big wide eyes, saying nothing.

"Okay," said Billie. "We're not here for business. Tell Daman that Billie's here to see him. I'm an old friend."

"Friend" was not exactly the right word, but it would do for now. It conveyed what she needed it to convey.

"Are you two from ALM? You don't look like the type."

"ALM? I don't know what you're talking about. Just tell Daman, will you?"

The boy considered and then muttered something to someone in the darkness behind him.

Billie knew there was nothing more to do than wait. Either Daman was still here or he wasn't.

The silence around them stretched like the shadows, punctuated only by the creaks and groans of the structures around them and the noise of pseudo-leather adjusting to a shift in the first boy's weight. Briefly, she wondered what ALM was, running the possibilities through her head. She could sense Dog moving uneasily behind her, becoming impatient, and again she reached with one hand to reassure him. Any sudden actions on his part could be dangerous right now.

They didn't have long to wait. A presence stirred the darkness and then a young man walked into the room, trailed by two others. Billie recognized Daman immediately, the way he held himself, the clothes, strangely out of character with his age, the hands clasped behind his back as he walked.

"Hello, Diamantis," she said quietly.

Daman stopped halfway across from them and looked her up and down. "Who are you? You're not Billie. What do you want?"

"Look closer," said Billie, and took a step forward.

The two who accompanied Daman—she didn't recognize either of them—stepped from behind him protectively.

Daman held up a hand. "No, wait," he said. "You . . . ," he said, addressing Billie, "come closer. He can stand over there," he said, gesturing at Dog.

Dog took the instruction and walked a few paces to the side where Daman had indicated.

Daman nodded and, returning his hand to its place behind his back, took another couple of steps forward, peering at Billie, a slight frown marking his brow. "Indeed, there is something familiar about you. Who are you really?"

"I'm Billie, Daman. Where's Pablo?"

Daman's frown deepened. "Pablo's not here anymore. What do you know of Pablo?"

"What happened?"

Again, he withdrew one of his hands and waved her question away.

"Talk to me," he said. "Tell me something."

"Uncle Pinpin," she said. "Uncle Jack. Outreach."

Daman narrowed his eyes. "Go on."

"No more. Just talk to me, Daman."

He grimaced, looking over at Dog. "And him?"

"He's a friend."

Daman stood, his lips pursed, breathing heavily through his nose.

"So what are you doing here? What do you want?"

"I need help to find Jack Stein. He's here in the Locality somewhere. Outreach has taken him, just like they took me back then. I have to get him back. It's important." The words all came in a rush as she tried to get them out before Daman cut her off. "I was hoping Pablo was here. He'd know how to find him."

Something dark crossed Daman's face, then disappeared again.

"If you are Billie, and I am not convinced yet, you will know some things—"

"Dammit, Daman. We're Family," she said.

He flinched and one of the other youths glanced at him quickly. Daman took another step, peering into her face.

"What did you say?" he said slowly.

"Didn't you always say that Family looked after each other?"

He blinked a couple of times in rapid succession and turned on his heel. "Come," he said, and headed toward the doorway from which he'd emerged. The other two youths stepped out of the way to let her follow. Billie beckoned to Dog, but Daman, as if sensing what she was doing, turned quickly to look over his shoulder.

"Not him," he said.

Billie knew better than to protest. What Daman said went, and she only hoped Dog would behave himself until she could convince Daman that it was all right to have brought him here.

Eleven

They sat across from each other in standard chairs, grown at comfortable locations across what had once been an open office space. It was strange for Billie seeing Daman, the others, in an environment like this. She guessed that they slept, ate, and did other things on other levels. She also guessed that the "private" rooms were also somewhere else, maybe below. Nobody had really screwed with the building's programming; nobody had constructed sculpted and mobile shapes across the walls and floors, turning the place into an animate wonderland. She scanned the formlessness, the ordinary, shaking her head.

"What happened to Pablo?" she said finally.

Daman was studying her, his hands folded in his lap, his blank expression punctuated by the occasional blink as if he was still processing what he was seeing. He seemed to shake himself back to awareness.

"We lost him about two years ago."

"How?" she asked.

"I don't want to talk about that," said Daman. The words were short, clipped. He stared at her for a couple of seconds, then rose and crossed to stand in front of her. Hesitantly, he reached out his hand and traced the edge of her cheek with the tips of his fingers, then withdrew the hand and clasped it behind his back.

"I can see Billie in you. Tell me what happened."

"I don't know," she said.

Daman shook his head and circled her chair, then walked slowly back to his own. He sat again, watching her face.

"I find that improbable," he said. "If you are Billie, then something must have happened. I need to know what it is. I also need to know who that person is you have brought here."

Billie sighed. "I'm sorry, Daman. That's Dog McCreedy. He's helping me. He doesn't come from the Locality. He's a pilot."

He clasped his fingers in front of his face, peering at her over the tops of his fingers. "And," he said slowly, "what happened to you?"

There was silence except for the building noises while Billie debated with herself how much she wanted to reveal. Finally, she took a deep breath, choosing her words as carefully as she could. "I really don't know. It had something to do with the jump."

A slight narrowing of Daman's eyes, and he said a single word. "Jump?"

"You know, on a ship. Jump space or something. Something to do with temporal energy. I can't explain it."

Daman muttered something to himself, his gaze pinned somewhere in the distance.

"What?"

"Like when you first step through," he said quietly.

She didn't get it.

"I know what you're talking about," said Daman. "I know exactly what you're talking about."

He seemed to take possession of himself once more and he leaned back.

"But that's not important for the moment. First, what are you doing here? Really?"

"I told you. Outreach has taken Jack. They've taken him somewhere here in the Locality. I thought Pablo might be able to help me find where they've taken him. But if Pablo isn't here . . ." Billie caught her lower lip between her teeth. "I don't know then. Is there someone else who does the things that Pablo—"

"You're sure it's Outreach?" he said, interrupting her.

"Uh-huh, I'm sure . . ."

"Hmmmm." His gaze took on that faraway look again. "You've got a system here, you have to. Perhaps whoever took over for Pablo—"

"Silas," said Daman distractedly.

"Perhaps Silas can help me find what I'm looking for. Let me use the system. Show me some of the routines."

"Why is this so important?" said Daman, frowning.

Billie didn't want to tell him about the whole mess with the ship and the alien homeworld. It just made her feel stupid. And she didn't want to feel stupid, particularly in front of Daman.

"Because . . ." She thought about it. "Because Jack's Family, Daman. Jack's Family too." And she heard the truth in her own words. "You're going to think I'm crazy but . . . Jack's been in contact with an alien race. They have knowledge about the jump drive, about the temporal energy, about other stuff, maybe more. Outreach wants to try to get it out of him. They want to keep the knowledge to themselves and use it to increase their power. There's another group too, who call themselves the Sons of Utrecht. But, right now, Outreach has Jack. We have to get him away from them."

"And then what?"

Billie met his gaze blankly. She didn't know. She hadn't thought that far.

Daman made a show of studying his fingernails. "I know quite a lot about Outreach," he said.

Billie sat forward. "Then you know why we've got to do this. Look at this place, Daman. Look at me. Look at you. Look at the Locality. Look at what it does to people."

He lifted his head slowly to face her. "Things are changing, Billie." It was the first time he'd used her name.

"What does that mean?" she said.

"Just that. Things are changing." He shook his head and whistled, low, through his teeth, and one of the youths who had accompanied him before appeared from the other side of the room.

"Bring the other one," said Daman. The boy disappeared again.

Daman said only one more thing while they waited for McCreedy to appear.

"People do things to themselves, Billie. Outreach helps them. Outreach simply helps."

They didn't have too long to wait. A couple of minutes passed and the boy led Dog McCreedy into the room. Dog shrugged his arm free and crossed to stand behind Billie's chair, placing one hand on her shoulder.

"You okay?"

"Uh-huh."

"Take a chair, Mr. McCreedy," said Daman, indicating a vacant seat in the cluster of chairs they were occupying.

Dog looked down at Billie, then nodded and sat, sprawling back in the chair, one arm draped over the side.

"So what is this?" he said.

Daman lifted a finger to his lips.

"Why are you here, Mr. McCreedy?"

"Dog," he said. "I'm here for Billie."

"And you're a pilot."

"Yeah, I'm a pilot. What of it?"

Daman watched him expressionlessly. "So what use can you be to her here?" He let the question hang while Dog struggled for an answer.

"I asked him," said Billie.

"Shhh," said Daman. "Let him tell me."

"I can do other things apart from fly a ship," said Dog.

Daman stood and started pacing, circuiting Dog's chair. "Perhaps you can. But why would you bother coming here? What can you possibly do in a place that means nothing to you, in a place where you can know no one?"

"I can make sure Billie's all right."

"And what else, Mr. McCreedy?"

Dog lost the slouch and tried to track Daman as he circled the chair.

"Listen, Jack and I go way back. It's half my fault that he's in this fix at the moment. I want to help."

Somehow, Dog had realized that it was important to convince Daman of what he was saying.

Daman nodded as he walked. "And how do you mean it's half your fault?"

"Well . . ."

Billie could almost see the thoughts racing through Dog's head.

"If I hadn't agreed to take him on my ship, if we hadn't done all those jumps, we wouldn't be here now. I kinda feel responsible."

Daman stopped and turned slowly. "Do you?"

Dog stood now. "Yeah, what of it? I don't see why we have to put up with this questioning from a kid."

Daman gave a low chuckle. "Not everything is always as it seems. You should know that." He turned away.

Dog gave an exasperated growl and retook his seat.

"Okay," he said. "Okay." He glanced across at Billie, a questioning expression on his face. She half lifted a hand and he gave a blink of understanding.

"All right," said Daman finally. "We will do what we can." He spun to face McCreedy. "But be warned, Mr. McCreedy. Billie has a place here. You do not. Bear that in mind."

"Call me Dog. And yeah, I get it."

Daman crossed back to his chair and sat. He leaned forward, fingers steepled in front of him.

"All right, Billie. I think you should tell me more. I want to know what happened and how it happened, in detail." He caught the look of protest on her face. "I have my own reasons. Just humor me. Then we can think about our next steps. I too am eager to speak with Jack Stein."

Billie saw that she had little choice if they were going to get help from Daman, and taking a deep breath, she began filling in the details of their story.

Later, Daman introduced them both to Silas. Silas was maybe thirteen, pale, with pinched features and a faraway look in the eyes. In some ways, he reminded Billie of herself at that age. He was no Pablo. Pablo had been full of self-confidence born of faith in his own genius, and the creative flair he mined to play with what he did. Billie could tell Silas was serious and damaged.

She knew Daman was different, special, and she'd never really subjected Daman's role in the Family to much thought. He found these kids, he looked after them, made sure they were protected, and yet, at the same time, he exposed them in ways no child should be exposed. She watched him as he explained to Silas what Billie needed. She remembered that old-man paternalistic stance and tone from her own time down here. She had respected Daman, looked up to him, just like the rest of the Family. And yet . . . there had been Pinpin Dan and the string of others, and Daman had allowed all that to happen. In some ways, he had engineered it. Should she hate him for it? She didn't know.

"I'm going to need your help on the system, Silas," she said. "I need to know what routines you've set up and what access bridges you've got going. How much entry to Locality systems you really have and the tools you've got in case we need to break into them."

Silas nodded gravely, glancing to Daman for reassurance. Daman gave him a quick nod in return. "Billie used to be one of us," he told him.

Silas looked at Billie, back at Daman, and then turned to look at her again.

"Okay," he said.

The lights in the room stuttered, flashing shadows across the pale young face. Silas and Daman barely seemed to notice. Dog was glancing around the room.

"Good," said Billie. "Show me where you're set up, Silas."

"Anywhere," said Silas. He could manipulate the system from any wall in the place, within the limits of how well the structure still functioned. They were far enough up Old that it shouldn't be too much of an issue.

"Have you got a room we can use?" she asked.

Silas gave one of his big serious nods.

"Show me," she said.

She looked at Dog and then at Daman, making sure that Daman would look after him. Daman gave her a brief half smile and Billie turned back to Silas, who reached for her hand and led her toward the back of the building. Billie, for now, didn't want to be interrupted, and she was grateful for

the flickering, empty space that would separate them from
the others. The last thing she saw was Daman placing a hand
on Dog's shoulder and steering him away into a different
sort of darkness—a darkness populated with the shades and
shadows of her own past.

Twelve

In the back of the vehicle, Jack worked his jaw, swallowing back the flat, metallic taste of blood trickling into his mouth. The explosion of pain had dulled to a deep throb, hard and bruised. His face was going to be uncomfortable for a couple of days. He prodded at the place gingerly with his fingertips. Thorpe sat up front. Beside him, crowded close was the guy who'd hit him. He was watching Jack, smiling knowingly at Jack's proddings. He didn't say anything; he didn't have to.

"So what now, Thorpe?" Jack said. "I don't know what you think you're going to do with me."

Thorpe peered back over his shoulder, turning slightly so that he could look at Jack full in the face. "What now is that you'll be taken to a place we've prepared for you. I suggest you don't try any more foolish stunts, Mr. Stein. We'll only find you again and bring you back. And we'd prefer to have you in one piece." He glanced significantly at the man sitting beside Jack and then returned his focus to Jack. "We really don't want to make things any more uncomfortable for you than they have to be."

Jack narrowed his eyes. Yeah, right.

He looked away from Thorpe and turned to watch the streets outside, trying to work out where he was. The last time he'd been spirited away, they'd taken him to a holding facility in one of the parks toward the upper end of Mid, but this time, they seemed to be heading in a completely different direction. Of course, the Locality had changed in the interim, so much of what they passed was unfamiliar. The direction was clear, though. They were heading up toward New. He could feel Thorpe watching him from the front seat, assessing, but he wasn't going to acknowledge it. And Sharkey . . . Sharkey had been in on the setup. It was the last thing he would have expected. Maybe they hadn't given him any choice. It still didn't excuse it, though. A certain class of the Locality's population was supposed to stick together.

Jack's thoughts turned to Billie. He hoped she wasn't doing anything really stupid. Would she come back here to the Locality looking for him? Who knew . . . especially with McCreedy in the picture? Inwardly, he sighed. He seemed to spend half his life digging her out of trouble. Of course, half that trouble was his own fault, but still . . .

Gradually, the streets and buildings grew cleaner, slick and hard like the facade that Outreach wore as a mantle, disguising the reality that lay within. Jack pressed his teeth together tightly at the thought and immediately winced, regretting the action. There was a dull pounding growing in his head, echoing the throbbing in his jaw. Damn them. Damn Outreach and damn McCreedy and damn the aliens as well. What was it about the Locality that maintained such a hold on his life? Whatever he did, he just didn't seem to be able to escape it.

The vehicle turned, veering into a side street and heading away from the Locality's center. Wherever they were taking him, it was out toward the edge, out near the very walls that separated the population from the outside world. Not many people ventured out that way. The vast, shiny, semitransparent walls reminded people of the hive nature of the existence they led. Jack had been that close only once or twice during his whole time in the Locality. People lived out near the walls, but their buildings faced away from the outside, looking inward. Mainly, there were offices, and storage facilities, the occasional maintenance station, rather than residential complexes. Most of the living spaces were nearer the Locality's spine, where the ceiling panels were far above, giving the illusion of real sky if you half closed your eyes and forgot about the armies of tiny builders working within.

They pulled up in front of a blank wall on an empty street. Jack tilted his head to try to get a better look around Thorpe's shoulder, but there was nothing to see. No people, no doorways, nothing. It would be stupid to try to make a break for it here, and he doubted whether they'd let him get away with a similar performance again. Thorpe got out of the transport and stood by the door. The guy next to Jack got out, crossed behind the vehicle, and opened Jack's door, gesturing with a tilt of his head for Jack to step out. With a grimace, Jack complied and stood, verifying his first impressions as the door closed and the transport took off up the street.

"This way, Mr. Stein," said Thorpe, walking toward the wall closest to the Locality's outer edge. "Your new home, at least for a while."

The other man, Madsen, made to grab at Jack's arm, but Jack wasn't going to give him the pleasure. He slipped from the grasp and stepped quickly after Thorpe, joining him in front of a featureless expanse of wall.

Thorpe was looking up expectantly, and a moment later, the previously smooth surface broke in a thin line, revealing a wide door that slid back out of sight. Thorpe stepped through the doorway, and taking the obvious cue, Jack followed. Madsen quickly brought up the rear. Almost soundlessly, the door slid back into place behind them, merging with the rest of the wall until there was nothing to show that there'd ever been a door there at all.

They stood in a small passageway, dimly illuminated, leading farther into whatever this complex was. If it had existed before, back when Jack lived in the Locality, he'd had no knowledge of it. He doubted that it had been here back then. It would have shifted down and away toward Old. No, this place was new.

Thorpe led the way, walking briskly down the corridor, coming to a junction, and then turning right. Jack followed without a word, not giving Madsen an excuse. Even the smallest victory was a victory right now.

The next corridor ended at a door, which opened at their approach, and Thorpe stepped through and crossed slowly to the center of a small room set with a table and chairs. He turned and placed a hand on the back of one of the chairs.

"I'll take you to meet the people in a moment," said Thorpe. "But for now, I just want to say something. We are all here to do a job, Mr. Stein, nothing more. We are very interested in achieving results as soon as possible. I know that this is inconvenient for you and you may resent your presence here, but it would not be a good idea to take out those frustrations on the people you'll be dealing with. You've made things difficult for us in the past, but we're prepared to forgive those lapses of judgment. What's past is past. All that matters is the now. And, of course, trying to escape would be foolish. There's no way out." He removed his hand from the chair and turned, stepping across to a door on the other side of the room. "This way. I'll show you your accommodations."

Accommodations, was it? Nice.

Completely ignoring Madsen behind him, Jack stepped around the table to join Thorpe on the other side.

Leading him down another corridor, Thorpe spoke conversationally over his shoulder.

"Jack, I know you might not agree with what we're doing, but think of it this way. In the end, we're working for the common good. Whatever benefit we gain from this exercise is good for all of us in the long run. The potential benefits are enormous."

"And you really believe that, Thorpe? Or is that just some sort of corporatespeak meant to salve your conscience? I don't buy it."

"I'm sorry you feel like that, Jack."

"Yeah, well. You don't have to make me feel better. If it's trying to make you feel good about yourself, I hope it's working."

Thorpe lapsed into an unimpressed silence.

He led them to another room, much larger than the first one, where two other people awaited them. The first, a thin-faced woman with dark hair cropped short and deep-hollowed eyes, stood with her hands clasped in front of her. The second, standing slightly behind, a man, slightly overweight and with a round, flat face and button nose, watched Jack with interest as he entered the room. Jack could feel himself being studied.

"And who are they, then?" said Jack.

Thorpe turned to face him. "These are Doctors Lagrange and Hart," he said, indicating first the woman and then the man. "They will be monitoring and working with you over the days to come."

The woman nodded, but the man made no response, just kept watching him intently. Jack was starting to become uncomfortable under that gaze.

"And there," continued Thorpe with a wave of his hand, "is where you'll be staying."

Jack turned to look where Thorpe was indicating. For the first time, he noticed a row of chairs fixed in place, facing one of the walls. The wall itself seemed to shimmer, and then, an instant later, disappear. The surface had become transparent, revealing another set of rooms beyond. Doorways led from a main room that sat directly in front of him. In the room's very center sat a sleep couch, a small table beside it, some inducer pads. The whole setup was uncomfortably familiar. Jesus, they'd gone to the trouble of replicating his old working office from the Locality. Even the sleep couch was the same design, the same color, everything.

He turned to Thorpe. "And what's this supposed to be?"

"We thought you'd be more comfortable in an environment you were used to," said Thorpe. "Anything you want to change, just let us know."

Jack could see exactly where this was going. "Yeah, Thorpe, for starters, how about letting me out of here and disappearing from my life? How would that be?"

Thorpe gave a little smile and shook his head, not bothering to grace him with a response. "Let us show you the rest," he said.

As a party, they trooped through a doorway and another immediately after, which led into the room that had been revealed through the wall. They stepped through, and Jack scanned the room quickly. It was good, damned good. It even smelled like his old rooms.

Across the other side lay a bedroom, bathroom, kitchen area, living space, all designed to look like his old place.

"You can, of course, program the facilities just like you would an ordinary apartment," said Thorpe. "Now, is there anything you'd like to know?"

Jack's resentment was growing, along with a sense of resignation. For now, he knew, there was little option except playing along.

"What do you want, Thorpe? What do you think I can do?"

"We know about your abilities. We know about your contacts, Jack. Dr. Lagrange and Dr. Hart will fill you in on the program, what we hope to achieve."

"And what if I refuse to play along?"

"Then you will be here longer than we'd hoped."

No matter what Thorpe was saying, Jack didn't believe Outreach would have any plans to let him free any time soon. He remembered what they'd done to Gil Ronschke. They had a way of making people disappear and then keeping them disappeared. Jack ground his jaw and let out a deep breath. "I don't know where you guys think you have the right—"

Thorpe held up a hand. "I have to leave you in the capable hands of the good doctors now, Jack. I hope you'll be comfortable. I wish you every success."

He walked past Jack toward the outer door, Madsen trailing behind. Just before stepping from view, Thorpe turned.

"Sweet dreams, Mr. Stein," he said.

Jack suppressed a growl. Smart guy.

Jack looked at the pair he'd been left with, then turned away from them. The man was still scrutinizing him like a specimen, and he did not like the feeling it gave him.

He walked back out to the office space, the room with the sleep couch, and looked around. He could almost imagine himself back in his old office, almost. There was one thing that stood in the way of the complete illusion. Apart from the slightest differences in layout, differences that could be written off as whims of programming, the opposite wall was incongruous, slightly shiny, almost metallic. Vague traces of reflection moved in the surface, mirroring the room, mirroring Jack and the pair behind him. Beyond that wall, Jack knew, lay the observation area, the fixed chairs. He was going to be watched, observed, by who knew how many, and the thought didn't make him comfortable at all. It looked like, in the meantime, all he was going to have for company was his smudged reflection in a vaguely mirrored wall. Great.

He turned to look at the doctors. "Okay," he said. "You two want to leave me alone for a while? I need some time to get used to the idea."

He pushed past them into the bedroom and sat on the edge of the bed, his elbows on his knees, his face propped in his hands, not even looking at them.

They left in silence, at least granting him that much.

After they had gone, he gazed out through the doorway into the office space. The end of the bed gave him sight into the other room, and across to the opposite wall. He could see, in the wall, his own blurred shape, sitting and looking, staring at his own predicament. He really didn't deserve this shit, did he? Meanwhile, what about Alice, and more important, what about Billie?

Fat lot of use you turned out to be, Jack Stein.

Thirteen

The boy led Billie through a maze of interconnecting rooms and then stopped in a doorway. The room beyond was small, containing a bed, a worktable, and a couple of chairs; that was it.

"So this is where you work," she said.

Silas let go of her hand, walked into the room, and sat on the edge of the bed before nodding slowly, big important nods.

"So, what do you do here?" asked Billie.

"Stuff," said the boy with a shrug. This wasn't Pablo. This was nothing like Pablo.

"How do you get to the systems, then?"

Silas pushed himself up from the bed and walked over to the desk. He placed his hand flat on the surface, waited a moment, and then pointed at one of the walls. A screen flickered into view, and *flickered* was the right word. When Pablo had been in charge of programming their building, the systems themselves were always in top condition. Now . . . it seemed things had really changed. This kid—she caught herself; she was thinking of the boy as just a kid, with the emphasis on *just*—was clearly not up to the same level as Pablo had been, or maybe he just had different priorities. Again, she wondered what had become of Pablo.

She crossed to the bed and sat on the edge where Silas had been a few moments before.

"Can you access Locality plans?" she asked.

"Um . . ." There was uncertainty written all over his face. Great.

"Or, maybe you can give me access to the system?"

The boy was chewing at his lower lip but, after a couple of moments, nodded. He beckoned her over.

A couple of spoken commands, and Billie placed her hand, palm down, on the table surface.

"Billie," she said.

The system showed it had registered her name, and she reached back and pulled over a chair.

"Search," she said.

Silas stood there watching her, saying nothing.

As soon as she had put in the request, she left the system to do its work, and turned to face the boy. The screen would notify her once it had retrieved what she was looking for.

"How long have you been doing this?" she asked.

Silas shrugged.

"Okay, then, what happened to Pablo?"

Another slight shrug and a shake of the head. Billie sighed.

"Look," she said. "It's okay to talk to me. I grew up here. I grew up with Daman and Pablo and the others. I haven't been back for a while, but that doesn't change things. We used to be in another building. Did you ever see it?"

Silas again shook his head, watching her warily, his pale face and dark eyes making his expression look even more wary.

"It was different," said Billie. "You should have seen it. Pablo had programmed the whole thing. There were shapes and things moving all over the walls and the floor. He changed the way the building worked too. It was like there were crystals, buried in everything. When you turned on the lights, everything sparkled. I guess it got too old," she said.

For the first time, the boy looked interested.

"How can you do that?" he said.

"It's not easy," said Billie. "But if you want, I can show you some stuff. Maybe you can work it out from there."

This time, the nod held a little more enthusiasm, but the kid was still withdrawn. She could feel it. There was something buried deep inside this boy and it reminded her of things inside herself—things she'd rather not dwell upon.

"How did you wind up here?" she asked.

"Don't remember." He shook his head and took a step back.

"That's okay," said Billie, turning back to look at the screen.

The system was nearing the end of its search, layering results in boxes one on top of the other. A moment later and a small tone announced it was done. Billie had the option. She could use voice command, but she wanted to manipulate the images directly, drag and tap while she thought. It helped her focus what she was doing. She stood and made to cross to the wall, but Silas stopped her, placing a hand on her shoulder.

"Wait," he said. "Look."

He leaned over, touching the table, and dragged his finger across the surface. On the screen, one of the boxes changed position, floating across the other images.

"Uh-huh," said Billie. "Nice. Did you do that?"

"Yes," said Silas.

Okay, maybe the kid wasn't as useless as he seemed. But then, she should have known better. Daman always did things for a reason, and fostering a person's unique talents was one of the things he excelled at. Sometimes that was out on the streets, sometimes enclosed and locked away and safe.

As she played with the grids and maps in front of her, Billie thought some more about the way things had been, down here in Old with Daman and the rest of the crew.

They'd been into all sorts of things, willing to take on just about anything if it had a payoff and allowed them to survive just a little better in the confines of their urban enclosure. Through it all, Daman had looked after them, planning, building a network of connections, and using them whenever it made sense to do so. The Family, Daman's crew, had certain advantages in the Locality. Often, the young were beneath notice. Who paid real attention to kids, after all? Sometimes, the things they did were not that good, but they were things that most of them were doing in one way or another anyway. Daman just made sure nobody really got hurt in the process. Now, thinking about it, Billie wondered exactly how you measured what hurt was. Whatever the answer, it was better than winding up dead. And here she was, back again.

She glanced at Silas and wondered what it was about this kid that made Daman want to give him an extra level of protection, shielding him from the outside world. She understood why he'd done it for Pablo, but why this one? She knew better than to even try to find out.

Turning her attention back to the schematics, she scrolled and panned, looking at the Locality from all directions, zooming in and out, focusing on this area or that, seeking some sort of clue that would point her in Jack's direction. After a while, she sat back with a sigh. She was never going to find him like this. Think, Billie. If you were Outreach, where would you put him?

She had another thought then. Back when Jack had been working on the Outreach case before, he'd gone out to the Residence. That was where Van der Stegen, the big boss, had lived. The Residence, unlike the Locality, was a fixed community of buildings designed for the wealthy and powerful, disconnected from the Locality's urban sprawl and its denizens. Would Outreach have taken him there?

No, she didn't think so. It didn't make sense.

What about Warburg? He was the Outreach executive who had employed Jack in the first place. Perhaps he was a possibility? Maybe.

"Where are you, Jack?" she said to the screen, zooming in once more on the schematics.

"Huh?" said Silas.

"I'm looking for someone," said Billie, without turning around.

"Who?"

Billie surprised herself then, struggling to know how she could explain Jack. What was he to her? What was their relationship . . . really?

"Um, his name is Jack Stein. We kind of work together. He's a sort of detective. Anyway, he's disappeared and we think they've taken him here somewhere."

"Who are 'they'?" asked Silas. He was becoming very talkative all of a sudden.

"Outreach Industries. A guy called Thorpe," she said, finally turning again to look at the boy.

"Why aren't you looking for him?" he asked.

"What?"

"Well, if he's taken Jack, if you look for him, you might find Jack."

Damn, the boy was right. She grimaced to herself. Stupid, Billie. She wasn't going to get anywhere looking at schematics of the city. She needed to be able to narrow the possibilities down. The way to do that was to find Thorpe. If she understood anything about Outreach, it was that they wanted Jack because he knew something about the aliens. It wouldn't be like Jack to give that up in a hurry. So, wherever he was, he was likely to be there a while, and until Outreach got what they wanted, Thorpe was likely to be involved.

She knew the answer, but now she wanted to give the boy some credit. "So how do I find Thorpe?" she asked.

"I don't know a lot about buildings and stuff," he said. "But I know about finding out things about people."

He moved over to stand beside her, and Billie gave up her chair. It made sense. One of the things Daman used was information, and information about people was generally the most useful of all.

A few hand motions and a picture appeared on the wallscreen.

"That the one?"

"Uh-huh," said Billie. The face was different—it was an old picture—but it was the same guy.

"Okay," said Silas. "Let's see."

A file bled into view beside the picture and Silas tapped it open. Together they scanned the contents.

"There's not much there," said Billie.

"No."

"Either he's clean or we don't really know about him." Silas shrugged.

Normally, there'd be something more. Daman ensured that the crew kept detailed files on most of the people they interacted with, notes, times, places. Outreach was not immune from his attention. In fact, from what she remembered, Outreach always warranted particular attention. He used to call it his insurance. Briefly, she wondered if he still did.

Thorpe was clean. There was nothing they could use.

"So what now?" she said aloud, more to herself than to Silas, but the thought was there.

"Easy," said the boy. "His office is here." He pulled up a

map of the Locality and zoomed to a building at the far end of New, pinpointing the floor and then the room itself.

"So?" said Billie.

Silas was really starting to come out of himself, and he looked at her like she was stupid. "We follow him. I can tap into the security system and we can send some of the others to watch. I can send them an alert when he leaves or when he arrives. If they use a transport, I can map it. Easy."

"And what good will that do?"

"If this guy Jack is here and he's important, then Thorpe is going to go there, isn't he?"

"We don't know that for sure. He could go offworld, go on another assignment."

Silas planted his fists on his hips and sighed. "That's what you think?"

Billie grimaced. She didn't know. Perhaps this kid was right.

"Well . . . ?"

"All right," she said finally. It was the best chance she had right now. "We need to talk to Daman."

Dog looked from one face to the other, clearly trying to follow the silent something that had passed between Daman and Billie. Silas stood in the background, still looking slightly pleased with himself.

Daman rubbed his chin. "So, if we do this, it will have implications for Outreach," he continued.

"Yeah," said Billie. "They're not going to like it at all."

"But what if we locate Jack? Wherever they have him, it's going to be secure."

Billie frowned. She hadn't really thought that part through.

"Let's just find him first," she said.

Dog cleared his throat and Billie turned her frown on him. "What?"

"Well, the old Dog is not entirely useless," he said.

"What?" she said again.

"I've got one or two things back on the *Amaranth* and you know—"

"Just tell me, Dog," said Billie, her frustration finally getting the better of her.

Dog took the rebuke sheepishly and then spread his hands wide. "I've got firepower. We need to get into a place, I can supply weapons, other stuff, whatever we need."

"And you think that's smart?" she said.

"No, I'm just offering—"

Daman lifted a hand. "He may have a point, Billie. We don't know how secure whatever it may be is going to turn out being. Silas is good, and even I can do a little something, but you never know. They own these systems. You know that."

"And I'm pretty good too, Daman," she said.

"Yes, you are, Billie. You always were, but we still don't know."

Billie turned away from him and walked to the other side of the room. She stood for a couple of seconds before facing him again and walking slowly back.

"They own the systems," she said, fixing Daman with a steady gaze. "What else do they own?"

Daman held her look with difficulty, and then his own gaze slipped away.

"If you upset Outreach and they find out it's you, what do you think will happen? What do you think will happen to you and the rest of them here?"

She couldn't help it. She needed to find Jack, but she felt something for the younger inhabitants of Old. This was where she'd grown up, if she had ever needed to grow up. At times like this, she felt almost as if she had always been old, that she'd never really been a kid.

"They can't afford to," said Daman simply. "I'll be all right. I'll always be all right."

And maybe, just maybe, she thought, Daman knew what he was talking about.

Fourteen

Jack had only two choices: he could play along, or he could pretend to play along. It was that simple. As he knew from his time in the service, misinformation could be just as powerful as information, if fed the right way, and damned if he was going to give these bastards what they wanted. What *he* wanted was simple too. He wanted Outreach out of his life, but for now, he couldn't see any way to make that happen. No way was he going to be bonding with either of the good doctors. They spent most of their time peering at him through that one-way mirrored wall anyway. He couldn't exactly see them, but he sure as hell could *feel* them.

Stretching, Jack got up for another circuit of the small complex of rooms. He'd not given them the pleasure of slipping into dreamstate yet, but it couldn't be too long before it came upon him involuntarily. After they'd finished probing and prodding him, sleeping was the last thing he felt like doing. What he really felt like doing was ripping their damned heads off, together, but that wasn't going to happen either.

Wishful thinking, Stein.

Muttering to himself, he gave a quick wave to the reflective wall and forced a grin before turning away. If he thought about it, they probably had ways of watching him wherever he was in the faux apartment and office and that was enough to give him even less comfort.

He walked into the bathroom, feeling even more discomfited with the implications of his last thought. Some things were private, dammit. A mirrored cabinet sat above the sink, a shower unit in the corner, just like in his old place. He pressed the cabinet edge and the mirror slid out of view. It was a cabinet, nothing more. Inside, patches sat in neat rows—unlike in his old place . . . well, not anymore. Oh, the patches were right, but the old Jack would have had to rummage around until he found what he was looking for. He poked at the ordered stacks with one finger. They were all there, anything he might want. Stims, analgesics, even recreationals . . . maybe he should just wipe himself out for the duration with a good selection. No. Not yet anyway, until he had worked out exactly how he was going to play this. Even through the patches, he might risk dreaming and he wasn't ready for that yet.

Next stop was the kitchen. There he had just about everything he needed too, and again, it was just like his old apartment. A coffee unit sat to one side. He hit the brewing control, knowing without thinking about it that the result would be rich and strong, just as he liked it. Out of half-remembered habit, he glanced out the window to watch the world while he waited, realizing as soon as he'd done it the foolishness of the action. There was no window, only a blank wall. The illumination from above was graduated, giving the illusion that more light was actually coming from the direction of the wall where the window should be. Oh, they were good—too damned good. He really did have to be careful. Old habits were still old habits and it seemed that everything about this place had been designed to trigger the layered memories and patterns that lay deep within him.

As the coffee finished brewing, he poked around, investigating. A full bottle of bourbon sat on one shelf, and an array of ready-cookeds sat on another. Well, that was one thing they'd gotten wrong. Jack Stein would never sport a fully stocked kitchen. Still, compared with everything else, that was minor. For the hell of it, he reached for the bourbon, cracked the seal, and took a healthy sniff before replacing the top and shoving it wistfully back up on the shelf. Not yet with that either.

The coffee was ready, and he grabbed the mug to accompany him on his next stop. The bedroom had everything he might expect too. He sat on the edge of the bed and reached back with one hand, testing it, then leaned forward, cupping his mug with both hands, and shook his head. The bed was just as he liked, firm, with not too much give. They'd done a damned good job; he had to grant them that. When he called up the wallscreen, it showed a system linked to all of the Locality's options. Entertainment, vids, news—it was all there. He killed the display, the comforting smell of the coffee the only thing to accompany his sense of unease on his next investigative pilgrimage.

The living area mirrored the layout of his old apartment except for the lack of windows. As with the kitchen, there was the faintly graded illusion of windows, and two almost indistinguishable lighter patches on the walls, working on his subconscious. He glanced around. There was the couch, a couple of chairs, the shelves along one wall.

Jack stopped dead, his mug halfway to his lips. On the shelves sat a collection of items, bits and pieces shoved there in seemingly random confusion, just as he would have done himself back then. One single object stood out among the clutter, glaring at him across the compact space, its presence almost like a slap in the face. The small blue bottle, an antique piece, had been one of the items crucial to his first case with Outreach, drawing him into the visions of Gil Ronschke strapped into a chair after disappearing from the mining station on Dairil III. Jack took a deep breath, hesitating to reach out with his senses and *feel* the thing. How had they gotten it? How had they known? Jack bit his lip, staring at the object, his thoughts racing.

Slowly, slowly, he placed the mug down and crossed to the shelf. His lips pressed tightly together, he reached out to the bottle. This one small object had been filled with memories and cues that had dragged him into another place with his first dealings with Outreach. He was still wondering how many of his abilities had deserted him.

One touch. One fleeting touch.

There was a tingle deep in his guts, but that was it. It was the same piece, the same small blue bottle that had been back in his offices way back then. He could feel it. Outreach must have been planning this for years.

Suddenly, Jack felt deeply uneasy. He couldn't be that important to them, could he?

Despite his very best efforts, Jack did eventually dream. The time shift traveling from world to world, the adrenaline burn, the tension, and the frustration all caught up with him and he gradually succumbed to the subtle fingers of Morpheus. One minute, he was lying back on the bed, watching an old vid on the wallscreen with one arm behind his head, trying to ignore that they were observing him even now, and the next . . . waves of darkness had swept down upon him without his even realizing it.

He stood in an open field, the smells of exposed countryside unmistakable in the air. Jack looked around himself suspiciously. Open country and pleasant landscapes were not exactly where Jack Stein was supposed to be. He knew he was dreaming. The ur-reality of the dreamscape held an undercurrent that constantly plucked at the lower layers of his awareness. There was something vaguely familiar about the gently rolling fields, about the grassy sea that washed about his ankles, about the tissue-thin brushstroke clouds like finger trails across the pale blue sky. He'd been here before, hadn't he?

Deep within, Jack felt a sigh growing, but didn't let it form. Not right now, Jack. You don't need to be dreaming— at least not like this.

He tried to will himself out of the dreamstate, but knew very quickly that his effort was wasted. This was definitely one of *those* dreams, and he was along for the ride.

"Okay. So what?" he said, but nothing, no one, answered him. It looked like he was going to have to work this one out for himself, regardless of his vaguely independent subconscious.

The way he was facing was as good as any, so he started to walk.

A few paces farther on—he wasn't sure how many—Jack became aware that his feet were no longer in contact with the ground. Flying and floating were fairly standard parts of the dream iconography, but in his lucid dreams, he usually had to will the act, or it came as a response to something else. This was different.

As he walked, his pace increased, every step taking him even farther above the ground. He looked down and behind, watching the receding fields, trying to pick out anything that might give him a clue about where he was supposed to be. He could see clumps of tiny trees in the distance. They were far away now, but still close enough for him to determine that they were normal trees and not the strange arboreal structures, the cathedral trees, on the alien homeworld. Which was good. He didn't want to be stuck in a vast echoing room in semi-darkness with a bunch of silvery animate coatracks right now.

Farther and farther, the ground receded; faster and faster, his steps took him up and away until the landscape was rushing away into the distance, the individual features blurring into a skein of colors.

It wasn't long before Jack found himself suspended in the heavens, floating far above a world that was clearly not his own. No familiar oceans, no fondly recognizable swirling cloud masses, but there was something vaguely familiar about the planet all the same.

Jack stopped walking, hovering in empty space, and waited. It was slightly ironic that he was such a lousy flier in the real world, slightly uncomfortable with heights, but here in the dreamscape, far above a slowly rotating world with nothing beneath his feet, he felt almost completely at ease. The dream reality was a funny place.

The world below him turned, Jack hovered, stars around him burned brightly in the blackness and Jack started to become impatient. He tried for a moment to will himself back down to the planet's surface, but failed. He tried the other direction without success. Now it looked like he was stuck. He hung suspended for a couple of minutes that seemed like an eternity, the frustration building, when something started to twinge in his senses. A growing energy, a presence nearby, started to prickle at his extended awareness.

He tried pinpointing the source: nearby, but not anywhere in particular. Delving deep inside, he reached out, touched *something*, and drew back just as quickly. Whatever he had touched had the sensation of sharpness, something hard, cutting at him like jagged blades clawing his inner nerve endings.

What the hell?

The blackness wavered. The stars blurred, and almost directly in front of him, nothingness started to take shape and form, black upon black. One by one, behind the solidifying presence, the stars winked out of sight. Jack reached out again and immediately drew back. Whatever this thing was, there was something in it that clashed with his inner senses, setting his teeth on edge and grating against his nerves. This wasn't good.

Jack stretched out a hand foolishly. Whatever the black nonpresence was, it was far, far away, far beyond his simple mortal grasp. The thing was fucking huge. The realization came to him the next instant and a chill started to grow, taking form alongside a suspicion about what he was really seeing.

Keeping one part of his awareness on the ebon half-seen shape, Jack turned his attention to the world below. Down there, patchwork green spreading around it, was a darker, square shape. Its well-defined edges told of deliberate construction. Jack knew then, for sure, why this place had seemed vaguely familiar. He'd seen the world only briefly ever before, and at the time, his teeth had been firmly clamped together as he'd swept down toward the planet surface, his eyes half-closed, Billie beside him with her eager anticipation washing past his discomfort. This was Mandala. Not Mandala of the time when they had visited, but a long, long time before it had become a resort world, decades, even centuries before.

Something very bad was about to happen.

Jack turned back to the reflectionless ship. The sensation of deeply charged atmosphere built, even though Jack knew there could be no atmosphere here. He was just an observer here, compelled to watch.

Something like a vapor trail shot out from the front of the

shape, spearing through the blackness, ill defined, ill formed, and half-invisible, a shimmer, a feather touch across the void.

Turning his attention to the surface below, Jack watched. The regular shape on the planet surface showed no change, not from this distance anyway, but moments later, there was a response of sorts. A tiny speck appeared near the squared-off area and grew rapidly larger. As it swept toward Jack's position, its details became clearer, color, form: a silvery ovoid growing ever larger, glowing slightly at the tip, as it coursed through the remaining layers of atmosphere. A similar form flashed in from the side, and another from above. They were responding properly now, and the response was quick. Bright beams of blue white shot from several points on the ovoids' surfaces, converging on the shadowed shape, dazzling him with their brilliance. Jack continued watching, his eyes half-shut against the glare. Blue white splashed against black, fanning out across an invisible surface in radiating patterns. Once, twice, three times, the beams seared through the emptiness and met that unseen barrier. A moment later, the stygian form responded, that barely seen shimmer arcing across the void and another and another till the spokes touched the solid silver shapes. And in the next instant, the argent ovoids were gone, only spinning fragments showing where they had been. There was no sound, no feeling, no pressure. One moment there had been ships, the next just debris.

Jack swallowed. Jesus.

Slowly turning, but traveling with immense velocity, a piece of shattered ship spun past him, then another. In the next instance, a smaller bit flew by. As he tracked it, he realized this wasn't a piece of metal or misshapen strut. Though silver gray, ruptured along its length, it was the shape of one of the aliens that had become so familiar to him over the past few weeks.

He had just witnessed a battle—one in which the alien creatures hadn't had a chance. Maybe this had been the moment of destruction of the City of Trees, the alien city on Mandala, the archaeological site he and Billie had visited. It sure as hell looked like it.

In the back of his head, a chorus of voices swelled like a wave.

"You see, Jack Stein? You *see*?"

He saw.

This was history.

Fifteen

Outreach Industries' new building was pink. Billie stood across from it, staring up at walls that looked like they belonged on the outside of a cake. It was still an impressive structure, reaching up toward the ceiling panels at the glitzier end of New, but it was pink. It was nothing like the glass and metal monolith that had once housed the corporate nerve center that ran the Locality, granted, but pink? What the hell were they thinking?

Next to Billie stood one of Daman's crew, an older kid called Freddie. Freddie leaned back against the wall, one leg propped up, his hands shoved into his pockets, his dirty blond hair tousled. He was more than just a kid, she thought. More like a youth, older and nonchalant, hanging around just killing time. They'd talked about it, all together, and decided that Freddie was the right choice. One of the younger members might draw too much attention if there was any real following to be done.

"He's in there now."

Silas's voice came from a spot in the wall just above her head, pitched low so she and Freddie were the only ones to hear it. Silas wasn't Pablo—that much she knew—but when he'd said he was good at finding out stuff about people, he wasn't wrong. In some ways, she thought, his talents extended far beyond anything Pablo had ever done. That trick with the talking walls was something. Wherever she was in the Locality, not only could Silas find her, but he could talk to her too, simply sending a program pulse to one of the local bits of scenery. She wondered what else he could do to manipulate the Locality's facilities.

"You ready, Freddie?" Billie said to her companion, trying hard to suppress the grin that the involuntary rhyme brought.

Freddie narrowed his eyes, clearly picking up on her expression, but he only gave a brief nod. Billie turned her attention back to the building across the street. She knew she was taking a risk being here, but in her new form, with her new apparent physical age, she doubted that Thorpe would recognize her. Maybe he'd seen her since the transformation. She didn't know, after all, how closely Outreach had been monitoring her and Jack, but she didn't think it would have been long enough to stick.

"He's not moving," said Silas.

"Great," said Billie. If he could do this, what else could he do? Why couldn't he just locate Jack if he was in the Locality, and lead them directly there without having to go through this whole find-and-follow thing? She wasn't going to have that conversation out on the street, though.

People came and went from the building's wide entrance. It was hard to keep track of the individual figures and after a while, they all started to blur into one another. Billie was becoming bored, and quickly.

"Now?" she said.

"No," said Silas.

Freddie just looked like he was dreaming, half watching the passersby, not even acknowledging her presence.

This was pointless. There were other kids positioned at strategic crossover points along the Locality's length, but how did they have any idea where Thorpe might go? Maybe they should just enter the building and see what eventuated. They should have thought about this some more, but it had seemed like a good idea at the time.

"This isn't working," she said to the wall. Freddie glanced at her, but said nothing.

"Wait," came Silas's voice. "He's moving now. He's coming down."

Billie turned slightly away from the street, masking her face from the other side, but still allowing her a view of those who came and went.

"He's nearly at the entrance . . . no . . ."

"What?" said Billie.

"He's going down further. Lower levels. Wait, he's outside now."

Billie turned, scanning the street. But then there it was, a white anonymous vehicle, heading slowly up the street and toward the port area. Of course, he wasn't going to take the shuttle, not someone like Thorpe. She and Freddie could try pursuing by shuttle, but she doubted that would do any good. If he was heading toward the port . . .

"Keep following him," she said. "We need to work out what to do. Is there anyone up front, near the port?"

"Uh-huh," Silas answered. "Tina and Sean."

"He's in a ground transport. Tell them to look out for it."

Billie screwed up her face, thinking about the options. There weren't very many of them for the moment. She'd had this picture of seeing Thorpe and following him right to wherever they had stashed Jack, but it didn't look like it was going to work like that. She was leaning back against the wall, her hands behind her, fingers drumming on the smooth surface, while she thought.

They waited for another ten minutes. Billie's frustration threatened to take her over until Silas reported some action.

"He went to the port. He got out of the transport and went across to a flier. The flier left."

What if he was going to the spaceport? What if he was going offworld again? They'd have no other leads.

Billie growled to herself. How did Jack put up with this stuff? He had to spend hours and days following people. She knew he did; she'd seen it.

Right now, it looked like they had no other option than to hop a shuttle and head back down to Old until something more happened.

"Is there any way to tell where he was going?" Billie asked of the wall.

"No," said Silas.

"Okay, Freddie," said Billie. "Let's go back."

All the way back to their building, she was thinking, trying to work out a better way of doing this, but apart from the possibilities she'd already considered, she came up blank. Freddie hung on a railing beside her, face half-concealed behind his hair, looking like he wasn't paying attention to anything, but she could see the watchfulness in his eyes, a watchfulness that was painfully familiar from her previous life. She dismissed those memories and concentrated on the matter at hand. She had to find Jack. Maybe Dog had some ideas.

When they arrived, Freddie simply faded into the shadows, leaving her to seek out Silas and Dog on her own.

She found Silas, back in the small room toward the building's rear, but there was no sign of McCreedy.

"Hey," she said, hanging in the doorway. "Where's Dog?"

Silas shrugged. "With Daman, I think."

Billie nodded. She could find him in a minute. For now, she wanted to run her idea past this kid.

"If you can track Thorpe," she asked, "why can't you do the same thing with Jack?"

"No signature file," he said.

"Huh?" She didn't understand.

Again, Silas shrugged. "It's easy to do if you have the information. We know a lot about these people. Outreach, other people. We have the files. Daman always says we have to know as much as we can about them."

"So how many files have you got?"

"I dunno. Maybe two hundred."

"Huh. So why can't you make a file on Jack?"

Silas frowned, thinking. "It's not that easy," he said. "I need recent stuff. Trace patterns collected by the Locality."

"But we used to live here," she said. "There must be something."

"Maybe," Silas said, his frown deepening. "I don't know. I might be able to find it, but I don't know."

Billie sighed. "Well, I'll let you think about it for a while. I need to talk to Dog and Daman."

She left him there puzzling over what he was going to do.

Wandering through the complex of old offices, she eventually located Daman. A broad reception area had a number of couches and chairs spread across an otherwise empty area. Daman sat forward in a chair, his elbows on his knees, his fingers steepled in front of his face, seemingly deep in thought. Daman's eyes barely flickered, registering her presence. There was no sign of Dog.

"Daman?"

He looked up from his thoughts.

"Any joy?" he said.

Billie shook her head and moved to prop herself on the back of a couch.

"No, and I think maybe it's stupid. How are we going to follow this Thorpe guy anyway? We don't know if he's still going to be involved with Jack. He's done his job, hasn't he? It could be anyone else from Outreach. I asked Silas if he can try to get a fix on Jack himself."

Daman lowered his hands and plucked at his lower lip. "Yes, that might be possible, but I wouldn't be sure. We only really started collecting records when Silas joined us. Before then . . . well, we had files, information, but nothing like the signature traces that Silas is working with."

"Is there anyone else you can use?" Billie asked him.

"It's difficult," said Daman. "Trust only goes so far, and with the sort of people we might employ it goes far less than with most. Hmmm. Our access to the true hierarchy within Outreach is limited."

Billie gave a heavy sigh.

"Though it is worth exploring," said Daman. "But locating where they have him is only one part of the problem. We need to work out how we're going to get him away once we know, and as much as I can rely on some of our contacts, that is probably a step too far."

"So where's Dog?" she asked, looking around.

Daman shook his head distractedly. "He said he had some things to do, that he'd be back later."

Billie frowned at him. What could Dog possibly have to do in the Locality? He knew no one, knew nothing about the place, unless it had something to do with the person he thought he'd seen. Perhaps he'd gone back to the shuttle to get some things after all. Still, it didn't feel right. She pulled at her bottom lip, thinking about it. What was Dog McCreedy up to now?

Daman had drifted away and had a faraway look in his eyes. He seemed to remember that Billie was there and moved back into the conversation as if she'd never changed the topic. "I suggest we let Silas explore what he can do. We keep an eye on Thorpe and see if he leads us anywhere useful. Meantime, I will think about our other options."

"Daman," said Billie.

"Hmm?"

"Thank you for this."

He blinked a couple of times before responding. "I have my reasons," he said.

He had always been like this, giving up only as much as he needed to. What went on in Daman's head would always remain a mystery, she suspected. Though she had some thoughts of her own.

"Tell me about Outreach, Daman."

"What more do you want to know?"

"Well . . ." Billie thought for a second. "Who is it now?"

"It is not so very different from when you were here. There have been changes. But Warburg still heads the board. The Van der Stegens have a continuing presence as well."

"The old guy?"

"No. He seems to have faded into the background. Anastasia Van der Stegen is the dominant force now."

Billie remembered her. She hadn't liked the woman at first sight, and she'd tried hitting on Jack too. At least Jack had been smart enough to see through the ruse at the time. Warburg she didn't know much about, except that he was the one who had hired Jack initially, hoping for some reason that he'd blow the case. Same old players, sort of. She hadn't really understood everything about what Warburg had been trying to achieve back then, but she understood enough to know that the man had very few moral principles.

"Do you know any of them?" she asked.

Daman stood and walked around to the back of his chair before answering, his hands clasped behind him. When he finally spoke, he was facing away from her.

"I've come across Warburg once or twice, but no direct dealings. It was always through someone else. He tends to keep to himself, insulated from most of their overt activities."

He turned back to face her.

"He has other people to do everything for him."

"So what about them?" said Billie. "Can we get to any of them?"

Daman lifted one hand. "I'm thinking." He used the hand to rub at one cheek and then moved around the chair to re-take his seat. "I was running through the possibilities. The problem is, just as we know them, they know us. People like Warburg are not stupid. Remember, Outreach owns this city. We exist, we survive, in part, because they allow us to exist. It suits their purposes."

Daman gave a heavy sigh before continuing. "I share a portion of responsibility, but it's a joint responsibility. I keep the Family safe. Billie, you know that."

She was a little surprised to hear him talking like this, almost as if he was seeking her approval. She sat back, catching the inside of her bottom lip between her teeth. As long as she could remember, Daman had always been there, unquestionable. Now, suddenly, she was starting to see him in a new light. Despite herself, she recalled some of the things that she had done, that the other kids had done, certain that Daman had let them happen in full knowledge of what was going on. She tugged at one ear, pushing that chain of thoughts away with a grimace. She didn't want to think about that, about any of it. They had more important things to worry about.

Sixteen

Jack woke, his heart still racing. The group unconscious of the alien race was not done with him, it seemed.

Yeah, he'd seen. He'd seen all right, but he didn't know why.

Every time he'd entered into that weird joint dreamspace, the aliens had had a reason, some sort of message or purpose for him. He still couldn't figure out why the aliens would be dreaming of him while he was dreaming of them. That part was still too strange. They could have found a better choice, surely.

He rubbed splayed fingers back through his hair and checked the time display. It was very early morning. He'd slept right through the night. He still felt like crap, but he was a little rested at least. He needed coffee and a shower. Falling asleep in his clothes didn't do much for his general aura of health and well-being.

He pushed himself up from the bed and stumbled into the kitchen, setting the coffee to brew, leaning back on the counter, and considering what he had dreamed while he waited, before the details faded as they were sometimes wont to do, even though, over the years, he had trained himself to retain as much as he could.

One by one, he picked through the sequences, turning them this way and that, but there was nothing hidden or obtuse he could identify. It was simple; the aliens had given him a brief history lesson. So what was the point? Yeah, the City of Trees had been half wiped clean. Yeah, the power of destruction had been huge, but he knew all that already. What did it have to do with his current situation? And more to the point, what could he do about it? That stuff was centuries in the past. Still, he couldn't believe that the fading alien race didn't have a purpose in what they were showing him.

Do you see, Jack Stein?

He saw, but he didn't get it.

He reached for his coffee and, taking his first sip, washed it around in his mouth, cupped the mug between his hands, and considered.

In the room nearby, with their monitoring equipment and their clinical fascination, the good doctors were probably watching him. Or maybe they were just recording for later analysis. Briefly, Jack wondered if they had a way of telling that he'd been dreaming. One way or another, he guessed he'd find out soon enough.

If Jack was going to use what he had, he had at least to make a show of playing along with them. Some of the questions they had asked him yesterday had shown clearly that they knew he had been dreaming and when he was dreaming. He could use that. He walked across to the reflective wall and tapped on it a couple of times with his knuckles.

"What is it, Mr. Stein?" It was the woman. He couldn't even remember their names. They were just the "good doctors" now.

"I'm ready," he said. They wanted a dream session; he'd give them a dream session.

"Ah, very good, Jack," said the male doctor. "We are particularly interested in anything you can find out about the temporal-dispersion device. Anything further you can provide on the history of the alien species would also be useful.

If you can try to steer your dreams in that direction, that would be good."

Yeah, he bet it would.

Jack took his time going through the ritual of removing his clothes and carefully folding them one by one on the nearby chair. He then climbed up on the sleep couch, reached back for the inducer pads, and affixed them to his temples, all the while feeling the discomfort of the doctors' unseen gaze upon him. He might be a specimen to them, but he was a specimen with his own mind. Thankfully, there was no way they could read his thoughts—at least not just yet, as far as he knew.

As the gentle waves of the inducer drifted through his mind, subtly pressing his awareness down through the layers of consciousness, he crossed his hands on his naked chest, the feeling of determination resting hard and solid within him. The blackness swept up to cover him, folding him away in that place that existed deep within him, sparking the currents that flowed to that dream place where Jack worked best.

Jack was back. Back on the alien homeworld, that was, back in the large echoing room with the artificially constructed sleep couch and the clusters of immobile alien creatures, silver-skinned and motionless in the gloom. He thought of this as the dream room now, because it was here that he wound up every time he and the aliens dreamed each other. He still hadn't come to terms with the way the whole thing worked, how they *could* dream each other. All he knew was that it seemed to work. And then he had to go into that routine where he dreamed he was lying on the artificial couch and slipping into another layer of dreamspace. How far could the whole thing go? Could he dream he was dreaming he was dreaming and so on? Was there a risk that he might become buried in recursive dream layers, so far down that he could never find his way back? No. Stupid, Stein. Thoughts like that were not going to help matters at all.

"Hello," he said to the immobile shapes. He knew they were there in their own version of unconsciousness, somewhere back on their homeworld, and that this place was just their mental construction to help him feel at home with the necessary process of their communication.

He looked dubiously at the nearby sleep couch. No, he didn't need it. He didn't need any of this anymore. They were good, but this was simply unnecessary by now.

"Can we get rid of this stuff?" he said, waving an arm to indicate the room, the couch, everything that surrounded them.

Nothing happened.

Drawing his inner senses tight, he focused on willing the environment away. For an instant, it seemed to be working; the walls shimmered, became insubstantial, and then solid again.

Dammit. He tried once more.

This time, the reaction was different. One of the aliens swung a leg forward, and then another, using its awkward stepwise gait to move closer to him. Its trunk bent forward, pointing the top of its central shaft down toward him.

"Hi there," said Jack.

Now he felt really stupid. Talking to the silver lizard-skinned coatrack, knowing it had no means of talking back to him. Perhaps he should just climb up on the sleep couch and get this over with.

"Look, I don't need this stuff anymore," he said. "Talk to me. Just talk to me."

"J . . . ack." The familiar multivoiced chorus swelled and died away in the back of his head.

"St . . . ei . . . n. Too. Hard." The echoes flowered and wilted. No, they were right. This was too much hard work.

"Bring back Billie, then," he said. It had worked before. Why not now? And with that thought, she was there.

"Hello, Jack."

He spun to face the voice. Propped on the edge of the sleep couch sat Billie, the young Billie, all of twelve years old, with her blond bobbed hair framing the pale aesthetic features and her shadowed, faraway eyes.

"Hello," he said.

"What can we do for you?" she asked, cocking her head slightly to one side.

It was still unnerving talking to Billie in her earlier form, but it was better than some of the other choices the aliens had offered him in the past, perhaps unknowingly, but still . . .

"I don't know," said Jack. "I'm worried."

"Yes?" said Billie.

"I had a dream last night. I think it was one of *your* dreams. I saw a battle above Mandala. Some kind of black ship blew away three of yours. It was total destruction. The other ships didn't have a chance. What can you tell me about that?"

He looked around the room, but the aliens that surrounded them were still unmoving. If his words had prompted any reaction, it wasn't evident. He turned his attention back to the dream simulation of Billie. Maybe it wasn't a simulation, but some sort of simple holographic projection. But that didn't make sense within a dream either. It didn't really matter. If it allowed him to communicate, then that was good enough.

"That was history," said Billie. She looked away.

"But then why were you showing it to me? We've been through that before."

There was a long pause. "We know," she said finally. "But before, you did not see the risk. Before, you saw, but still you came."

"The risk?" asked Jack.

"You will come again, Jack Stein," said Billie.

Not if he could help it. No way was he getting on another jump ship and hopping across the galaxy. Nothing could make him go through that again.

"Not likely," he said.

"Very likely," said Billie. "Not you, but your kind. You will come again."

Billie twirled a finger in her hair, watching him. She was starting to fade.

"Wait," he said. "So what? Why is that important?"

The room around them faded with Billie's image and Jack thought he was losing the dream. The next moment, Jack was floating, suspended in cold space, star fields stretching out in every direction. Bright pinpoints clustered together, and as soon as he focused his attention on one of them, he rushed toward it. It wasn't a star, as he'd first thought, but something much, much more than that, a collection of stars and dust and other things all bound together in the familiar shape of a galaxy. He flew closer, toward the center, where the stars lay thick, only separating from one another as he drew even closer. There were planets, worlds, rings of debris, and he saw them all. They varied in intensity and hue, numberless around him. It was a magnificent sight, but he still didn't know why they were showing it to him.

One star grew larger in his field of vision until Jack could make out the individual bodies accompanying it.

"Here," a deeply swelling voice proclaimed inside his head.

"What?" said Jack, his speech floating away like a vapor streak across the blackness. "What am I supposed to see?"

A shadowed shape flew up from the planet's surface, dark and lightless like the ship he had seen in the battle before. It was followed by another, and another. They whispered past him, silent in the void, but as they swept by, even at the great distance, he felt the chill, the jagged cold cleaving at his inner senses, filling him with a current of dread that trickled to his very marrow.

One after another, they passed him. One by one, they radiated the fear, impossible to resist, and still they kept coming.

"Tell me what I have to do," said Jack.

"There is nothing you can do," said the voice. "Nothing." It sighed and drifted away into mere echoes, deep within his mind.

"Nothing . . ."

Jack sat up, his heart pounding. That cold dread was like nothing he'd ever felt and he could still taste its presence flowing like an oily stream through his bones. Bad, bad, bad.

"Jesus," he whispered to himself.

"What was that, Mr. Stein?" said the male doctor's voice.

"No, nothing," said Jack, remembering where he was. "Just making the transition. Coming out of it. Give me a moment or two."

"We don't want to lose anything of the dream experience," said the "good doctor," concern evident in his voice.

"No," said Jack. "We're fine. Just let me collect myself."

He swung his feet off the couch and padded into the bathroom, not caring what they thought he was doing. He needed to take a piss. He stood staring down at the stream as he did so, thinking. What was he going to tell these guys? He hadn't quite worked out what he'd really been seeing, though he had a vague suspicion, let alone the story he was going to tell them. He flushed, washed his hands, and said,

"Mirror." The wall above the sink became reflective, showing him his own, younger face looking thoughtfully back at him. He leaned forward and touched the hair at his temples, strangely missing the gray. He pulled back a bit, studying either side of his face critically.

Quite frankly, he was feeling a little weird. He turned on the water and leaned over to splash his face. His image blurred through the wetness, Jack felt even stranger as he stood upright again. He reached up with one hand and wiped the back of it across his eyes, getting rid of the remaining water. A dark shape stood in the mirror behind him.

"What the—?" He spun to face it.

Maximilian Aire stood behind him in the doorway, completely naked, his gold jewelry offset against his dark skin, his fleshy jowls looking slick and shiny just like the top of his head.

His gaze was penetrating.

"What the fuck are you doing here?" said Jack, taking a step backward.

Aire's face creased into a grin that was followed by a deep belly laugh.

"Ah, Jack Stein. You see what happens when you mess with things you know nothing about."

This was what he had been thinking about before: He was still dreaming. He'd woken in his dream, but only in his dream. Perhaps he'd invoked this by thinking about it. Still, it was damned unsettling. Aire had to be here for a reason. Jack thought he'd left the Sons of Utrecht far behind in Balance City, but apparently not. The unseen hand of the SOU had no logical place in his dream, but sometimes dream logic was obtuse.

"Come on, Aire, tell me what you want."

It might be a dream, but things happened in his dreams

with a purpose. Jack had threatened the big leader of the political group when he was looking for Billie, and he was pretty sure that Aire had had something to do with the death, the so-called suicide, of Dr. Heering from the university, but he'd been unable to prove it. It looked like he wasn't done with it yet.

"You are looking for something I want," said Aire, his deep voice still sounding amused and his expression matching.

"And what might that be?" said Jack.

"The way home," said Aire.

Jack stared at him. What was that supposed to mean? Jack became aware of a cold wind on his back, and looking back over his shoulder, he was not surprised to see that the walls had disappeared. Instead, he stood at the edge of a high cliff, leading down into darkness. The craggy sides looked vaguely familiar. He turned back to look at Aire, but the big black man had disappeared, as had the rest of the complex. In front of him was forested landscape, tall trees in an even line densely packed and blocking his view. It was light enough that he could see everything, but behind him, when he looked over his shoulder, the murk still obscured any view of what sat beyond the cliff, or what lay hidden at its bottom. Strangely, Jack felt little unease standing precariously on the cliff edge. He should be on the verge of quaking by now. He leaned over the edge, peering down, seeing if he could penetrate the gloom. Nothing.

Above him, thick clouds boiled in the sky, dark and pregnant with threatened storms. Again, the cold wind buffeted him from behind, rocking him on his feet. The next instant, another gust blew him back and the ground beneath his feet started to crumble. He watched as dislodged stones fell, slowly turning end over end as they dropped to be swallowed in the darkness.

And then he was falling.

Jack sat up, his heart pounding.

"Jesus," he whispered to himself.

"What was that, Mr. Stein?" said the male doctor's voice.

"No, nothing," said Jack, remembering where he was. "Just making the transition. Coming out of it. Give me a moment or two."

He swung his feet off the couch and padded into the bathroom to take a piss, not caring what they thought he was doing. He stood staring down at the stream as he did so, thinking. What was he going to tell these guys?

"Jesus, no!" he said aloud. "Mirror."

His reflection stared back at him, slightly wild-eyed. Nothing stood in the mirror behind him. He turned to look over his shoulder. No Maximilian Aire. No landscape. He looked back. No cliff. So far so good.

Flushing and washing his hands, he walked warily back into the pseudo-office, his heart still pounding. If he didn't know better, he'd be thinking that he was starting to lose his senses. Reaching for his clothes, he pulled them on slowly, still deep in thought.

For a while, he'd suspected that his dream ability was changing. Back in the days of the original Outreach case, things had been different—kabbalistic symbols, ancient rhymes, mystical doorways; all that stuff seemed to have faded from his subconscious awareness. The dream sequence he'd just been through harkened back to some of those earlier dreams. The feeling within him, that edgy, taste-of-the-precipice feeling in his guts, was the same too. He'd even suspected that the alien beings were subsuming his talent, taking it over and guiding it with their own dream presence, though now he wasn't so sure. Perhaps the visions were products of circumstance, of the energies and presence within which he moved. But why the hell had Aire been naked? He shook his head, almost as an effort to remove the image from his brain.

"Mr. Stein?"

"Yeah, yeah. Give me a minute to order my thoughts."

"Very well. Just tell us when you're ready."

Seventeen

They made several more abortive attempts, but still Thorpe had led them nowhere. Billie was becoming tired with this, and some of the crew were starting to grumble. She didn't know how Jack put up with these endless hours of watching and waiting. There had to be something else they could do. Dog had returned a couple of hours after she'd noted his absence. Despite her quizzing, he told her nothing about what he'd been up to. Billie filed it away. He hadn't been gone long enough to make it to his shuttle—at least she didn't think so—and he'd returned carrying nothing more than what he'd left with. She didn't like this secretive behavior from him at all.

There were frustrations on other fronts as well. Despite her suggestions, Silas hadn't been able to put an effective trace on Jack. He'd managed to find enough to put together a signature, or a "kind of" signature, as he'd put it. He'd set it loose in the Locality's structure, but so far, it had drawn a blank. Jack had to be here somewhere; she just knew it. Outreach was pretty good at keeping its secrets.

Daman had made a few discreet inquiries, but so far, he'd come up with nothing too. He'd seemed withdrawn and thoughtful when he'd broken the news. Every few hours, their task felt more and more hopeless.

Dog tried to keep their spirits up, but even that was starting to wear thin, especially in light of his mysterious excursion. She was in no mood for it, and she even snapped at him once or twice. He'd backed away, palms held up, and left her to it.

"Got something." Silas's voice came from nearby. She knew he was off in his back room, but his voice made it seem he was standing right beside her and she jumped.

"What is it?"

"Thorpe's back. He's on the move. Somewhere new."

"Where?" said Billie.

"Hold on."

One of the nearby walls started to flicker and move, the smooth surface replaced in a moment with a multidimensional representation of the Locality. A bright dot was moving, high up in the structures, and then down, lower. She tracked it. It traveled down the Locality's main arterial route and then did a sharp turn to the right, heading toward the Locality's westward side. It was about halfway up New.

"Is there anyone up there?" she asked.

"Close," said Silas, "but too far away."

"How soon can they get there?"

"A few minutes. Maybe ten."

She kept her attention on the marker, willing it to stop, willing it to slow, so they could get someone on it. A few moments later and it did just that, out near the Locality's outer wall. It stayed still for about a minute.

"Is there anything there?" she asked.

"Not anything special," said Silas.

The bright dot was on the move again, and then, suddenly, it vanished.

"What was that?" said Billie.

"I don't know. I don't know. Wait. . . ."

The seconds dragged by.

"I don't get it," said Silas. "I've lost him. One minute he

was there and then he wasn't. That can't happen. It doesn't happen."

Billie chewed her lip, staring at the map, her hands shoved into her back pockets.

"Is there any way he can get outside from there?" she said. Maybe there was some sort of hidden gateway out from the Locality that only Outreach knew about.

"Nuh-uh. Not there. I know all the ways in and out."

"So what happened, Silas?"

"I don't know," he said. He sounded upset, as if he'd let her down. She needed him to keep it together.

"It's okay," she said. "We just need to work it out. I'm coming back to see you."

She wandered back through the corridors, still chewing her lip. Just when she thought they had something, it looked like it was gone.

Silas sat behind his desk, staring down at the surface, his lips pressed together in a thin line. He didn't look up at her as she entered.

"What happened?" she said.

He shook his head.

"Silas, just think. Something must have happened. Could something have happened to your routines?"

He stood and turned away from her, then turned back and kicked at the desk. "Should have worked," he said petulantly. "Always works."

"It's okay," she said. "We'll figure it out. We know where he was when it happened."

He nodded slowly, venturing a glance at her face, and then looking away again quickly. Shit, she hoped she'd never been like this. Maybe she had. She walked over and put her hand on his shoulder. "Show me the place again," she said softly.

"Should have worked," he said quietly.

"It doesn't matter now. Just show me."

A couple of touches on the desk and the same map bled into being on the wall. Silas zoomed in on the spot where Thorpe had been a few moments before.

"And there's nothing there?"

Silas shook his head.

Dog appeared in the doorway, hanging around the frame. "What's going on?"

She waved him down. "Is there anything Thorpe could do that would block the trace?" she asked Silas.

Again, the boy shook his head. He was sulking now.

She turned to Dog and spoke. "We found Thorpe, and then he just disappeared."

"Disappeared where?"

"We don't know."

"And what was there?"

Billie sighed. "I asked that. We don't know. Nothing."

"So . . ."

"So what?" said Billie.

"So let's get up there and see," said Dog.

She glanced at Silas. "Silas already has some of the crew going there, haven't you?"

Silas hesitated, then gave a brief nod. He still refused to meet their eyes.

"So we wait," said Dog.

It took about ten minutes for the crew to check in. Silas monitored their progress on the map. When they were close to the spot where Thorpe had disappeared, he finally spoke. "There. What's there?"

One of the younger kids' voices came from the desk. "Some buildings. A street."

"What else?"

"Huh, that's weird."

"What is it?"

"I dunno. It's kind of like a wall, but it's curved. It reaches up and then goes in."

Silas and Billie both peered at the map, trying to see what the kid was talking about. There was nothing there.

"You sure about that?" said Silas.

"Course I'm sure," came the voice.

Silas was frowning. "There can't be anything there," he said. "I'd see it."

"Listen," said Billie. "If they had some way of shielding, that would explain it, wouldn't it? That would be why Thorpe just disappeared. He went inside something and whatever it is has to be shielded in some way."

"Yeah," said Dog.

"So what do we do?" said Billie, turning to look at him.

Dog grinned. "We go up and knock?"

Billie made a sound in her throat that she hoped effectively showed how unimpressed she was with the suggestion. His grin faded.

"Silas, keep them there. Watch to see if anything happens."

Silas nodded. "You hear that?" he said.

"Uh-huh," came the kid's voice.

"We wait too," said Billie. She was thinking fast. "It would make sense. If they wanted to keep him hidden, they'd put him somewhere that was really hidden. We don't know who else wants Jack right now. It might not be only Outreach. The same thing happened with the tablet. Other people were interested in that too, and Outreach tried to get it. If they think Jack's got something like the tablet, then Outreach might want to keep him all to themselves, don't you think?"

"Yeah, I guess so," said Dog. "I think I see what you're

saying. But maybe they just want to keep him out of the way where his friends won't find him." He looked significantly in her direction with a lift of his eyebrows. He walked into the room and stood next to her, his hand creeping around to rest on the small of her back. "So again, we wait," he said.

Billie moved to sit, looking for somewhere that was not Silas's desk. Dog had no such qualms; he simply propped himself on the desk edge, ignoring Silas's look and crossing his ankles. He lowered his face to watch her through his hair, a little half smile playing on his lips.

Dog's sense of timing could be a lot better, she'd decided. It was pretty clear what he was interested in, but right now really wasn't the time.

They waited for about half an hour, Dog watching her and Billie sitting on the edge of a chair, her legs jiggling up and down with impatience. She hated waiting. She had always hated waiting. Dog's looking at her was making her feel uncomfortable too and she turned away so she wouldn't be so aware of it, choosing to watch the map instead, though it told her very little.

A full half hour it took before anything significant happened.

"There's a ground car," came one of the kids' voices from Silas's desk. "It's stopping."

Billie leaned in toward the source of the voice. "Is anyone getting out?"

She could hear another sound, a regular thumping.

"What's that noise?"

"They're playing," said Silas as if that explained everything.

She guessed it did. They had a ball or something. Kids played together on the street. It would look less suspicious than if they were just hanging around doing nothing.

"No," came the kid's voice. "He's just sitting."

"Can you see inside?"

"No, the windows are dark."

"How many are there?"

"Hard to tell, but maybe only one."

They waited for about another ten minutes with nothing happening, the anticipation killing her. The regular sound of the ball or whatever it was thumped out from the desk, grating on her nerves.

"Something's happening."

There was a pause.

"Hey, that's weird."

"What?" said Billie.

"The wall kind of opened up. Two men just came out."

Billie glanced at the map. The bright dot indicating Thorpe had reappeared.

She leaned in even closer to the desk, her heart pounding.

"Two of them? Describe them to me."

"They're both pretty old. One has dark hair, thin, wearing a dark suit."

Thorpe . . . it had to be Thorpe.

"The other one is kind of big. Really short hair. He's wearing a dark brown suit."

Billie's heart sank. Neither of them sounded like Jack. Well, the thin one maybe, but it was Thorpe. The map clearly showed Thorpe as being present, one of the pair, meaning that the other one had to be a bodyguard or something. The whole thing with the magically appearing door and the shielded wall gave her enough confidence to think that they'd found where Outreach was holding Jack, though.

"Thanks," she said. "You've done enough for now."

"Silas?" The voice was questioning.

"Yeah," said Silas, looking at Billie for confirmation before continuing. "Come back," he said, but only after she'd nodded.

Billie looked significantly at Dog. So what now?

He raised his eyebrows, waiting. He was giving her the lead, just like he had done from the very start. She stood, shaking her head at him.

"What do you think?"

Dog ran his fingers through his hair, pushing it well out of his face before turning to Silas.

"Can you get us in there?" he asked.

Silas was staring at the map, his bottom lip thrust out.

"Dunno," he said.

Billie crossed and gave him a reassuring touch on the arm. "What do *you* think, Silas?" she said.

He shrugged. "Dunno. It shouldn't be like that. I should be able to see it. If I can't see it, I can't touch it."

She knew exactly what he meant. Programming ability was directly limited only by the levels of access. If a system was denied to you, it might as well not exist. That's why bridging capacity was so important.

"It's got to be programmed from somewhere," she said. "There might be a way in from the central Locality core, some sort of gateway."

"Maybe," said Silas, but he sounded doubtful.

"Why don't we just bust in?" asked Dog. "Easy."

Billie turned. "What makes you think it's so easy?" she said. "The Locality is different. If Jack's in there, we don't want to make a big noise getting him away from there. We want to try getting him out before they know he's gone. Remember, there's only one way out of this place that we can use. It's a long way from there"—she tapped the map—"to there, up to the port. And that's our only way out."

She'd already thought that part through. She imagined

that if they wanted to, Outreach could seal up the port as tight as a trap, and then they'd be no better off than when they'd just arrived.

"Yeah, I guess," said Dog. "So what?"

It was already quite late in the day and she could feel the pangs of hunger starting to grow, interfering with her thought processes and putting her even more on edge.

"I need to eat," she said.

Dog looked vaguely incredulous. "Now?"

"Uh-huh, now."

She dug her handipad out of her jacket pocket. "Here," she said. "Go and pick something up. Do something useful. I'll wait here and do some work with Silas."

He snorted and shoved the handipad into his pocket. "Any preferences?"

"Yeah," she said. "Molly's would be good. Silas?"

The young boy gave a big nod, his face lightening.

Dog stood there as if waiting for something.

"You'll find one easy. Head up toward Mid. Just go, Dog."

He shook his head and left them there, muttering as he went. She watched his retreating back as he stepped into the corridor outside. Was there something else he was about to do? For the moment that was the least of her worries. Besides, with Dog out of the way, maybe she could concentrate now, despite the burgeoning hunger.

"Okay," she said to Silas. She moved around to his side of the desk. "Can I use it?"

There was a moment of hesitation, but then came a half-reluctant acquiescence.

"Show me," she said.

It seemed like an age before Dog reappeared, bearing brown bags and drink containers, but in the meantime, Billie and Silas had not been idle. Together, they'd been exploring the Locality's neural pathways, probing and peering with their on-hand tool sets as well as some that weren't immediately apparent. When Billie and Jack had left the Locality that first time, she'd taken the precaution of burying some of her own tools and routines deep within the Locality's infostructure. It didn't take her long to remember where she'd hidden them, and then in less than five minutes, she'd unfolded the masking layers to make them available again, disguised, but present. Despite Silas's current familiarity with the network and the comparative sophistication of her own tools, they'd so far drawn a blank. When Dog appeared in the doorway, half struggling with his burden, it was a relief. She waved him over.

"I didn't know what to get," he said. "So I got some burgers and some fries and some drinks."

"Perfect," said Billie, waving toward one of the bags with an outstretched hand.

He tossed her a bag and she half ripped out the burger, spilling fries all over Silas's desk. The boy looked at them detachedly, then reached for one, munching on it slowly. Billie was already halfway through her burger when he plucked another from the desk and lifted it to his mouth.

"So, any luck?" asked Dog.

Billie wiped her mouth with the back of her hand, peering through the remains of the bag for a napkin or something.

"Nope," she said, growling and reaching for an as-yet-unopened bag and again searching for something to wipe her hands and face with.

"What do you mean, nope?" asked Dog. "It took me ages to find the place."

She shrugged. "What do you expect? These guys don't

want it to be found, do they? It would be pretty stupid if they left it out in the open in a system sense too."

"Yeah, I guess so," said Dog. "So what do we do?"

Billie reached for the unfinished half of her burger, not caring about the mess for the moment. She was still hungry. As she took another large bite, she shrugged.

Dog pushed his fingers back through his hair, looking decidedly unimpressed.

"Silas has got an idea," she said around a mouthful of food. Damn, she'd missed these things. She hadn't had a Molly's for ages.

"I think I can build something that will get us in." There were traces of uncertainty in Silas's voice.

"How?"

"I'm not sure. . . ."

Billie waved her hand at Dog and gave him a frown, then swallowed what she was chewing. "Silas says he can do it; he can do it."

"Okay," said Dog.

"It's going to take a bit of time," said Silas quietly. "I have to work it out."

"Yeah, okay," said Dog, finally reaching for one of the brown sacks. "What do we do until then?"

Billie looked at Silas. "You've got the system monitoring Thorpe anyway, right?"

He nodded.

"Then we should go and get some rest. If Silas is going to take a few hours . . . we need to get in there really late at night or early in the morning when no one's around. That would be best. Is that okay, Silas?"

Again he nodded.

"You're not going to need any sleep?"

He gave a slow shake of his head, looking vaguely pissed

off with the suggestion. She could relate to his response. She'd been just the same. If there was a problem to solve, she wanted to solve it and she didn't want to stop until it was done.

"Okay," said Billie. "We should probably go back to the hotel and try to get a couple of hours of sleep. I'll let Daman know what's going on."

Dog was watching her speculatively, slowly chewing as she left the room to seek Daman out.

Eighteen

All the way back up to the hotel, Dog was very quiet, more quiet than usual anyway, and Billie wondered what was going through his mind. She decided not to press him until they were back in the relative privacy of their room.

As they stepped from the shuttle, Dog suddenly grabbed her arm.

"Back," he hissed, pulling her into a doorway.

"What?" she said, glaring at him.

He motioned for silence. "Just wait," he whispered through closed teeth, pressing her back into the corner and angling his face around the doorway so he could get a view up the street.

"What?" she asked again. She'd had enough of his little secrets.

He spoke without breaking his position at the doorway's edge. "Can't be seen right now. There's someone up there. We need to wait until they're gone."

A couple of seconds passed and still he hadn't budged. "Shit, they're not moving."

"Who, Dog? What's going on?"

"I'll tell you about it later," he snapped.

She'd had enough. If he had to stay out of sight, that was his business. She wanted to get back to the hotel. She made a move toward the roadway. Dog immediately whirled, grabbed her shoulders, and pushed her back against the wall, hard.

"Stay," he said.

Billie threw her weight against him, anger flaring inside her. She wasn't the dog here. "No!" she said.

At that moment, someone stepped out through the door. Without hesitating, Dog wrapped his arm around her shoulders, pulled her close, and planted his mouth firmly on hers.

Billie's hands were up, flat against his chest, pushing him back. In the instant it took the other man to pass, smile, look away, and step out onto the street, Dog's eyes were watching.

She shoved him away from her and stood back against the wall, glaring, her hands planted on her hips.

"What are you doing? What the hell are you doing, Dog?"

Shrugging off the question, he ducked his head around the doorway's edge.

"They've gone," he said. "For now. But we'd better be careful."

"Dog?"

"Not now, Billie. Please."

She ground her teeth together and took a deep breath.

"Come on," he said. "Back to the hotel. I'll tell you more there. Okay?"

"No," she said, shaking her head. "Tell me now."

Dog sighed, glancing around the doorway again before turning back to her.

"There's a couple of SOU guys here," he said. "They know I'm here."

Billie frowned. "How? How could they know you were here, and what's it to them anyway?"

He shook his head. "I can't explain now. Just trust me. I can't afford to run into them. There's some stuff I'm tied up in back on Utrecht. If we're going to get Jack out, we can't afford the complication."

It just didn't add up. She narrowed her eyes. "I don't believe you."

"Dammit, Billie, later," he said. "Come on. They clearly know we're here." He reached for her hand.

Reluctantly, she let him lead her toward the hotel, his stride quick, his movements alert and watchful. He'd said "we." Why would the SOU be interested in her anyway?

They marched rapidly through the lobby and to the elevators. Once inside, Dog spoke their floor number, and the elevator, recognizing his voice, shut the doors and sealed them away.

"Shit, I wish I had my gun," Dog muttered quietly to himself.

And that was really going to make her feel comfortable.

The elevator stopped at their floor and Dog got out, heading straight for the room. Billie followed more slowly. Maybe he was right. Maybe she didn't need to worry about it. Whatever Dog was involved in . . . well, she could guess, but why it would follow them to the Locality was a different matter. Right now, though, she had no choice but to trust him. He'd gotten her here, hadn't he? And she suspected that it was a bit more than her attempts at manipulation that had managed that. Dog and Jack went back a long way.

He was waiting for her at the doorway.

"So," he said finally when he had shut the door firmly behind them, "Silas is going to call when he's got something?" He was clearly changing the subject.

"Uh-huh," she said. She kicked off her shoes, stripped off her jeans unself-consciously, and climbed into the bed. When he didn't move, she frowned.

"What is it, Dog?"

Slowly he took off his jacket and draped it over a chair. "I don't know. Just . . . something I . . . no, it's not important."

What was with him?

"Come on, Dog McCreedy," she said, patting the bed beside her.

He sat on the edge of the bed and pulled off his boots and then removed his trousers, his back to her, his hair obscuring any view she might get of his face. He took his time laying out the trousers before turning back to the bed. His dark T-shirt he left on. Lifting the covers, he slipped into bed beside her and lay with his fingers linked behind his neck, his gaze upward, staring at the ceiling.

"I don't know," he said. "It's strangely immediate. All of a sudden, we might be actually getting him out. I guess I didn't figure it out that far."

Billie frowned as she lay back, propping herself on one elbow, watching him. "Isn't that what we're supposed to be doing?"

"Yeah, of course," he said. Then, "Lights," and she couldn't see his face anymore as the room plunged into darkness.

They lay like that in the dark for several minutes, neither saying anything, the only thing to disturb the silence the sound of their breathing, which seemed unnaturally loud around them. Sleep seemed a million miles away, but Billie knew it would be smart to get some if they could.

Dog moved in the darkness, turning to face her. She could feel his warm breath on her skin. Strangely, she felt suddenly awkward. She turned to lie on her back and then again onto her side so that her back was facing him. Dog shuffled closer, his weight creating a dip in the bed that angled her slightly more in his direction. His breath was stronger now, closer. Billie's heartbeat had sped up and she could feel it in her chest, her ears.

Dog cleared his throat and one hand came up to rest on her shoulder. She didn't move away. She could smell his skin, his scent. Was this going where she thought? Should it? She hunched her body back, pressed tightly against him and snuggling into his chest. Dammit, Billie. Now was as good as any time. She wanted it to happen. She really did. She reached back with one hand, finding his hip and pulling him closer to her so he was tight against her back. She could feel his chest, his abdomen, touching her. That wasn't all she could feel. His growing hardness was pushing up against her buttocks, no mistake there. Knowing exactly what she was doing, she let her hand slide from his hip and across his erection, then back up till she gripped it within her fingers.

Dog gave a little groan, then pulled back.

"Billie, you're sure?" he said, almost a whisper.

She turned, reaching for his face. "Shut up, Dog. Come here." She kissed him then. Without any further hesitation, he kissed her back. She liked the taste of his mouth, the feel of the roughness of his chin against her cheek.

Still holding on to his face, she brought her legs up and then straddled him, bending over him to maintain the contact with his lips. His penis was hard, so hard pressing up between her legs. She shuffled a bit, feeling it, repositioning so that it was more comfortable. Then, letting go of her grip on his face, she sat upright, pulling her shirt above her head, reaching for his hands, and guiding them to her breasts.

Together they gave a half sigh, half groan.

Yes, she wanted this. Yes, she was sure. Silly man.

"Lights," she said, and the room flooded with brightness. She looked down at Dog, blinking against the glare. A few strands of his hair trailed across his mouth and she moved them away with her fingertips, coming back to trace the shape of his lips.

His eyes had adjusted now and his gaze traveled from her face to her breasts, to her belly.

"Oh God," he said. "Hang on."

He moved his hands away, shuffled back, and pulled off his shirt, tossing it to the side of the bed. At the same time, Billie swiveled, lifted one leg, pulled her underwear down, and discarded it, then reached to do the same for his.

"Oh God," he said again as she took his erection between her hands. "Wait," he said.

He turned, pushing her down on the bed beside him, and traced his fingers over her shoulder, her arm, the flat of her stomach, watching appreciatively, and then moved in close to place featherlight kisses on her skin. Each one brought a shiver, deep within. It was never like this; it had never been like this. She lay back, letting him do what he would, and drifted away with the sensations.

As much as it felt good, she wanted more. She wanted him inside her, wanted his heat and his own want. She pushed him away, onto his back again, and straddled him once more, reaching down, lowering herself slowly onto him, feeling a sigh escape from her lips as he filled her. It hurt, a little, but it felt good too.

She leaned forward, bending over him, letting him reach her breasts, and cupped the sides of his face with her hands.

"Dog McCreedy," she said, almost as a whisper. "You are different from everyone I've ever known. So different."

Then she closed her eyes, to lean back and surrender herself to the moment.

She watched him as he came, the pain/pleasure contorting his features. She'd seen the look before, many times before, but this time it was different. This time, it was special and good.

She sat there watching him, feeling him inside her as he lay there, his brow sweaty, and his breath deep and slow. She reached to wipe some of the moisture away and then once more to trace his lips.

It was different when you wanted it too.

There was nothing to fear about what they'd just done, no need for prophylactics, and no fear of disease. The body's chemistry and enhancements saw to that. And there was nothing to fear in other respects either. Billie felt good. She felt better than good. She hadn't come, but that didn't matter. Not now. Not this time. The revelation about how great this could feel was just about enough, and there'd be time.

Gradually his erection subsided, growing smaller inside her, and she swung herself off him, to lie next to him, still watching. She reached over, grasping some hair between her fingers and curling it around them. He did, she realized, look like no one she'd ever been with.

"Wow," he breathed.

"Uh-huh," she said. "That was nice."

His eyes were closed and he opened them to look at her. "Nice? Nice? I would have thought it was a little better than nice."

"Yeah," she said, and smiled. "It was just a word, Dog McCreedy."

He grinned and turned back to face the ceiling, slowly closing his eyes.

She watched him for several minutes as his breathing slowed. He had gone to sleep. Really, she didn't mind. It was good to lie here and just watch him.

Silas's call came just after midnight. Billie had drifted to sleep despite herself and when the insistent tone woke her, she felt fuzzy but kind of warm. The noise was the familiar sound of her handipad, chiming through the layers of sleep.

She frowned, trying to remember where she'd put it, and then remembered that Dog hadn't returned it to her. It was still in his jacket. She brought the lights on and jumped out of bed, heading for where he'd laid his clothes, and rummaged around in his pockets.

Dog was awake, just, and he cracked one eye and was watching her. "Hey, what are you doing?" he said.

Billie found what she was looking for and flipped open her handipad. "This," she said. "Yes?"

Dog had been definitely suspicious. It was weird, given what they'd been up to mere hours before. She filed that away for later consideration. Maybe he was just always suspicious. Maybe he had more reason after the events out on the street a few hours before. Still . . .

"I've got something," Silas said from her screen. He looked worn-out.

"It's ready?"

"I think so," he said. "I think it will work."

"We'll be down soon," she said, and closed the handipad.

Dog was still watching, but the hard knot of suspicion had been replaced by something softer.

"Come on, McCreedy," she said, tossing him his trousers. "We've got things to do."

He grinned then, lifting his hands above the covers defensively. "Okay, give me a minute. I'm wiped out. I think you've broken me."

Billie snorted. "Yeah, right," she said, reaching for her own clothes. Really she should shower, but right now, what they had to do took priority. She pulled on her clothes and stood waiting impatiently while Dog got himself together. All throughout, he was giving her little half glances, trying to disguise the looks, but none of them slipped past her. Inside, it brought a smile.

The hotel staff looked surprised to see them leaving at that hour, but there was no comment, and it was only minutes before they were out on the street and down to the stop to wait for the next available shuttle. They never stopped running.

A few minutes later, they made the change at Mid-Central and, a short time after, reached the section of Old where Daman's building sat. It was funny that she thought of it as Daman's building.

Nearly dragging Dog inside, she raced up the steps and through the connecting offices and hallways to where Silas had his room. He looked up as she entered, his exhaustion evident in his pale young face, his eyes red-rimmed.

"*Hi,*" he said, then didn't pause for her response. "I've got the answer. I think it's going to work."

Nineteen

Billie was conscious of Dog watching her as she spoke to Silas, but of something else, something drifting below the surface. She couldn't quite identify what it was, and that troubled her. That something was chewing at Dog in ways she couldn't work out. She didn't have time to address it now, but she would, later, along with a whole lot of other unanswered questions that had started to grow in her thoughts: What happened now? Where did they go from here? Was that just a one-off?

"Show me, Silas," she said.

Silas held up a small square piece of nondescript substance, thin, slightly shiny, a touch of gray iridescence in its flat surfaces. He turned it this way and that. Billie reached for it, but he held it out of her grasp.

"Don't drop it," he cautioned, and then held it out to her again.

"What is it?"

He pointed at the desk as soon as she'd taken it from him. "I grew it from there."

"Okay," said Billie. So what was a bit of his desk going to do?

"It's programmed inside. I don't know if it will work, but I think it might. I tried one before. You have to put it on the wall where the door is. The routines will pass across and get into the wall."

"And then?" said Dog from his position by the door.

"The wall goes away," said Silas simply.

Billie turned the flat square over in her hands. It was like some sort of virus. She looked at Silas with a new respect. He'd said he had an idea, but she hadn't expected anything like this.

"That's it?" said Billie.

"Uh-huh."

She turned to Dog, slipping the square away inside her coat. "We may need some others with us," she said. "We don't know what's in there."

He nodded in confirmation, but there was still something shadowing his eyes. "So let's talk to Daman," she said. "One of the kids from before would be good. They can tell us where the door is. Maybe a couple more for support."

"And more," said Dog.

"What?" said Billie.

"We need some hardware," he said. "This time we really do."

Together, they stood on the empty street, alert to any sound or movement that might indicate they had company. Outreach had been too overconfident this time, it seemed, trusting on their programming to safeguard this place, whatever it was. The boy pointed out the place where Thorpe had emerged, and Billie nodded. The ceiling panels and the streetlights cast a vague steely light along the empty roadway, gleaming in gray shades against the curved surface that masked whatever lay within. Billie looked up and down the street, listening to be sure. Dog was hanging back in the shadows, leaning against a building, half-masked in a doorway. They'd better move if they were going to get this done. Standing around out here in the open was more than suspicious. She looked to each of her companions, checking they

were ready, and then dashed across the street, up to the place
where the door was supposed to be. Reaching into her
pocket, she pulled out the small square and slapped it
against the wall, then stepped back. The patch stuck, fading
into the surface of the wall itself, until there was no sign it
had been there, and then . . . nothing. Billie stood there,
watching, her arms crossed, her teeth firmly closed together,
her jaw muscles tight. Nothing.

She was about to vent a growl of frustration when it
changed. Where moments before the patch had been, the
wall started changing color. Bit by bit, and then faster, it
pulled back from the spot, a large hole growing where once
there had been solid wall. She waved the others forward.

"Quick," she said. She hoped that Silas had put some lim-
iting routine into it. She didn't want it to eat the Locality itself. She toyed with that thought for just a moment before
dismissing it. Nice idea, Billie, but not yet.

It wouldn't be long before Outreach was alerted to what
was happening and they'd be swarming down on the place
with everything they had, or at least enough to stop them in
their tracks. She jumped through the opening and beckoned
the others to follow.

Dog hung at the entrance, holding back from stepping
through. "I'll keep an eye out, guard the rear," he said to her.

She didn't have time to argue. "Okay."

They were in a small entranceway, low reddish light illuminating bare walls. A corridor ran off straight ahead. She
checked for movement, but as yet, all appeared still. Striding rapidly, she headed down the corridor, the others keeping step behind. The passageway turned to the right and led
them quickly to a larger room. There were chairs, monitors,
and a large window looking into another room. The lighting
was so dim that it was hard to make out what lay on the other

side of the window. There was a large squarish shape in the middle of that room, a chair, a cabinet, but apart from that, it looked bare. Other doorways led off behind. No one was in evidence, either here or in the rooms beyond.

"Shit," she muttered, conscious of their ever-dwindling time. If Jack was anywhere, he had to be somewhere behind that window. She turned around quickly, looking for some way in. There, a door!

"Open," she said. Nothing. She scanned the surrounding wall for some sort of panel, something that would control the door. The other kids were standing around her, glancing nervously up the corridor they'd just come from and the adjoining one that ran off into darkness. As much to keep them occupied as anything else, Billie waved for one of them to go and check it out. He crept off up the passageway.

Billie dug into her pocket and pulled out her handipad. It had been a while, far too long, but she thought she still had the tools. She thumbed it into life, opened a series of links with a couple of quick taps, calling her routines into operation, staring down at the device as they went to work. They had to be good enough. They always had been.

"Yes," she whispered as the door slid open. She stepped through, debating with herself. She could light the place up, but that might bring attention. No, they had to be quick and quiet. A couple of steps took her into the room proper. She waved her companions off to the adjoining doorways, then stopped, familiarity hitting her. She knew what this was. She knew exactly what this was. This was Jack's old office, or something like it. Damn them.

"Here," came a hurried whisper from one of the doorways.

Billie was there in an instant, her heart in her throat. It was darker in this room, but she recognized it too. This was

Jack's old bedroom, the old apartment. And in the bed lay a sleeping form. She crept over to the bed, leaning over to see. Jack!

Crouching down, she gently placed a hand over his mouth and then shook his shoulder.

Jack's eyes flashed open, his body going into immediate fight mode, his eyes wide, and then they widened more as he recognized who knelt beside him.

It took him only a moment to comprehend, and he quickly nodded beneath her hand. She pulled the hand back.

"Billie," he whispered.

"Uh-huh."

"But what . . . ?"

"Shhhh," she said. "We have to get you out of here. We haven't got much time."

"Jesus," he said, swinging his legs out of the bed. "This is you, isn't it? This isn't another dream."

"Yeah, Jack, it's me."

"It's just that—"

"Shhhh," she said again. "You can tell me later. Get dressed."

Jack reached for his clothes and quickly pulled them on. The other two were watching the doors, nervously glancing back into the bedroom and outside again.

"Okay," said Jack.

"Go," said Billie. She walked rapidly through the fake office, out into the observation room, Jack and the others close on her heels. She hissed up the adjoining corridor to alert the other boy that they were done, waited a couple of moments while he crept back down, and then they were heading back up the corridor toward the hole in the wall that would take them back to the outside. The wall was already starting to repair itself and the gap was significantly smaller.

She poked her head out, but the way seemed clear. Where was Dog?

Dog was gone.

How could he be gone?

"Dog?" she said quietly in a forced whisper.

"Who?" said Jack.

She waved him down. There was no sign of Dog at all.

It would wait. Right now, they had to get the hell out of there.

"Come on, Jack," she said, walking briskly away from the complex and up an adjoining street. He needed no prompting at all and was walking beside her, matching her pace, looking sideways into her face.

"Damn, but it's good to see you, Billie."

"Yeah," she said, still worried about Dog, but more worried about getting them all back to the relative safety of Old. After that, they could work out how they were going to get out of the place, out of the Locality and away. And after that, she could worry about what had happened to Dog. Maybe he was already back in Old waiting for them.

All the way back, Billie was conscious that at any minute, Outreach's minions might sweep down upon them. She spent as much time looking nervously out of the back of the shuttle as she did looking at Jack, checking that he was okay, his face, his body, his hands. The clothes were different, not what he'd normally wear, but that was all. He actually seemed fine, though it was still hard to come to terms with the younger-looking face, the missing gray in the hair. Dammit, he really was attractive if she thought about it, but her thoughts weren't going in the direction. He was Jack.

The kids who had accompanied them to the hidden complex had split off and caught another shuttle, and in one case gone off to do something else; she didn't care what. More important was that they not be seen as a group. The likelihood of drawing attention would be too great that way.

They got off the shuttle about a block from the building, again, Billie thought, to divert attention, just in case. All the way along, Jack clearly wanted to talk to her, but she was determined to make him wait, giving him little frowns every time he tried to open his mouth. The only thing she told him was where they were going. His silence could last only so long.

Jack looked around, seeking signs of familiarity. Billie had led him back down into Old, and she had had kids with her. That meant only one thing—Daman. His memories from back then, of his interaction with Daman, were not that comfortable. Any tool they could use to get out of this place was worth it. But then? He watched Billie as she strode off across the lobby, gesturing him to stay.

Outreach was sure to be watching the port area, and that presented a problem. Maybe Daman would have some way to get them out.

Daman. And that was another interesting thing. Jack was really looking forward to finally meeting him again, despite the less-than-positive memories, just to confirm his own suspicions as much as anything else. Had Daman been used by Outreach? Had he known more than he'd let on back then? There was only one way to find out.

Jack cast his eyes around the lobby, wondering. This place looked nothing like the old building that had been used by Daman and his crew. There was no sign of the fancy programming, the skill and expertise. The place was decrepit, falling apart. The old building had been impressive, designed clearly to intimidate and inspire awe and distraction both. There was none of that here. None of it at all.

Jack headed toward the stairway that Billie had disappeared up, as he decided that was the better choice than trying to use the elevators. She'd indicated he should stay where he was, but he'd had enough waiting. He didn't even know which floor he was supposed to go to.

The second floor was quiet, disturbed only by the creaking of the building's structure itself and the sound of his own breathing. He thought it wise not to call out for Billie, remembering his first visit to Daman's center of operations. On that occasion, he'd wound up on the street, nursing a throbbing head on a slow climb back to consciousness, and he really didn't want a repeat of that.

The third floor was not much better. Traces of light came from somewhere near the rear, showing vaguely along the end of a corridor. This floor didn't look promising. Once again, he made for the stairs.

On the fourth, he found someone. Two boys stood at the top, watching him suspiciously.

"Where's Daman?" he said.

One of them gestured toward a passageway on the right.

"And Billie?"

The boy shrugged. Jack would find her with Daman, he guessed. Maybe it would be good for her to spend some time preparing the way up front.

He turned and walked up the corridor that the boy had indicated.

He emerged into a broad area, scattered with couches and chairs, far better maintained than the rest of the building appeared to be. He walked slowly to the center, looking around. There was no one there.

It took only a moment before someone did emerge. It was Daman, older, but still the same Daman that he remembered. The anachronistic clothes, the stance that didn't quite go with his body—all that had remained the same. Daman walked from the darkness and stopped a few paces from Jack, his hands clasped behind his back. That was familiar too.

"Ah," said Daman. "The famous Jack Stein."

"Ah," said Jack. "The famous Diamantis."

Daman waved his hand. "All right. Fair. Take a seat, Jack. You seem to have had some changes since last we met."

"Yeah, one or two," said Jack, sitting. He gave a humorless laugh. "Listen, thanks for helping Billie. Thanks for helping me."

Again, Daman waved his hand. "Nothing, Jack. I would expect the same from any of my people. Besides, it suits me to do so."

Jack nodded. "Okay, I can get that, but we still have a problem."

Daman cocked his head to one side. "Which is?"

"We need to get out of here. Outreach are going to have the Locality sealed up. Unless you know some other way . . ."

Daman crossed to a couch and sat right in the middle, folding his hands neatly in his lap. "And what is their agenda, Jack? What do they want with you?"

Jack sighed. "You don't want to know. I wouldn't worry about it."

Daman stood and walked slowly to stand right in front of him. "Agendas are a funny thing, Jack." He leaned to look from one side of Jack's face to the other, then turned around to resume his place on the couch. "Interesting."

"What?"

"Interesting that it should affect you like that. Billie I can understand, but with you it's totally the other way. The implications are troubling."

"Ah," said Jack, understanding at last what he was talking about. "The change."

"Yes, of course."

"And you know about that, don't you, Daman?"

He nodded slowly with his young/old face. "Yes, I do. When did you come to that conclusion?"

Jack thought for a moment. "I don't know, really. I started putting it together after we'd been through the jump. You were . . . I don't know . . . well, different. I don't know another way to put it. And there were obvious connections to Outreach. Back then, I just didn't have enough information to string it all together. How could I?"

Daman gave a short silent laugh. "How could any of us?" he said.

"So how old are you really?" said Jack.

He took a few moments before answering. "I was forty-seven when they strapped me into their device. Attached to a mining crew, but administrative. I'd had my share of questionable dealings. That was one of the reasons I was out there. And, like so many of the others, I had very few attachments. No one to really worry about me if I disappeared."

"Yeah," said Jack. "I thought it was something like that."

"Anyway, I went through the experimental jump space, and then, you know the result . . . intimately."

"So why didn't Outreach just get rid of you?" Jack asked.

"Good question. Mainly because I had some information on them. Information that, at the time, would have been very damaging to their position in the marketplace. It was well safeguarded, and it was my insurance. Since then, things have moved on. My position has changed. I am, in some small ways, useful to them, as they are to me, so we survive together, never quite allies, but both of us with some common agenda."

"Jesus," said Jack. "That's got to be some sort of uneasy relationship."

Again the little laugh. "Yes. In more ways than you can imagine, Jack."

"Oh, I think I can imagine," Jack said. "How do you sleep, Daman?"

Daman's eyes narrowed, just for a moment, and then he looked away. He gave no response to the question. Nor was Jack expecting any.

Jack looked around the room, expecting some sign of Billie by now. He was starting to become concerned. He considered asking Daman, and then thought better of it. She'd show when she was ready and not before.

Twenty

"So," said Jack, "can you help us?"

Despite the previous barbed comment, Daman seemed happy to entertain Jack's needs for the moment. "I don't know," he said. "It won't be easy. But maybe you should think about more than that. What about Billie? What does she want?"

"I don't know," Jack replied. "Maybe you should ask her."

Daman sat forward again. "Yes. Maybe I should."

As if she had known they were talking about her, that Jack had been thinking about her, Billie appeared in the doorway, looking slightly sheepish and more than a little reserved. Daman waved her in. She hesitated, then, taking the signal as encouragement, walked over to one of the couches and stood behind it, avoiding Jack's eyes as she crossed the half-empty space. What was going on?

"We were just talking about you, Billie," said Daman.

He stood, walked over to where she was standing, and subjected her to the same scrutiny that he had given Jack.

"Hmmm, interesting."

She frowned. "What?"

"Just the randomness of the effect," he said, turning away from her and moving back to his seat. "So, why do they want you, Jack?"

Billie stood for a couple of seconds, still looking

uncomfortable, then, realizing she was going to get no further encouragement, crossed to another of the chairs and sat, perched on the edge, leaning slightly forward with her arms folded across her chest.

Jack thought for a moment, wondering how much he should tell Daman. He really didn't know how much he could trust him, even if Billie did, and the links to Outreach were more than a little worrying. How much had Billie told him anyway? He realized that he wasn't really sure.

Still, they'd gotten him out, hadn't they?

"We went there. We followed the artifact and we went to the alien homeworld. Billie had gone looking for it with this professor from the university on Utrecht, but something had gone wrong with their navigational stuff and they were lost. I came across this guy called Dog McCreedy, a pilot I kind of knew from before, and he and I went after them and we found them more out of luck than anything else. One of the results, however, is what you see, what happened to us."

Daman was looking very interested. "And was there any pattern to how the effects manifested?"

"Not that I can tell," said Jack. "Dog and I went one way, Billie and Antille the other. Maybe it has something to do with the sequence of jumps. I don't know. That's for someone like Antille to work out."

"So, again, why do they want you?"

Jack sighed. "When we were on the alien world, we came by a device that counters the effects of the temporal buildup. Again, we were lucky. Dog had gone on his own private shopping expedition and 'acquired' one of these things. We don't know how it works. Nobody knows how it works. Outreach might access the thing with Dog's ship, but they don't understand the underlying technology. Of course they need working copies if they're going to be able to use the jump technology over great distances or for multiple series of jumps."

"Again," said Daman, the hint of impatience creeping into his voice, "why do they want you?"

Jack, in truth, had been avoiding the real reason, avoiding talking about what was going on between him and the aliens, but it seemed Daman was too smart for that.

"I am in communication with the aliens."

There was a lengthy silence as Daman processed the information. Finally, he spoke. "How?"

"I don't really understand it. We sort of dream each other."

"And Outreach knows this."

Jack nodded.

"I see." Daman spent a few moments thinking it through before asking his next question. "Why don't you just give them what they want?"

Jack spread his hands. "Don't you think I've thought about that? It's not that easy. There's a lot more at stake than simply giving Outreach what they want, or at least I suspect as much. The coatracks—"

"Coatracks?"

"Yeah, the aliens. Anyway, they keep showing me stuff about another alien race. These other aliens aren't very nice at all. Not someone you'd like to meet alone after dark."

"So?"

"So I think they're trying to warn me. If Outreach gets what they want, they'll be looking for anything they can do to get ahead of the game. That's how they work. Just say, in the process, they get involved with these other aliens. It's possible. Then what? From what I know—dammit, Daman, from what you know—nothing about what Outreach does shows any concern for the consequences outside their own interests."

Daman stood. Billie was watching them, following the conversation as it flowed from one to the other, and was simply observing, not reacting.

Daman turned away.

"And so, you're just going to run away, Jack Stein. Is that it?"

The words hit Jack like a slap in the face.

What Daman was saying was true. It had always been true. If the problem grew too big, he ended up running away. That was what had happened the last time he'd been in the Locality. He'd run away from the services as well, and other parts of his former life. The difference with the Locality was that he'd taken Billie with him.

But what other choice did he have? How could he—how could any of them—do anything about Outreach?

And anyway, what right did this . . . kid . . . have to make moral judgments about Jack's actions?

Jack stood. "Okay, Daman, if you're not going to help us, I'm going to find my own way out of here. Billie?"

She was staring at him. Still she said nothing.

He turned to look straight at her, a frown growing on his face. "Billie?"

She was chewing at her bottom lip, appearing to be on the verge of tears. "No, Jack. You didn't tell me some of that stuff."

He regarded her questioningly. "What stuff? You knew about the aliens. You knew about what happened to the City of Trees. We talked about that. The rest . . . well, how could I have?"

"But you never said anything about what Outreach wanted."

"Dammit, Billie, I just told you, didn't I?"

She shook her head. "Maybe . . . but I think Daman's right."

Jack strode across the intervening space. "So what do you suggest we do, Billie? Huh? What the hell are we supposed to do?"

"Something, Jack. Just something." She held his gaze, daring him to deny her, looking at him as if she expected him to come up with the answers.

The problem was, he didn't have any.

He turned away from her, feeling defeated, and walked back to his chair, lowering himself back down slowly, considering a range of possibilities that he couldn't touch. What the hell was he supposed to do? Outreach had all the resources and he had always been little more than a pawn to them.

Daman had resources. He looked over at him, thinking.

"What, Jack?" Billie asked.

"I don't know," he said. "Just give me a second."

Daman had resources, and he had access. What else did he have?

"How much have you got on them, Daman?"

"Some, enough, maybe. Enough to hurt some of them."

Jack rubbed his chin as he considered. "That's part of it, okay. But it's not enough. We need more. The way I see it, we don't have one problem; we have several—well, more than one anyway."

Billie sat farther forward in her seat. Daman also leaned forward, a touch of interest on his face.

"Go on," he said.

"Well, there's Outreach and the Locality," Jack said, holding up one hand to count the pieces of the problem on his fingers. "Then, well, there's Outreach and the aliens."

"Okay," said Daman. "And . . . ?"

"Well, this may not mean much to you," said Jack, "but there's the SOU as well."

"SOU?"

"Sons of Utrecht," said Jack. "They're after pretty much the same thing as Outreach. We might be able to deal with Outreach, but I can't see any way we can do anything about the SOU. They're off in Balance City, for a start. Whatever we can do here isn't going to touch them."

Billie had suddenly sat straighter in her chair. She was frowning.

"And we can worry about them later," she said.

Jack sighed. "Yeah, I guess you're right."

"They're not going away," she said.

"Yeah, and that's part of the problem," he said. "You know . . ." He went quiet again.

Billie waited. Finally, she lost patience with his thinking process. "What?"

"I was just thinking. It's the same as the artifact, really. You know, give them what they want, but don't really give it to them."

Daman frowned. "I'm not sure I understand. What artifact?"

Jack nodded. "Yeah, of course, sorry. We were involved in a case back in Yorkstone that led to this whole thing with the aliens in the first place. Billie and I were looking for this ancient alien stone tablet, which wasn't a stone tablet. The SOU were after it. Outreach were after it. It was supposed to contain the directions to the alien homeworld. It did, as it happened. The real one did, anyway. The thing was, the one everyone was after was a fake. Our friend back on Utrecht Dr. Antille had provided a copy that was just a bit off. It would never have taken any of them anywhere. They didn't know it. Everyone thought it was the real thing."

"So how's that the same?" asked Daman.

Jack clasped his hands in front of him, still playing with the thought. "Outreach wants to get the information that will allow them to build this temporal disperser, this thing that allows you to get through the jumps without the consequences. Only, it's my suspicion that what they want goes beyond that. I haven't got any confirmation of that right now, but I think I'm probably right."

"Like what?" said Billie.

"Remember Van der Stegen?" said Jack. "He was a big thinker, always looking at the links and tangents to things, the possibilities. How else do you think he came up with all those ideas about kabbalistic links to the physics of the wormholes? I think he'd look at the City of Trees and see more than the creatures that built it. I think he'd also see the creatures that destroyed it. Two sides to everything."

"I don't get it," she said.

"Okay, look. Why were Outreach and the SOU so interested in getting to the alien homeworld? It was for the technology, right? They thought that the knowledge they could get from the aliens would put them ahead of the game, let them steal a march on the competition. Imagine how much more advanced the technology potentially is from the race that could destroy our first aliens. How much more of a lead could that give them?"

"Okay, yes," said Daman, standing. "They're some interesting conjectures, Jack, possible, but as you say, you've got nothing to prove them apart from what's in your gut, or wherever it is."

Jack still couldn't get used to the voice, the turns of

phrase, that came out of that so-young mouth. He shook the thought away.

"My gut's been pretty good up to now," said Jack.

Daman looked at him for a second, then turned away and walked across the room, toward one of the doors leading into shadowed darkness beyond.

"Hey," said Jack, but Daman waved his protest away.

"I'll be back. Continue that line of thought while I'm gone, Jack."

Jack made to get up, a growl of protest rising inside him, but Billie shook her head. "He'll be back like he said."

Jack pressed his lips together and closed his eyes. Yeah, okay. It was so easy to forget he wasn't being talked to by some arrogant kid. He opened his eyes again.

"Okay, so how'm I doing?" he said to Billie.

She grinned.

"Where's Daman gone?"

Billie shrugged.

"So, what happened to you anyway, Jack?" she asked.

He took a few minutes to fill her in on the details of what happened back at Dog's apartment, watching as her lips became pressed together in a tighter and tighter line. He could almost sense the anger threatening to burst free.

"What, Billie?" he said.

"Dog's been with me all the time," she said. "He's been helping to find you." Her face was hard. "He brought me here."

Jack stared at her. "I thought I heard you say something about him back there, but then I thought I'd imagined it. I knew you were with him. I left a message with Antille to warn you off. I guess it didn't get through."

She shook her head slowly.

"What is it?"

Again, she shook her head. And then it hit him. Without knowing how he knew, he *knew* what the something else was. He stared at her.

"Billie?"

She lifted her hand. "Don't, Jack."

He frowned. "Billie . . . ?"

"Jack!" She glared at him.

Jack dropped his gaze, looking at his hands as he bunched them together into a tight fist.

He took several slow breaths before continuing. Mc-Creedy. McCreedy would keep.

"Where is he?"

Billie shrugged.

"Well . . . ?"

"Dunno."

He stared at her for a couple of seconds. She was clearly processing. That would keep as well.

"And then," he said finally, "I was stuck, had nowhere else to go, and so I went to see if I could find . . . shit! Alice . . ."

"What?" said Billie.

"I found Alice, the librarian, remember? She put me up at her place. Took care of me. Shit, I've done it again. I need to let her know that I'm okay."

"What have you done, Jack?"

He shook his head, annoyed with himself. "Same old thing," he said. "I wind up at Alice's place and then I disappear. She's going to start getting a complex if I'm not careful."

"It wasn't your fault." There was a hidden message in those words.

"Maybe so, but still . . ." He lifted his gaze to meet her eyes, delivering his own message.

He could call Alice, but somehow, he didn't think that would be a good idea in the current circumstance.

"I have to let her know," he said.

"I can do it," said Billie. "I liked Alice."

"Yeah, so did I," he said. "Still do."

"So, I'll go up and let her know."

"They're likely to be monitoring her place. You'd have to be careful."

Billie shrugged. "I can take care of myself. You've got to let me do it, Jack."

"Yeah, I do. But maybe we can send one of the other kids instead."

"To do what?" said Daman from the doorway, having reappeared without their noticing.

Jack explained about Alice and what he needed. Daman nodded. He disappeared briefly and returned a few moments later. "Done," he said.

Well, there was some relief in that, but Jack was still feeling guilty.

Daman moved into the room and over to the couch he had occupied before, crossing his hands neatly on his lap. "So, how far have you gotten?" he asked.

Jack gave him a questioning look.

"You were heading down a path about Outreach and the aliens and giving them what they wanted without giving them anything. Wasn't that it?"

"Yeah, right," said Jack.

"You likened it to the artifact or whatever it was they wanted before, but I don't think you're right."

"How so?"

"Because if you give them information that's false, about the device or whatever it is, they're going to know pretty quickly." Daman sat there looking smug for a moment. "An organization like Outreach, with the amount of resources at its disposal, isn't going to waste time in developing whatever it is you give them. They'll test it. You've already said that you had one of these things from the alien homeworld. They already have something to compare it against. It's not that easy to fool these people. Besides, if you get in touch with them to deliver any information, false or otherwise, you'll be putting yourself, and ultimately Billie, at risk again. They'd immediately track you down and have you again."

What Daman was saying made sense.

"How sure are you that they have this original device?" asked Daman.

"Oh, I'm sure about that," said Jack. "McCreedy's given it to them, or at least given them access."

Daman frowned. "McCreedy? Dog has?"

"Yeah. He's in Outreach's pocket."

Daman looked at Billie questioningly, but she refused to meet his eyes.

"I see," said Daman, and looked back at Jack. There was something in his tone that made Jack distinctly uncomfortable. He knew there was something going on with Outreach that he was only guessing at, but it seemed that Daman knew all about it. He swallowed back what he was feeling.

"So what do we do?" said Jack, standing and running his fingers through his hair. "I don't see what options we have."

"I really don't know, Jack," said Daman.

"What about Hervé?" said Billie.

"What about him?" Jack didn't see what Antille had to do with it.

"Well, you know. He was going to publish his results, get them out so everyone could use them. Can't we do that?"

"It's not the same," said Jack. "He had what he was going to use. We don't . . . or at least I don't. The knowledge is out there somewhere, and I'm not even certain I can get it. It all depends on the aliens. And that needs me to dream. I'm not sure I want to get that knowledge even if I could. As soon as I do that, I become a liability, because then I *do* have exactly what Outreach wants."

"Are you sure?" asked Daman. "Is that what they really want? Isn't that just a means to an end? You suggested as much yourself."

Jack sat again, feeling defeated. Again, Daman was right. No matter how he thought about it, he couldn't see a way out of the maze of possibilities, nor could he see how he, Jack Stein, could do anything that would block Outreach from achieving what they wanted. Whether he gave them what they wanted, or he didn't, it was going to do very little to stop them in the long run. How could he be so useless?

Billie was watching him, and now he felt uncomfortable meeting *her* gaze.

"I don't know," he said.

"Come on, Jack," said Daman, standing. He walked over behind Billie and briefly touched her shoulder. "Come with me, Billie. Let's leave Jack here to think about things for a while. I have one or two ideas of my own."

Billie stood, following Daman out through one of the shadowed doorways, leaving Jack alone with his thoughts.

Jack really didn't know what good that was going to do. The only thing he felt in his guts right now was emptiness centered on a building knot of anger against Dog McCreedy, and that last wasn't helping matters at all.

Twenty-one

Spiders. He was dreaming about spiders. The Locality was crawling, and in more ways than one. Jack frowned. He wasn't supposed to be dreaming. More to the point, he wasn't supposed to be asleep. Had those bastards from Outreach done something to him? He flexed his dream arm and his dream fingers, turning his hand to look first at the palm and then at the back. The small dark hairs stood out in fine detail against his pale skin, marching over the ridgelines of his sinews and veins. The hyperreality cut through his vision and he squinted against the nonexistent glare. The hairs were moving of their own accord. There was no breeze, no motion in the air.

Jack lowered his head and shifted his attention. He was outside the Locality, staring down at it. The slick, rainbow-glossed surface crawled with motion not its own. Spiders. He knew they were spiders, though he couldn't see them.

He willed himself closer, and this time his dream perception obeyed. The Locality neared as he swept downward, the pulsing life force present in its walls apparent to his inner senses, if not to his dream-fed sight. He could feel the hundreds of thousands moving within its walls, but more than that, he could feel the Locality itself and its living being. Weird. Maybe this was a dream, just a dream, but the acuteness of his awareness, his lucidity, gave the lie to that. Come on, Jack, why are you dreaming this?

His focus narrowed involuntarily, zooming in on one of the individual panels in the Locality's surface. The smooth hard square wasn't; it was supposed to be smooth and hard, but it wasn't. A slight ripple flowed through it, reminiscent of the motion of the hairs on the back of his hand a few moments before. Somewhere near the panel's center, a point of light grew and expanded, then faded again. Once more, the point appeared; it spread and died, synchronizing with the beating of his heart. The light turned to dark, black blood pulsing through the Locality's skin.

Hesitantly, Jack reached out, drawn to touch, drawn to feel, the pulsing rhythm, but before his fingertips were yet inches from the surface, the pulsing ceased. The panel surface bulged slightly at the spot; a slight hollow, the barest depression, formed at the very center of the bulge, and then the edges drew back. A couple of feet away, another bulge slowly formed, like a bubble rising through an iridescent mud pool. This time, Jack could see the motion contained within. He could not only see it; he could feel it, plucking inside him with a regular, beating pulse. As he watched, another bulbous form swelled in the opposite direction, then another and another. Though he fought against the urge, he felt his hand drawn toward one of the newer pulsing mounds, the motion throbbing in his fingers. He had lost full volition, and his hand drew closer and closer, his fingers outstretched, his palm stretched flat. Fear trickled in through his pores and washed into the back of his mind. He clamped his teeth together, fighting against the force that was pulling his hand like an offering.

Something multilegged stirred within the panel, struggling and then pulling itself free, it seemed to sup the air with invisible sensors. The next moment, it became aware of Jack's flesh, a real offering. Twin fangs emerged from the front and plunged, each instant drawn out like an eternity, and buried themselves in the back of Jack's hand.

Almost, Jack cried out, but his capacity for voice had been washed away by his anticipation of what was to come. His veins filled with chilling, intelligent ice, scuttling through the pathways of his body, through his arms, across his chest. His breath caught, and the next moment, the frigid awareness flooded through his neck and up into his brain.

Finally, Jack cried out.

"Jack. Jack, wake up."

Jack cracked his eyes, trying to focus. A blurred figure was kneeling beside him.

"Billie?"

"No, Jack. It's Alice."

He opened his eyes fully. Alice was crouched down beside him, one hand on his shoulder, a look of concern on her face.

Jack reached out and gently touched her cheek, not sure whether he was still dreaming.

"Alice?"

"Yes, Jack. It's me."

"But how did you . . . ?"

Alice stayed where she was, not moving back now that he'd woken. Her hand had slipped to the top of his arm.

"They tried to discourage me from coming down here to see you, but I was having none of it. Here," she said, slipping one hand under his shoulder, "sit up."

Jack did as he was instructed, sitting up, and rubbed his

fingers rapidly across his scalp, working his mouth to get the saliva flowing again.

"Weirdest dream," he said. "Spiders."

Alice frowned again and then her features softened.

"This is beginning to be a habit, Jack Stein."

"What's that?"

"This little disappearing act you pull every time you show up."

"Yeah," he said, gently rubbing her upper arm with one hand. "Sorry. It's not you. I didn't have much choice in the matter. The Outreach boys again."

"Yes, I figured it was something like that." She reached out with both hands and held the sides of his face. "Here, let me look at you. Did they hurt you?"

He grunted. "I've had worse."

They were alone in the broad meeting area. He must have fallen asleep on the couch while he was thinking. The tensions, the frustrations, of the last couple of days and the loss of sleep—they must have taken their toll without his realizing the true extent.

"Daman and Billie?" he asked.

Alice got to her feet and sat on the couch next to him.

"I saw them briefly. It was a little strained until Billie gave me the nod of approval." She gave a brief laugh. "That Daman is a strange one."

"More than you can imagine," said Jack wryly.

"Anyway, Billie had apparently looked in on you, seen you were asleep, and decided to leave you to it."

"Okay," said Jack. Finally, he turned to look at her properly. "How about you? You all right?"

Alice nodded. "Yes, nothing. I haven't seen any sign of

the Outreach people. That doesn't mean they haven't been around, of course."

Jack thought for a moment. "Perhaps you really shouldn't be down here," he said. "I don't know how safe it is."

"No, Jack. Not this time," she said. "You're not getting rid of me that easily."

Jack shook his head. He couldn't seem to clear his mind of the image of silver spiders.

"So, I see your visitor has found you," came Daman's voice from one of the doorways. He walked into the room, giving Alice a brief look of acknowledgment. He was followed closely by Billie and another kid Jack hadn't seen before, a pale young boy who reminded Jack somehow of Billie seemingly all those years ago. There was a nervousness about him that made Jack uneasy. He watched as the boy took one of the chairs farther away from the couch. There was something? . . . He couldn't put his finger on it.

"Have you gotten any farther with your thoughts?" asked Daman.

"Not really," said Jack, still watching the kid.

"Well, Billie, Silas, and I have been discussing things," said Daman.

Silas. That must be the young kid.

"As we see it," Daman continued, "Outreach remains a problem, and as there is no easy way to get you away from here, we need to find something that will take their attention away from you for the short term. If we can keep them distracted, give them something to focus on, we might have a chance to slip you out, right under their gaze."

Jack sat forward. "And how do you propose to do that?"

Daman steepled his fingers in front of his face. "It was

Billie who came up with the idea really. Silas thinks he knows how to implement it."

Billie nodded. "It was Hervé who gave me the idea," she said.

"You haven't been in touch with him?" Jack asked, worried.

"No," said Billie. "Not like that."

"So, what?"

She took a deep breath. "Daman knows a lot about Outreach, stuff they might not want generally known. If we had a way to get that out where people could see it, where they couldn't help seeing it, then Outreach would want to stop it, wouldn't they?"

"Uh-huh," said Jack. "But I don't see—"

"Wait, Jack," she said, a hint of annoyance now in her voice. "You can program the Locality, right?"

Jack nodded slowly.

"Silas knows how to do that in lots of ways."

He shook his head. "I still don't see—"

"We get the files and we program them into the Locality itself. Think about Scenics and the ceiling panels and the advertising logos—all that stuff is the same," she said. "We can do that. We can do that not only with the ceiling. We can do it to the walls; we can do it with the buildings and the streets. We put the message right out there where everyone can see, where everyone has to see." She was sitting up straight, the enthusiasm slipping into triumph in her voice.

The kid called Silas was watching Jack intently. Jack returned the gaze.

"You can do this?" he asked him.

Silas returned his look blankly and then looked away. What was it with this kid?

Alice tapped the top of Jack's leg, distracting him. "It could work, Jack. I've probably got access to more stuff we could use too."

"How?" asked Daman.

"The library," said Billie and Alice simultaneously.

Daman nodded. "Yes. Even if it doesn't stop them," he said after meeting the eyes of both of them in turn, "it will certainly get their attention."

"Yeah," said Jack, standing, starting to pace. "It will do that."

He crossed to where Silas sat. "You're *sure* you can do this?" he said, and reached out to touch Silas's arm.

Silas shrank back from the touch, almost scrambling out of the way, but not before Jack's fingertips had brushed across him.

Jack drew in his breath sharply. A lance of cold certainty embedded itself in his chest. The slightest touch. He drew back, staring at the kid. The boy was echoing his look, eyes as wide as Jack's must be.

He glanced at Billie and she gave him a questioning frown.

Jack gave her a slight shake of his head. She didn't need to know what he'd just felt. Jack didn't really want to think about the implications of what he'd felt either. Whatever it was, it wasn't good. He turned away from Silas.

"Okay, let's do this. It still doesn't do anything about our other problem, though."

"What problem?" said Alice, looking concerned again.

Jack sighed. "Doing this might slow Outreach down a bit, and even if it works . . ."

"Look," said Daman. "We know things about Outreach that Outreach doesn't even know."

Jack shook his head. "I'm not debating that. It's a good plan. Let's infect them with their own disease. Yeah, I can buy that. But that's not what I'm worried about. It's not going to slow them down getting to the aliens and I'm not the only one who can make contact with them. How long is it going to be before they have someone else who can do exactly what I do? Shit, they might already be working on it. They probably are. And they've already gotten a head start with the stuff that McCreedy has given them."

He paused, turned, and started a fresh circuit. All faces in the room were watching him as he paced.

"Jack, stop for a minute," said Alice.

"What?"

"Outreach are bigger than all of us—we know that," she said. "But there are others out there just as big."

"And that's half of the problem," said Jack. "Even if we can do something about Outreach, which is doubtful, then there are others just as eager to step into the gap and take advantage of whatever the aliens have to offer. The SOU is just one example."

Having voiced it, he crossed back to the couch to sit beside her, feeling defeated. The others in the room mirrored his slumped shoulders, staring into space, considering. They needed some sort of bright idea and it didn't look like it was going to be forthcoming from any of them soon. How the hell could they put up any real sort of fight against the Outreach behemoth, against any of the corporate machines?

"So what do we do?" said Billie, finally breaking the silence.

Jack looked up, met her gaze, and felt somehow that it

was his fault that they had run out of ideas. He turned away again. It was strange, but he thought the accusation would have been harder to take if the expression had come from her younger face.

He looked across at Daman, sitting primly, his hands still folded neatly before him; over at Silas, who could almost have faded completely into the background; and finally at Alice. They weren't going to get anything else done that night. He turned his attention back to Daman.

"So, I guess you've got somewhere for us to sleep?" he said.

Twenty-two

Billie had protested that she didn't feel like sleeping and had headed off to one of the other rooms, Jack guessed to keep on picking Silas's brains, though the kid had looked half-dead on his feet by the time they were done. He knew, though, that Billie wasn't going to let go of something until she was satisfied.

When one of the younger boys appeared to lead Jack to another section of the building, pointing out a programmed bedroom where once had sat an office, and the nearby facilities, which were probably original, Alice had followed. The boy left them and faded off into the shadows, ignoring Jack's thanks. There were a couple of beds in the room, and looking at them, he felt a twinge of discomfort, wondering what might have taken place back here, what the room might be used for most of the time. Nothing stirred his senses, though, so he let himself relax, at least a little.

Alice watched him, waiting, as he stood in the room's center.

"Come here, Jack," she said finally, reaching for his hand and pulling him toward one of the beds.

He let himself be led, allowed her to ease him down, her hands applying gentle pressure to his shoulders, pushing him down to sit on the edge of the bed. She stood in front of him, looking down at his face, a slight smile quirking the corners of her mouth.

"I don't know, Jack," she said. "Do I have to do every-thing?"

She helped him off with his shirt, then, turning, removed her own, leaned down to slip off her shoes, and then stood and eased off her trousers. Jack sat and watched, taking in her shape, the paleness of her skin, the slight dusting of freckles on her shoulders.

"Come on," she said, turning, lifting him to stand, and then reached for his trousers.

No, she didn't have to do everything. He helped her re-move the trousers, dropping them to the floor and stepping out of them, feeling slightly stupid with the awkwardness of the action. She watched him in return, and then stretched around behind her, unclasped her bra, and slipped it off too, not a trace of self-consciousness in the action.

"Come here," she said, pulling back the covers and slid-ing into bed.

Jack really didn't need to be told twice. As he climbed into the bed beside her, he reached up and pushed her hair back from her cheek.

"Hi there," he said, for the time being forgetting about where they were. For a while, at least, the universe con-tracted into a tiny bubble that contained no one else, and not even Outreach could puncture the skin.

Later, Jack lay on his back, staring up at the mottled ceil-ing, one arm supporting his head. Alice lay beside him, one finger tracing patterns through the hair on his chest.

"So what are you going to do, Jack?" she said, almost in a whisper.

"I really don't know," he said, after a pause while he thought it through. "Sure we can distract Outreach in the Lo-cality, but that only goes so far." He drew in a deep breath and held it for a couple of moments before letting it out slowly. "And I don't care if Outreach or the SOU get to the alien homeworld. They will eventually. Anything we do to slow them down only delays the inevitable. Somehow, I don't think the aliens are going to be much use to us."

He made a noise deep in his throat. "You know, I've got to find something else to call them apart from 'the aliens.' I can't go on calling them coatracks either. That's just stupid."

Her fingers stopped moving on his chest. "What about Silvers," she said. "Every time you said anything about them, you called them silver."

"Yeah, that works," he said. "Okay, the Silvers don't really seem to care about anything—all they've done so far is give me warnings. From everything I've seen, they're in decline, a failed empire or something like that. They're kind of like this old relative that doesn't know much or care about what's going on in the outside world anymore. Though I don't see how we could be related."

"So, if they don't matter," said Alice, "who or what does?"

"I don't know," said Jack. "Should I be more worried about what some alien race might or might not do to us, or about what people like Outreach are doing to their own? For all we know, the other aliens—let's call them the Blacks— might be some fairy story meant to frighten the children. And dammit, we are the children in this relationship. Outreach is the biggest kid of all."

Alice's fingers were moving again, tracing little patterns across his chest and abdomen. The light touch of her nails made his abdominal muscles spasm involuntarily and he grabbed for her hand, holding it in place.

"So, can you ask them?" she said, content for the moment to let her fingers lie within his grasp.

"Ask who?"

"The Silvers."

"Yeah, I guess I could," he said. "But I'm not sure it would do any good. Their consciousness is so . . . different. I'm not sure what really matters to them either, if anything does."

"And you?" said Alice. "Does anything matter to you, Jack?"

He gave her fingers a little squeeze. "Some things do," he said. He turned on his side, burying his face in her hair and drinking in the smell of her.

After a while, they slept. Jack dreamed of black and silver diamonds, attacking each other on a chessboard. Every time the pieces swept across the playing surface, one after the other, the silver ones fell.

But it was just a dream.

"Oh," said Billie from the doorway.

Jack opened his eyes. She was standing at the room's entrance, a mixture of emotions on her face.

"Billie? What is it?" He felt Alice stir beside him.

"I want you to see something," said Billie. "Doesn't matter. I'll come back later."

She looked confused.

"No, wait," said Jack. He leaned over the side of the bed, feeling around for his clothes. He pulled his trousers on under the covers and then got out of bed, pulling on his shirt. Alice opened her eyes slowly, and looked at him, a dreamy smile appearing on her face.

"Jack?" she said.

"It's fine," said Jack. "I'll be back soon. Take your time."

Billie avoided his eyes as he crossed the room to join her. "What have you got to show me?"

For the first time, Billie met his eyes. "We've done something," she said, a slight grin coming with the words.

Jack padded after her. He knew that tone of vague triumph in her voice. Billie clearly thought she'd done something pretty clever.

He scratched the back of his head, following as she led him through the network of rooms to a small office space near the back of the floor. The kid, Silas, lay curled up on a couch at the rear of the room. Jack glanced around, but could see nothing that warranted Billie's sense of expectation. She held her finger to her lips and pointed to Silas. Jack nodded.

"We worked pretty late," she whispered. "The stuff Silas did to get you out of there gave me an idea. I wanted to see if we could do it first."

Jack was about to ask what, but Billie hushed him before he could. She leaned over to the flat desk in the room's center and touched a couple of places on the top. Nothing seemed to happen. Jack glanced over at the wall, seeing if he was supposed to watch something on the screen, but the wall remained blank. He turned back to Billie and frowned. She grinned and shook her head, then nodded at the desk.

Jack watched. Still nothing happened, but then a moment later—the lights were low—he noticed a subtle change in the table's surface, right near the edge. A pulsing discoloration throbbed through the hard material.

The ripples of darkness coalesced, drawing ever closer to a single point, and then formed a single, circular mark that spread out slowly. The surface bulged toward the very center of the mark, then drew apart like an irising lens. Something silver poked out of the hole and then something else.

"Shit," Jack said under his breath, and stepped back. Fucking spiders. Just like the dream.

Billie was grinning like an idiot now, watching his re-action.

The thing pulled itself free of the hole and sat rocking slightly above the black space, its oval silver body sus-pended by four legs that straddled the hole. Not eight legs— four. Four legs, Jack. Keep it together. The thing was a machine.

"What is it?" he whispered to Billie.

She touched something else and the spider melted back into the table surface.

He frowned at her, but she glanced in Silas's direction, then came toward Jack, grabbed his arm, and dragged him out of the room.

"So?" said Jack in a more normal voice. "What is it?"

"So," said Billie. "When we had to get you out of that place that Outreach had you in, Silas did something. He pro-grammed a piece of the desk to contain a code that infected the wall's programming around that place. It made it draw back into a doorway that let us get in."

Jack didn't really understand what she was talking about, but he let her continue.

"So I was thinking about what Hervé wanted to do with his research, and how we could get the information out in a way that Outreach couldn't stop it. If we could program it into something that could infect anything with the data and routines, they couldn't stop it, could they?"

Jack shook his head. "I don't get it."

Billie gave him one of her looks. "We're stuck here, right? We can't get out. Outreach monitors the transmissions and the networks built into the Locality. Any links to other sites are guarded. I can get in and out of systems, but it's re-ally hard to get from one place to the other. All of the chan-nels are monitored by intelligent routines that are faster than

a person can think. The only way we can really shift information from Outreach is to carry it somehow. That thing's
my bug," she said, and grinned again.

"Bug?" said Jack.

"Uh-huh," said Billie. "They used to talk about bugs in
the systems. Things that weren't supposed to be there that
stop things working the right way. Bugs are like insects, and
insects used to be one of the ways diseases got carried and
transferred. I read about that stuff. So, that's my bug. It car-
ries the disease. Only it isn't a disease. It's the information.
When it gets somewhere else, it transfers the information
and the code for building more bugs. They go out to other
places and so on. Outreach could never stop it. Every system
in the world would have bugs. Outreach could never keep
the information to themselves. Everyone would have it."

"Yeah, okay," said Jack, running his fingers back through
his hair. "I can see how that would work. There's plenty of
people who have the technology now to get to the Silvers."

"Silvers?"

"Yeah, the aliens. Alice thought of the name," said Jack.

"Oh," she said, looking away again, her enthusiasm
seeming to suddenly fade.

Jack set his jaw. "Listen, Billie, have you got a problem?"

Billie said nothing, just shook her head.

"Okay, then. We should go and tell Alice what you've
come up with and then we can talk to Daman."

"There's one problem," said Billie quietly.

"And that is?"

"We need to get the stuff, the information, to give the
bug."

Jack frowned. "But what about the research that Hervé
did? That's what got us there in the first place."

"Nuh-uh. I thought about that. We don't have it. Hervé

has it. We can't get it from him. They'd know straightaway and it's different. It's not the real information. It would have to be decrypted," Billie said.

"Well," said Jack, starting to walk back to the room where Alice still waited for them, "we have to get it from somewhere else."

"And where do we get it, Jack?" said Billie, following behind.

"Um." Jack stopped in his tracks. "The only other people who have it are Outreach."

"And Dog," said Billie.

"Yeah."

"And Dog's gone," she said flatly, but he could tell she was masking what she was feeling about that particular statement.

He let it pass and continued walking. "So we get it from Outreach."

They'd reached the makeshift bedroom. Alice sat on the edge of the bed, fully dressed.

"Get what?" she said.

Billie was hanging back in the doorway, watching Alice. Jack looked at Billie and then back to Alice.

"I'll let Billie explain," he said, and stepped aside to let her pass. He thought that was the wisest course of action, under the circumstances.

Twenty-three

Daman was more than interested in what Billie was proposing, but he too saw the dilemma. The only ready source of what they would need was right in the heart of Outreach Industries itself, probably somewhere within the corporate headquarters up near the far end of New. He'd asked Silas to check for appropriate access points as soon as the boy was awake, but Silas had drawn a blank.

He and Billie sat side by side on the couch, Daman on another, and Jack perched on the arm of a chair. They were all looking at him as if they expected him to come up with the answers.

"Jesus," he said. "I don't know. How do you expect us to get into Outreach? We'd be better off trying to find McCreedy, wherever he might be."

Billie scowled. "How, Jack?"

"I don't know. Send people out after him. Look for him. Find him. I like those chances better than taking on Outreach head-on."

Alice appeared from the back rooms. "Find who?" she asked.

"McCreedy," said Jack, turning to look over his shoulder at her as she entered the room. He frowned, despite his urge to smile at her. "But I don't like those chances either."

"You find people. That's one of the things you do," said Billie, her eyes narrowed now.

"And what, you're expecting me to find Dog? Is that what you want?"

A mix of emotions passed across her face and then she averted her gaze. "If we have to," she said.

Jack pushed himself up from the chair. "Don't get me wrong. I'd love to find McCreedy, believe me," he said, not even bothering to mask the hardness in his voice.

There were noises from below. Jack turned in the direction the sounds were coming from. Daman frowned.

A kid shouted, the words indistinct. Then a man's voice drifted up. Another shout, and then silence.

"What the . . . ?" said Jack.

Daman was on his feet, a look of real concern on his face. He grimaced and made for the door leading to the way down. He was halfway across the room when one of the older boys burst in, panting.

"They're here," he said. "They got Will. You better get out."

"What?" said Daman, almost spitting the word.

"Down below. They're looking for him." The boy nodded in Jack's direction.

"Shit," said Jack. "Which way out, Daman?"

"Go!" Daman said, pointing at one of the side doorways. He strode out the main door, dragging the boy with him.

"Shit, Billie, move," said Jack. "Alice?" He held out a hand.

Billie was on her feet. "Silas?"

The young kid, looking wide-eyed, huddled in the corner of the couch, his arms wrapped around himself. He shook his head.

"Silas!" said Billie, in one of those pissed-off tones so familiar to Jack, but the kid didn't move.

"Forget it," said Jack. "He'll be fine." He made quickly

for the door that Daman had indicated, Alice a step in front of him.

Billie growled and then, giving up on Silas, followed quickly after.

As soon as they were through the door, Alice stood, looking first one way, then the other.

"Which way, Jack?"

He grabbed her arm. "This way," he said, taking the corridor to the right. He didn't need to confirm; he just knew. Alice didn't argue, nor, thankfully, did Billie. Jack strode quickly down the corridor, not quite running, but fast enough to get them to the exit and, hopefully, escape capture for the time being. With any luck, Daman could hold their pursuers off long enough for the three of them to get out of there and away. And Jack was good with luck, or he was supposed to be.

Jack had no idea where they were going. Nor was he certain who it was who was after them, but he had a pretty good idea that it was likely to be Outreach.

At the end of the corridor lay a gloomy staircase, leading down into the shadows, a little-used route to the lower levels, by the looks of things. Jack didn't hesitate; he took the stairs two at a time, heading for the ground floor. The sound of Billie's and Alice's footsteps on the staircase felt unnaturally loud in the small echoing space. At the next level down, he paused, listening, holding his hand up to stop them as the noise of their descent faded away. Everything had gone very quiet. There were no voices, no sounds of pursuit, nothing but the creaking of the building's structure around them and the rhythm of their rapid breathing. Jack decided to risk it. Gesturing for quiet, he took the next set of stairs more slowly, listening carefully as they went.

They had nowhere to go. They could lose themselves in the mass of crumbling doorways and decaying shells that made up Old, but it would last for only so long. If Outreach had found him here, it wouldn't be long before they tracked him down anywhere within the confines of the Locality. They had to know about Alice by now. They probably knew about Billie too, after the breakout at the facility they'd constructed. He just couldn't risk their finding either one. Right now, his chances alone would be no better than with the women. He needed time. He needed time to think, or for something to happen, for his inner senses to kick in and show him a way out of this.

They descended another level, creeping down stair after stair and pausing at the next level to listen. There were sounds again. A muffled shout from above. Jack froze, straining to hear. Alice was looking at him questioningly.

The next floor down, and they'd be at the lobby, or at least to the rear of the building at the ground. Jack closed his eyes, reaching out, trying to feel for threats. He shook his head.

"I can't tell," he whispered.

Billie gave him a frown.

Suddenly something sparked. That sharp chill worked in his guts and his breath caught. He lifted one finger, urging quiet. He raised the finger to his lips, held out his hand, palm outward, telling them to stay, then turned, taking each step at a time, slowly, senses prickling.

Somewhere below, there was someone waiting.

The staircase ended in a small enclosed area with a single doorway leading off. It was dark down here, the shadows pooling in the small space, making it hard to distinguish detail. Jack stopped a few steps up, straining against the gloom. There, half-concealed by the edge of

the doorway, stood a shadow darker than the rest. Old re-
actions, old patterns, kicked into place. Almost crouching,
trying to make himself smaller, taking the remaining stairs
silently, slowly, Jack crept down. One step from the bottom, he paused again, watching, making sure of what he
was seeing. He couldn't tell, but he thought there was just
one. One he could take. One he thought he could take. The
shadow moved, disappearing behind the edge of the doorway. Jack waited for a moment, then took the opportunity
and stepped lightly across to the doorway's edge, pressing
himself back against the wall, still reaching, trying to
make out the nature of the presence that lay mere inches
away.

"Right," said a man's voice.

Jack held his breath.

"No, nothing yet. You want me to check these stairs?"

Silence.

"Okay."

Jack glanced up, but Billie and Alice were out of direct
sight from this vantage point. The one-way conversation
told him that the guy was alone. He didn't know how far
away any of the others might be, but for now, all it mattered
was that the guy was alone.

A head appeared around the edge of the doorway. Jack
was ready. Both hands clasped together in a fist, his arms
upraised, he brought them down, hard, against the side of
that head. The man went down, sideways, momentarily
stunned, a deep grunt coming from his mouth. He fell back
against the other side of the doorway, slamming against the
wall and then dropping to the floor, another noise forced
from his lungs as he hit. Something dropped and skittered
across the floor. A gun.

Jack didn't think. He kicked.

His foot made contact below the chin, slamming the man's head back against the wall. Jack was ready for another, but there was no need. The faceless shadow slumped, not even a groan issuing from its lips. Jack listened, but there was no other sound. He crouched, feeling across the floor, and then his fingers made contact with the weapon lying near the base of the stairs. He pocketed the gun and stood again. Moving back to the doorway, he listened, assuring himself that there was no one else out there, feeling with every sense at his disposal. Then he returned to the base of the stairs and peered up.

Billie and Alice were crouched on the landing, huddled together, looking down. Once more, he raised his hand to his lips and then gestured them down. He turned back to check the unconscious form on the floor. Jack thought the man would live, but frankly, right now, he didn't really care.

As he stood, both Billie and Alice moved up close behind him. Alice glanced down at the body on the floor and then looked away again quickly. It didn't surprise Jack at all that Billie seemed completely unfazed. She stepped around Jack silently and poked her head around the doorway before Jack had a chance to stop her.

"Nobody there," she whispered.

"Shit, Billie," said Jack, pulling her back with a hand on her shoulder.

He looked around the doorway, but she was right; the way appeared clear for the moment. A wide room lay empty of any furniture. Another doorway led beyond and light filtered through from the front. Footsteps marked the ever-present dust. It appeared as though Daman and his crew didn't use this way much. Perhaps that was intentional. Jack

nodded to himself. Only one set of footprints. He quickly
stepped across the open space and pressed up beside the next
doorway, ducking his face quickly around the edge, and then
back again. He gestured to the other two and they too
quickly crossed to join him, flat back against the wall next
to him.

"What now?" whispered Alice.

"We go," he whispered back. He didn't know how long
the guy on the floor would be out. For all he knew, they
didn't have any time to waste. Briefly, he wondered what
was happening on the floors above them.

So, Stein, what now?

He still didn't have any answers.

He reached into his pocket and pulled out the gun, checking it. A medium-intensity energy weapon. The safety was
off. It was set to low, designed to disable, not to kill. He
upped the setting and then adjusted his grip.

"Okay, let's go," he said.

Out—they had to get out. The apparent silence might be
deceptive. The quick glimpse had revealed little. The wide-
open space had looked like the lobby, and it was likely that
somewhere out there others would be waiting for them.
Alice was watching him again for direction.

The sound of feet on the stairs behind them took away
the choices. Jack whirled, making quickly for the opposite door, ducked through it, and crouched, training his
weapon on the topmost step that he could see from his
position. He beckoned Alice and Billie over and pointed
to the shadows lying below the stairs. There was more
than one set of rapidly approaching footsteps. They were
moving fast, taking the stairs at a run. Jack concentrated,

giving just a brief glance to make sure that Alice and Billie were well out of sight.

"Stop!" cried a man's voice from above, echoing down the confined stairwell.

"Shit," said another voice, urgent, hurried.

Jack held his breath.

Feet appeared at the top of the steps, then small legs. More feet, larger legs, moving quickly. Jack kept his weapon trained, holding his fire. The legs didn't belong to any of the Outreach crew; it was Daman's kids, trying to get out. There was a bright flash; then one of the figures was tumbling down the stairs, not running. Jesus. They'd shot one of the kids.

Jack swung himself to the staircase bottom, gripping the gun with both hands now, giving the fallen kid only a brief look. The other figure had stopped his descent and Jack let his breath hiss out. It was Daman. He seemed frozen in place, staring down at the body below him.

Another figure appeared behind him, features grimacing, weapon in hand. It took only an instant for the man to register Jack's presence, for his expression to change, but by then, Jack had fired. The guy dropped, a neat hole burned into his head. Jack waited, but it seemed like there had been only one. Jack took the stairs two at a time, reaching Daman quickly, then moving past him. He checked the stairs above, but they were clear. Then he stooped to retrieve the other weapon, pocketed it, and walked back down to where Daman still stood, unmoving.

"Daman," said Jack, taking a grip on Daman's arm. "We've got to move."

Daman resisted, clutching the railing with one hand, still staring down at the unmoving form below them.

"Silas," he said quietly.

"Shit," said Jack, looking down. He could tell by the angle of the neck that there was no point checking. If the shot hadn't killed him, the fall had done the rest.

"Shit," he said again, increasing the pressure on Daman's arm. "Come on. We have to get out of here."

Jack glanced above again, but for now, there was no further sign of pursuit.

This time, Daman allowed himself to be led down the remaining stairs, past Silas's small, still form, and round the edge of the stairs, his face blank.

"Jack," said Alice.

Jack shook his head. He pulled out the other gun, handed it to Alice.

"Can you use this?"

He knew Billie didn't know how.

"Give it to me," said Daman, the words coming from between closed teeth.

Jack handed over the gun and Daman looked down at it, his jaw working.

Jack couldn't afford to wait around while Daman came to terms with whatever was warring in his head. They really did have to get out of there, and fast.

He moved to the open doorway and ducked around to take a quick look, but their way was still clear. He beckoned for the others to join him.

Looking afraid, Billie and Alice came over. An instant later, Daman followed, weapon held at the ready, the lack of expression still evident on his face, but his eyes hard. Jack checked around the door—still clear.

"No," said Billie.

She'd seen the body at the foot of the stairs.

Jack reached out and grabbed her arm.

"Not now, Billie. We have to go."

Her eyes were wide, but she nodded, the emotions battling inside her, threatening.

"Daman, over here," said Jack. "Keep an eye on the stairs."

Jack stepped out from the doorway and crossed the empty room beyond. The doorway at the other side provided enough cover and once again, he checked beyond it, darting his face around the edge and back again. This time he got a better look. Two men were standing at the lobby's street entrance on either side of the wide double doors. They'd been in uniform, not police, but some city functionaries. From the brief glimpse he'd gotten, it appeared they were armed. He looked back toward the stairwell, held his fingers to his lips, and then pointed to the other side of the doorway and waved the others forward.

Quickly, quickly, Billie, Alice, and Daman crossed to take up position where Jack had indicated. They were still in reasonable shadow here, so he might gain some element of surprise, but he wasn't sure he could take both of the men in one go. All it would take was for one of them to have the chance to raise the alarm.

Any thought of Jack's next actions were taken from him. Daman stepped from the doorway, gun held behind his back, a smile on his face.

What the . . . ?

"Gentlemen," said Daman, sauntering calmly to the lobby's center.

"It's that weird kid," said one of the men.

It was the last thing he said. In the next instant, Daman

had whipped out the gun and dropped both of them before they had a chance to do anything else. Good, clean shots.

"Damn," said Jack. "Come on," he urged Billie and Alice. "We'd better move."

Daman stood where he was, staring calmly at his handiwork, gun still held loosely in his hand.

"Where?" said Jack.

"This way," said Daman, seeming to come back to himself, and stepping quickly toward the front doors.

Twenty-four

The four of them were huddled in a structure at the far end of Old. It wasn't comfortable. The building noises only added to the tension sitting like a rough and tattered blanket between them. No comfort there. Billie was on watch, out by the main entrance. Daman was staring down at the floor in front of him, occasionally turning the gun still held in his hands. Alice sat with her knees pulled up, her arms wrapped around them, also staring at a spot in front of her. Jack was worrying about whether Outreach had some tracking capability on him. He thought that they were probably far enough down that the Locality's systems would work intermittently at best. The building groaned and he shifted as a trickle of dust fell nearby.

Come on, Stein. Think.

They'd lost Silas, and Jack didn't know how much Billie had absorbed of the kid's knowledge before they'd gotten out of there. He looked across at Daman, and as if sensing it, Daman looked up, met Jack's gaze, and then dropped his own to the floor again. From where Jack was, he had a view of Billie, sitting and rocking slightly.

Jack pushed himself to his feet and wandered over toward Billie, making sure to keep out of the direct line of sight through the doorway.

"You okay?" he said.

"Uh-huh."

He crouched down beside her. He could tell that she wasn't really okay, but that she was putting a brave face on it.

"We've got a bit of a problem," he said. "I'm sorry about what happened to Silas. We needed him."

Billie sighed. "Yeah."

"So, what do you think we should do, Billie?"

She looked up and held his gaze. "I can do it."

He knew better than to question her answer.

"Okay, but where? We need to get into Outreach, don't we?"

"Not for the first part," she said resignedly. "I can do that from the library with Alice."

That wasn't a bad idea. Perhaps Outreach didn't have tabs on her yet, or on Alice after all. It was worth the risk. It would give Jack an opportunity to talk to Daman and make some plans.

"Okay," he said. "When?"

She chewed at her bottom lip. "Now, maybe."

Jack nodded. He slipped back into the other section of the building, leaving her sitting there with her thoughts.

"Alice," he said.

She looked up. He couldn't read what was on her face, but there was a softness there too when she met his eyes. Jack almost smiled, despite their circumstance.

"You need to go with Billie," he said. "She can do the stuff with the Locality and she thinks she can do it from the library. Is that going to be okay?"

Alice stood, looking thoughtful.

"Yes, but what about you, Jack?"

"I need to talk to Daman."

Alice reached up and touched his cheek. "Be careful," she said.

"You too." He leaned over and kissed her on the forehead. "Go. We'll meet back here."

She slipped out to follow Billie.

Daman was sitting in the same place, not having shifted position at all. He had been watching them. Jack moved across to join him, crouching again.

"So what do you suggest?" he said.

Daman sighed and shrugged. "Our options are limited. I don't have ready access. It would be foolish to return to the building, and I don't know what's happened to the others."

He turned the gun over and over in his hands, watching the motion intently.

"Bastards," he said between closed teeth.

Jack waited, seeing if there was anything more, but Daman had gone silent.

"But you knew that," he said quietly.

Daman looked up at him with an accusing stare and then looked away again.

"Yes," he said just as quietly.

"So why?"

"Because somehow I knew that eventually a time like this would come. Because after what happened to me I was powerless. After what they'd put me through, I looked for ways to manipulate in return. I don't know, Jack."

"But the kids . . ."

"I know that too. Perhaps I was fooling myself that I was protecting them. Giving them a semisafe environment in a place that could never be safe."

"So why didn't you just try to expose what was going on?"

"Because I couldn't," said Daman. "Outreach owns everything here. How could I do anything about that? I needed to be in a position where I had enough resources, and in a way, I suppose, that became a trap of its own."

Jack shook his head.

Daman looked back at him, accusation slipping back into his expression. "What about you? You just ran away, Jack, What use is that?"

Jack sighed. "Yeah. Things have moved on since then, though. I kept Billie safe, didn't I?"

Daman's eyes narrowed. "Did you?"

Jack chewed on that for a moment. He didn't know.

"Okay, forget about that," he said finally. "We are where we are. What do we do now?"

For the first time that Jack could remember, the confidence that usually filled Daman's every action and word appeared to have simply slipped away. He was a tiny despot who had lost his empire and he was powerless without it. Jack waited.

"According to Silas . . ." Daman's voice caught for a moment, but he cleared his throat and continued. "The hub of Outreach's systems is protected in the same way that they shielded the place where they were holding you. It is not immediately visible from conventional scans of the city or its networks. We need to get right inside if we are to access what we need. Then, we probably need a healthy chunk of time in there to do what we want to. Without Silas, though . . ." He spread his hands wide.

"Billie can do it," said Jack.

"Yes, she probably can," said Daman. "She was always very good."

"And she still is," said Jack. "That much hasn't changed."

"We shall see. . . . In the meantime, we wait. Let's give Outreach something to think about before we storm the castle. As it is, they are going to be looking for us."

"Okay," said Jack, standing. "Meanwhile, I suggest we take watches, take turns getting some rest. We may need it."

Giving one last look at the gun in his hands, Daman nodded and stood as well, something unreadable working behind his eyes. He looked up into Jack's face.

"I'll take the first watch and give some thought about our next steps." He seemed as if he expected Jack to challenge the suggestion.

"Yeah, you do that," said Jack, turning away and seeking a patch of floor relatively clear of dust and debris.

It had been a long time since he'd last slept like this, and he doubted he'd get any real rest, but he lay down anyway, settling himself on his side, one arm crooked beneath his head, a position he knew would cause him to wake automatically once his arm had gone to sleep and started to hurt. He closed his eyes, listening to the creaks and pops of the decaying building, smelling the musty odor of the invisible builders, dead and dying and filling his senses with their last spark of life.

What now, Daman? What have you got coming, Jack?

There was a presence stalking through his consciousness, something palpable and cold. Jack stood in darkness, noises all around him, a deep humming felt in the very pit of his stomach rather than heard. A shadow loomed beside him, and then moved past. The thing radiated a chill presence and Jack caught his breath, hoping that whatever it was hadn't noticed him.

Where the hell was he?

He probed the space, using all his senses, seeking at least a clue.

The vibration continued, pulsing now inside, unsettling him right down to his bones. There was a smell too, something like crushed ants. He couldn't make out shapes; it was too dark. Wherever it was, it felt large. He could feel the space around him, and everywhere the chill. It wasn't cold, not really. The chill was a presence, something he could feel inside rather than on his skin.

Somehow, he knew it wouldn't be a good idea to say anything. He debated, but it looked like nothing was going to change in the immediate future, so he took a tentative step forward. Whatever lay beneath his feet was solid enough.

Another shape loomed up on him from the darkness and moved past. This time, Jack took a side step, moving out of the thing's way. He got the impression of something dark and spiny, all hard angles. No, he didn't think it would be a good idea to have that run into him either.

Why was he seeing this?

Slowly, he turned, seeking some clue.

Nothing but darkness and cold and that ever-present hum.

Okay, Stein, this isn't a very nice place. Time to go.

He closed his eyes and willed himself away. Slowly, carefully, he opened his eyes again. Nothing had changed.

Right. It appeared he was supposed to be seeing something.

A bright flash came from one side, momentarily dazzling him. Jack blinked, trying to clear the afterimage from his vision. There had been no noise accompanying the light. He frowned, turning toward the direction that the flash had appeared to emanate from, and took a few more cautious steps.

Come on, Jack. What are you looking for?

His toes met something solid, and he could feel the vibration now through his feet as well as through his bones. He reached out with one hand, groping through the gloom, the colors still floating through his sight, making it harder to see even dim shapes. Something solid, metallic by the feel of it, blocked his way. He ran his palm across the surface, testing. Small protrusions clustered midway along the surface, jagged and angular, and he withdrew his hand quickly.

Okay. What now?

What he really needed was some illumination. Sometimes in the dreamstate, if he concentrated on something enough, it would appear. He focused on light, on the thought of light.

A bright flash expanded from right in front of him, blinding him completely.

Shit. Good plan, Stein. Brilliant. How was he supposed to find anything now? He blinked rapidly, his eyes watering. Maybe this was just a normal dream, something conjured in response to the gloom and death surrounding his sleeping form, but he doubted it was the case.

Spots in front of his eyes, but he was starting to be able to make out patches of even darker shapes in the shapelessness of the darkness around him.

Behind him, a hulking presence grew. He couldn't see it, but he could certainly feel it. As it neared, the cold sensation radiating from it swept through his senses, almost numbing his capacity for thought. Most of all, though, he could feel its threat, and he felt that deep in his guts, right at the very bottom of his abdomen. Jesus, what was that thing? It was moving, alive, but like no other living thing he had ever encountered. Was it alive, or was that merely the impression he was getting? His urge to bolt away from the thing was growing, but he stayed, half-blind, rooted to the spot. The chill within, he thought.

Jack measured that chill and felt its shape, testing its boundaries, trying to contain it. It lived inside him, pulsing with a deep presence. He tasted it and then used the taste to form a probe, outside, feeling through the surrounding space, seeking its source. And then he found it. The cold and hardness was numbing, a center of dark intelligence, hatred, disgust. Vicious cruelty came from that source and sought his presence, feeling back along the length of the probe that Jack had sent out.

It knew he was here.

Jesus.

Jack took a breath and closed his eyes, trying to force the thing from him, trying to shove it back and away.

Jack's heart was pounding. He could feel the thing give, a little, and then it was pushing back against him with more vigor, with an intent that was unmistakable. The thing was trying to crush him, crush his mind and will, and swallow him, drain the very life out of him. It was too much. Jack fought, but it was far too much for him. He felt himself fading.

No. He could not let this happen.

He focused his will. Come on, Jack. You're not really here. He had to believe it, make that thing believe it, before it consumed him completely.

I am not here.

The tendril of cold hate was suddenly questing, no longer a certainty. The alien mind had lost him.

He felt it seeking.

Teeth firmly pressed together, Jack concentrated his will.

And then he was somewhere else.

"Jaaaack Steeeein," said the voice. It welled up inside and over him, one voice that was many voices combined into a single reverberating echo.

The voice swelled again.

"Jack. Stein."

This time it was clearer, more controlled.

Jack looked around, up at the sky, behind him, across open fields to either side, but they stood alone together, he and the alien being.

"Okay," said Jack. "What the hell was that all about?"

"You saw?"

"Yeah, I saw. So what?"

"You cannot defeat them."

Jack drew in a breath and let it out. "Again, so what? I don't have any intention of defeating them. I don't even know who or what they are."

There was a lengthy silence in which Jack stared at the Silver and though it had no eyes, it seemed to stare back at him. Impasse.

"Listen," said Jack. "I don't know what you want. Okay, I know, everything you've done in the past has been pretty good, but that's not the point. We're done. I found Billie. I found you. Now that should be the end of the story, shouldn't it? Why do you keep bringing me back here?"

"It is not we who bring you," said the chorus. "You come because you must."

Jack grimaced. "We're dreaming, right? We're both dreaming. So explain to me why you are dreaming me. I don't know what you can do anymore. You are thousands of light-years, or however far it is, away from us. You seem content to sit in your own little city and wait for whatever is going to happen to you. What interest is it of yours?"

Again, there was silence. Jack felt nervous challenging them like this, but he was getting a little tired of being constantly dragged back here in his dreams when he was supposed to be using them for something. At least they had dispensed with the constructed interlocutor. He doubted whether he could have stood for talking to a younger Billie this time.

He was about to speak again when the alien voice swelled once more inside his head.

"We are content," they said.

"Then why?" said Jack.

All that met his question was silence.

Jack struggled back to full wakefulness. His arm was numb and aching, but then he'd been expecting that. The hardness of the floor dug into his hip and he winced as he rolled onto his back and then sat up.

How long had he been out for? No handipad to check the time, but it felt like only about an hour or so. As he sat there, working his mouth and face, allowing full awareness to trickle back, he carried on the dream thought. What the hell did the Silvers want with him anyway? They said they didn't know. Well, he certainly didn't. The other place had to have been something to do with the Blacks, and why he was seeing them again too was a mystery. Surely seeing them once was enough to deliver the message. These were bad guys. You didn't want to mess with them. What more did he need to know?

Jack pushed himself to his feet and crossed to the doorway. Daman was squatting by the front entrance, half-hidden in shadow, but Jack's eyes were used to the gloom. Anyone from the street would have a hard time seeing him at first. Jack stepped lightly over to where he sat, making sure to keep out of the direct line of sight himself.

Daman glanced up. He seemed a little more settled now.

"That wasn't long," he said.

"Nah," said Jack. "Dream woke me."

"Isn't that what you're supposed to do?" asked Daman. "So, have you dreamed a way out for us?"

"Yeah, funny," said Jack.

"Well?"

Jack shook his head.

"No, nothing here either. I don't know whether Billie's

managed to do what she was supposed to, but I think it would take a couple of hours for it to filter through the city's programming anyway. The streets have been quiet."

"No sign of any of your crew?"

It was Daman's turn to shake his head. "They know how to lie low. They've been doing it all their lives."

It wasn't the only thing they'd been doing all their lives either, but Jack refrained from saying anything.

"Have you come up with any thoughts?" Jack lowered himself to squat beside him.

"Well, I have been considering. I've been thinking about alternatives actually, but I'm afraid I've not been too successful. We have limited numbers. We have two guns. It's not going to get us very far, is it? We might have had more of a chance if I had all my people, but it's going to take some time to get them together again and after what's happened, they're going to be scared. We don't even know how many managed to get away, or if Outreach took them either. For all we know, they may have. . . ." Daman bit his lip.

"No," said Jack. "I don't think so."

"We do not know," said Daman.

The echo of the dream still sat fresh in his mind, and it was unsettling. He frowned.

"The only other option I can see is to try and get you out of here," Daman continued. "Again, though, I am suddenly limited in what I can do. Perhaps with you gone, Outreach will leave us alone."

"I don't think that's likely to happen now," said Jack. "Especially after what Billie and Alice are doing. And thanks a lot for your support."

Daman snorted. "Wait." Further conversation was cut short by movement out on the street. He lifted one hand for quiet, inching closer to the door for a better view. "It's them."

Billie came charging into the building first, closely followed by Alice, both of them breathing hard. Billie was grinning.

Twenty-five

"You should have seen it, Jack," said Billie, her voice still breathless. "It started just after we got out of the library. The building across the street was playing a vid. You couldn't really see the faces in the bit we saw, but you could tell what was happening. It was so big. It covered the entire front of the building."

"Great, Billie," said Jack. "Did you see anyone? Outreach? Any of the kids?"

"There were some men in uniform," said Alice. "We walked right past them. They didn't even notice us."

"You're sure?"

"Uh-huh," said Billie. "They were too busy watching the building."

"And nobody followed you down here?"

She shook her head.

"The place is pretty empty, Jack," said Alice. "We didn't see anyone at all when we got to this end."

Billie ducked around the doorway. "Oooh," she said. "Come and look. It's starting."

Jack wasn't sure about moving out into the open, but he had to rely on the thought that the Locality's systems would be too far gone at this end of Old to be reliable. They all stepped out from the building's shadow to stare up where Billie was pointing. Far above them, spreading across the width of the ceiling panels, a stuttering image was taking shape. Jack recognized the face. It was William Warburg, CEO of Outreach Industries. Lines of text were scrolling beside it. Jack didn't bother trying to read what they were saying. The image would be better in New and Mid, farther up the city. All that mattered was that the information was there.

"Yes," he said, quietly, reaching out to squeeze Billie's shoulder. She turned briefly to grin at him.

On the side of a building, a couple of blocks up, vague shapes started forming. The image was shadowed, intermittent, but it was there. It showed a man and a child. More sets of blurry shapes formed on a building opposite, then another and another.

Jack looked up at Warburg's face and smiled. Take that, you bastard. He'd have a little bit more to think about now apart from Jack Stein.

Staccato text scrolled up the street away from them, word after word. They were just shapes to Jack. He didn't need to puzzle them out.

"Good, huh?" said Billie.

"Yeah," breathed Jack.

Daman had said not a thing. He was staring up the street.

"What is it, Daman?" said Jack.

"Look."

Jack followed his gaze. Someone was strolling down the street toward them, someone with a strangely familiar gait. Jack frowned. What the hell?

Billie saw him next. Her expression changed immediately. The pleased-with-herself look slipped away and was replaced with something cold and hard, something filled with anger and disbelief.

Jack dug in his pocket and pulled out the gun, checking quickly to see that the safety was off. He held it before him, making his intentions completely clear.

"That's far enough, McCreedy," said Jack. "What the fuck do you think you're doing? Come to perform another service for your Outreach buddies?"

McCreedy grinned, though his grin was uncertain. He glanced up at the ceiling, to the buildings on either side, and down at the street, then back at Jack. His gaze lingered for a moment on Billie, and then returned to Jack.

"Pretty impressive," he said.

"Yeah, what of it? What are you doing here?"

McCreedy had his hands shoved deep in his pockets and he pulled them out slowly, spreading them wide. "I came to find you."

Jack had the sudden impression that he was standing in an old Western, except one of them didn't have a gun, and what had become magazine city surrounded them. Instead of a noonday sun, the head of William Warburg shone down behind him. Jack felt like shooting McCreedy, felt like blowing that supercilious smirk right off his face, but he kept it in check.

Daman had drawn his weapon, holding it in an easy grip by his side, but Jack could tell he was ready to use it at a moment's notice.

"Not good enough, Dog. I think you'd better turn around now and forget you've even seen us."

He couldn't let that happen, though, could he? He couldn't trust McCreedy. Not at all.

Dog lifted his hands in a placating gesture. "You'd better get in off the street," he said. "It's a bit exposed out here, don't you think? You might not be worried about yourself, but what about Billie?"

The mention of her name was enough. Before anyone could stop her, she was charging up the street toward McCreedy.

"What do you care?" she said, pulling back one arm as

she reached him and letting fly with a fist. "What do you care?" She hit him once, twice, three times. Dog stood there and let her, cringing away from the blows but doing nothing to stop her.

"Billie," said Jack. "Leave him. He's not worth the effort."

Billie seemed to have lost the initial rush of fury, and she let her hands drop to her sides. She took one step back.

"You're right, Jack," said McCreedy. "I'm not worth it."

Billie, spat, a look of contempt on her face, then turned and stalked back to where the three of them stood. When she got closer, Jack could see there were tears in her eyes.

"Jack," said Dog. "Listen to me. I can help. I know what's happened. I know what's been going on."

Jack looked at the others. Alice had her arm around Billie's shoulders. Billie wasn't looking at Dog anymore. Her face was lowered, her mouth in a tight line. Daman was wearing a slight frown.

"Perhaps we should listen," said Daman quietly.

"Why the fuck should we?" Jack shot back.

"Because we don't have a choice," said Daman. "We have to use everything we can. We don't know what he has to offer."

"We can't trust him, Daman."

"Maybe so, but we should listen to him first before we decide. It might give us some options."

Jack grimaced. Daman was right, as much as Jack was reluctant to admit it. He turned back to McCreedy and waved him forward with his gun. Dog sauntered forward, hands back in pockets, looking only slightly contrite. Before they moved back inside, Jack asked him one more question.

"So what's to say you're not going to bring Outreach right down on top of us?"

Dog peered at him through messy strands of dark hair.

"I've got my reasons, Jack," he said. "You don't have to believe me, but you can believe that much. There's quite a lot about me you don't know. There are things I need to tell you. There's more than just Outreach involved here. There's more than just one player in this game."

"Yeah, and why should I believe you?"

Dog shrugged. "If you let me explain . . . I had to do what I did, Jack."

"That's gone, Dog. All that matters is right now."

Dog bit his lip.

Jack grunted and stepped back to let Dog pass. "Okay, inside. You know the stuff. One false move and all that."

Dog bowed his head, stepped between Jack and Daman, and headed for the doorway that Jack had indicated. Alice still had her arm around Billie's shoulders. Billie was glaring at McCreedy as he walked past, but he didn't meet her eyes. Jack wouldn't like to be on the receiving end of that ire and he could feel the fury burning in her.

Alice led her inside and Jack and Daman followed. McCreedy stood in the room's center, waiting for them.

"Where's your ship, Dog?" asked Jack as soon as he was inside.

Dog shrugged. "*Amaranth* is there where I left her."

"So why are you still here?"

Jack had pocketed his gun, but Daman was toying with his, looking as if he was deciding whether he was going to use it or not, just seeking a reason.

Dog pressed his lips together and ran his fingers through his hair. "I don't know. I've had a change of heart or something." He glanced at Billie, then back at Jack.

Jack pressed his jaw tightly closed, reading the implications in Dog's words and not liking them one bit.

"And?"

"And I decided it was time to make good."

Jack narrowed his eyes at McCreedy. "No, I don't get it, Dog. What made you change your mind this time? You thought it was worth setting me up with Outreach."

Again came the shrug. "I told you. . . ."

Frankly, Jack was starting to find the gesture annoying.

"Okay, McCreedy, try this," he said, stepping forward. "You set me up with Outreach. You sent them all your logs. What else did you—"

"Jack," said Billie from the side.

"What?"

"The logs. They contain the stuff we need."

He stared at her as the thought sank in. She was right. In all the excitement, he'd forgotten that bit. "Good girl."

"So, McCreedy, you can still get to your ship, right?"

Dog nodded.

"So you can get us the logs, give Billie access to them."

Dog swallowed and looked sour. " 'Fraid not."

"What do you mean?"

"Outreach. They wiped *Amaranth*. Everything on her. They gutted her soul. All records, logs, data, everything. All of it gone."

Jack frowned. "I don't get it."

"While I was with you, they got to the ship, got rid of my insurance. They know the way I work."

"What makes you think it was Outreach?"

"Who else could have done it?" Dog asked.

Jack turned back to the doorway, walked across, and looked out onto the street. The pictures and images were growing, spreading.

"So they know you're here," he said over his shoulder.

"Yeah."

"Well, I don't know what use you can be to us, Dog," Jack said slowly.

"Oh, there are things I think I can do," he said. "In the end you'll thank me."

Jack turned to face him. Dog held his gaze unflinchingly.

Daman, quiet up till now, broke the silence.

"How did you find us?"

"It wasn't too hard. I found one of your kids. Asked what had happened. I was looking for you anyway. It wasn't difficult to piece it together from there."

"And it won't be too hard for Outreach to do the same," said Daman.

He was right. They had to keep moving. Jack looked at each of their faces, then back at McCreedy.

"What can you do for us, Dog? Tell us exactly what you can do."

Dog grinned and Jack narrowed his eyes again. Dog McCreedy just didn't seem to know when his expressions were appropriate. The guy was genuinely dysfunctional. Dog continued, apparently oblivious to Jack's reaction. "Remember the armory on board the *Amaranth*? They only touched her systems. They didn't touch any of the hardware."

Jack thought quickly. Weapons would be good. If they were going to get into Outreach, a bit of extra help might be needed. The problem was that apart from him and Daman, he didn't have anyone else who could really use a gun. Billie and Alice were out. Besides, if you carried a gun, you were more likely to get shot. One of the reasons he hated the things. There was no choice; they needed McCreedy too. Let Dog be one of the ones to get shot. In the meantime, they could use his skills.

He turned to Billie. "Is there any way that Outreach could trace what you've done to the Locality's systems?"

"Nuh-uh."

"You're sure?"

She thought for a moment. "I think so."

That was a start. Perhaps they could still use the library for the time being. The problem was, if Outreach knew Alice was involved, which they did, then that could present a risk too. They were likely to be watching the library. If not now, then soon.

"Jack, can I relax a bit?" said McCreedy. "You're not going to shoot me."

Jack turned back to him with a hard expression. "Shut up, Dog. I'm thinking. And no, I'm not going to shoot you . . . yet."

"But I might," said Daman quietly.

The words had been said matter-of-factly, but Jack knew the truth of the threat that lay beneath them. McCreedy seemed to have caught the sense of it too. Jack gave Daman a querying look.

Daman gave a little shrug in return. "I'm not convinced yet."

"Okaaay," said Jack. He caught a brief look from Billie, an expression of . . . concern? He decided to process that one later.

"So what now?" Daman said.

"You got anyone who can use a weapon?" said Dog to Daman, ignoring the threat for now.

"One or two," said Daman.

"Can we find them?"

"Perhaps. Where did you see the boy you talked to?"

"Up near Mid-Central somewhere."

Daman nodded. "Yes. There's a couple of places up

around there they might go. I could try to find out if there are any of them around. I'm not completely sure where they might go, though."

Daman moved the gun from one hand to the other, scratched the back of his head, and then took charge.

"Jack, you need to find another building to hole up in. We've been here too long. Billie and Alice, you need to get back to the library. Find out what you can about Outreach's main building. You also need a system to grow the key, Billie. If the library's being watched, we'll find a system somewhere else. It's just that the library seems a safer option for the moment. Queries about the Locality itself should be comparatively run-of-the-mill from the library system. If they come from a private location, they might trigger alerts. You—" He gestured at McCreedy. "You get what you can, and can reasonably carry from your ship without setting off alarms all over the place. Meanwhile, I will go and see whom I can find. We are going to do this," he said with a statement full of finality. He looked at each of them and then nodded. It was still strange to see such authority coming from someone who on the surface looked so young. All the same, Jack was relieved that Daman seemed to be more in command of himself again. And not only of himself by the looks of things.

Jack studied him, half with respect and half with something else. Daman had been more than a simple administrator in a past life, he thought. But whatever lay in his history was beyond reach now.

"So, how do we find each other?" asked Jack, slipping into practicality. He could jump from building to building until they met up again, but unless they had somewhere clear to rendezvous, they'd lose more time.

Daman frowned. "Why not here?" he said. "You can keep

moving, Jack, but come back and check here. The odds of them finding you with a random search are limited. Eventually, we will all make our way back here, to this building. This will be our meeting point."

"Okay," said Jack. He looked at each of them in turn and they returned his gaze. He could feel determination there, vengeance maybe, but a drive that might just get them through this.

Daman left first, striding calmly out onto the street. Billie and Alice looked at each other, but Dog was the next to leave. He shot sidelong glances, first at Billie, then at Jack. As he slipped out the door, he lifted a hand toward Jack's shoulder, but Jack stepped back out of reach.

"We really do need to talk, Jack," he said in a low voice.

Jack shook his head and gestured toward the outside with his chin. He'd had enough of McCreedy's stories.

"Fine," said Dog. "Later." And then he was gone and out and up the street.

Finally, the women left too, Alice pausing to give Jack a peck on the cheek. Jack moved to the door and watched them as they walked together up the street, strolling, a couple of girlfriends out for a chat, though what they were doing this far down in Old would be a question. For a couple of minutes after they were gone, Jack watched the space where they had last been visible. He reached into his pocket, fingering the weapon, then looked both up and down the street. He didn't want to spend too much time out in the open, so he strode quickly across the main thoroughfare and ducked into a side street, keeping close to the walls, seeking the shadow of the surrounding buildings as he went.

Jack chose a building at random and headed inside, not bothered about the structure's safety at this point. There were bound to be weaknesses, the potential for chunks to tumble down from ceilings and crash into the floors below, but if he kept to the outer walls, he should be secure.

Already, Billie's handiwork was spreading farther, creeping to the inside walls; lines of text, unreadable for the most part in the crumbling structures, scrolled and sputtered into life, interspersed with images. The whole of the Locality was becoming alphabet city. Outside, the ceiling panels had moved on from William Warburg. Jack thought, wryly, that perhaps it was time that he moved on from William Warburg too. He had bigger things to worry about now. He could use the time to try to puzzle out the message delivered by the Silvers. Of course, the dream images could be suspect and were never clear-cut, but there was a purpose there somewhere. What he, Jack Stein, could do, however, was beyond his grasp.

He ran the dream through his head, tasting the sensations and images in his memory, briefly shying away from the touch of malevolence that rode with the cold. These Blacks were not nice creatures. That much he'd already gathered, but then he'd known that from the initial dream where they'd first appeared.

"We are content," the Silvers had said. Content about what?

Jack reached deep inside himself, looking for answers, but there were none there to find.

Just for once, he could do with an answer not couched in riddles.

Twenty-six

By the time Daman found him back at the building, Jack was still working through the dream. It nagged at the back of his thoughts even when he tried to push it from him. Seeing Daman with two others accompanying him gave Jack a welcome sense of relief.

Daman hung in the doorway, the kids with him mere shadows in the background.

"No sign of the others yet?"

Jack shook his head. He wasn't completely confident that they'd see Dog McCreedy again. He was far more worried about Billie and Alice and whether they'd managed to retrieve what was needed. After the breakout, the infection, everything else, Outreach had to be aware of both Billie and Alice as a threat.

Daman looked out onto the street, and then moved into the building proper, waving his two companions forward. Both boys were in their late teens, and had a hard-bitten look about them, something sly and calculating in the way they met Jack's gaze and held themselves.

"Matthias and Grigor," said Daman.

Jack nodded to them. He thought he'd seen one of them back at the building before the raid.

"Where did you find them?"

"As I thought. One of the places up near Mid-Central."

Jack paced across to the other side of the room. "Others?" he said without turning around.

There was a lengthy pause before Daman answered. "Some," he said.

Jack didn't like the implications. Outreach had always been cavalier about individual well-being and the effects of their actions. Now, though, they'd gone a step beyond. He turned back to face the three of them.

"They're not going to get away with this," he said, the words sounding as ineffective as he felt personally.

Daman didn't respond. He looked away, motioning for the other two to take up positions on one side of the doorway. He pulled out his weapon and checked it, ignoring what Jack had just said.

"So, now we wait," he said.

Jack watched him for a few minutes, leaning back against the wall, still running the options through his head. The boys sat against the wall impassively, staring down at the floor in front of them. Occasionally, one or the other of them would look up, glance at Jack, or at Daman, and then return to watching the floor.

How the hell had Daman collected his crew? He had to offer them something. Maybe it was like he'd said, and he gave them some sort of protection and security. Maybe it was just as simple as a sense of belonging.

Jack's thoughts returned to the Blacks. What had the Silvers said? That he couldn't defeat them? He pushed himself off the wall and started pacing again. Blacks. Silvers. Silvers. Blacks. None of it made any real sense. He was just one lone human with some extra abilities that he could channel. Why they picked him remained a mystery. What could he, Jack Stein, do against a hostile alien race?

If he hadn't been there and seen for himself, actually

stood in the alien city, he could have written it off as a series of strange, aberrant dreams, but he didn't have that choice any longer. He had more than touched the reality.

"They're coming," said Daman, bringing Jack back to the immediate.

He crossed the room to stand just behind Daman, giving him a view up the street. Billie and Alice were walking down one side, heads together, two girlfriends in conversation. Jack checked behind them, but there was no sign that anyone was following. They quickly slipped inside the building and out of plain view from the street.

"Any problems?" asked Jack.

"No," said Alice. "At least not that we can tell. There were a couple of city people up near the library, but they didn't seem to be connected to anything that was going on. I don't think they noticed us."

Jack nodded. Billie was looking at the two boys sitting by the wall.

"I know you, don't I?" she said to one of them.

He looked up at her blankly.

"Mattie," she said. "Right?"

He frowned. "Um . . ."

"They don't call him that anymore," said the other one, Grigor.

"Oh," said Billie.

"He's Matthias."

"Oh," she said again.

After a pause, she spoke again. "I'm Billie," she said.

Matthias narrowed his eyes slightly, gave a thoughtful pout, then shook his head.

"Used to live with Pinpin Dan," she said. "Uncle Pinpin. You knew him too."

The reaction was immediate. A hard sneer grew on his

face and he averted his gaze. There was a history there, for sure.

Billie persisted. "I looked kind of different back then."

Jack was more than a little uncomfortable with the direction the conversation was taking. "Billie, leave it for now."

She humphed and turned back to join them. As soon as she was facing away, Matthias looked up again, watching her, something cold and hard in his gaze.

Maybe he thought . . . no, Jack didn't know what he was thinking.

"Dog?" asked Billie.

"No sign."

Alice had her handipad out and was checking something on the screen. She motioned for Billie to join her and soon they were both huddling over the device, scrolling through and discussing options.

A couple of minutes later, Daman spoke. "Here he comes now."

Jack moved back to the doorway and pressed against the frame, his gun held up and ready. "Alone?" he asked.

"Yes," said Daman.

Dog waltzed in through the doorway, swinging a long black bag, which he dumped unceremoniously with the clatter of something hard in the room's center.

"So, you miss me?" he said with a grin and a flourish.

"Actually, not at all," said Jack. "But you're here now. Let's see what you've got."

Dog crouched down beside the bag and slid his finger along the top seal. "Let's see. This." He pulled out a medium-length beam rifle, hefting it in one hand. "I brought this along just in case. I figured that we might be able to use one, but I went for small and discreet with enough power to make a difference, for the most part."

Jack crossed and took the rifle, checking it. It would do
the job. He held it down beside his body, and pulled his coat
around it. The weapon was short enough to pass a casual
glance. Whether it would hold up under decent scrutiny was
another matter.

One by one, he went through the other weaponry Dog
had shoved into the bag. He tossed a couple of hand weapons
to Matthias and Grigor, and they both plucked them out of
the air, and immediately began to check them. Jack felt a
touch of relief. It looked like they did know what they were
doing, not that he'd had any reason to doubt Daman's as-
sessment.

"This little beauty," said Dog, still crouched beside the
bag, "I've saved for myself."

He held up a gun, small and evil-looking. It also seemed
to be made of some sort of synthetic, missing the standard
metallic sheen.

Jack frowned at it. "What's that?"

"New stuff," said Dog, looking pleased with himself.
"One of my contacts. It's small, but it packs a real punch."

He rummaged around in the bag again after shoving the
gun in his belt and withdrew three or four small gray squares.

"I also thought I'd bring these along. Never know when
they might come in handy."

Jack recognized them for what they were, compact,
deadly explosive charges that you could affix to a surface
and then program in a time sequence for detonation. As soon
as they were in place, they took on the characteristics of the
material they'd been stuck to, making them almost impossible to detect unless you knew what you were looking for.
Nice, but Jack hoped they wouldn't be in a position to have
to use them. Blasting their way into the center of Outreach
wasn't quite what he had in mind.

"There are a couple of spare guns in there," said Dog. "I brought them along in case we want to give Billie and your friend something."

Your friend? Jack gave a hard look at the presumption. "No, I don't think so."

Dog shrugged and kicked the bag over to a corner of the room. "We can pick them up later."

If there was to be a later. The way things were going, Jack wasn't too sure.

"Right," said Jack, meeting each of the faces in turn. "Shall we do this?"

"I suggest we leave separately in pairings that aren't immediately recognizable," said Daman. "If they have scanning going on, it will make it harder. Jack and Dog, Alice and Billie, Grigor, you come with me, and Matthias, get there by yourself. We should meet at the corner of Twelfth, and then head down to Outreach together again. I suspect that Outreach won't be expecting any of you to come right to them. They'll be expecting Jack, for one, to try to get away. He's hardly going to turn up on their doorstep."

"Then what?" said Jack.

"We get in, Billie does what she has to, and then we get out." He looked across at her and Billie nodded back at him.

Daman scanned each of them. "Billie and Alice, first," he said. "Then Matthias. I suggest I go next and Jack and Dog will follow. They provide the highest risk. If anything happens to them, we can still do what needs to be done. Wait five minutes before heading out. Billie?"

Again, she nodded, looked to Alice, then, with one last glance at Jack, walked out onto the street, with Alice in tow.

Daman appeared to be counting silently to himself. After what was close to five minutes, he pointed to Matthias, who pushed himself to his feet, shoved his weapon in his pocket, and followed the other two out of the building. Once more, the counting, and then Daman waved to Grigor, and together, they joined the others outside, heading up to New and Outreach.

After they had gone, Jack, pressed up against the doorway, and watching them disappear up the street, spoke without turning around.

"I don't know why you think you have the right, Mc-Creedy," he said. "But you're useful, for now." He didn't look at him. "Just remember that. I'm not going to forget."

There was a pause before Dog said anything. "What's the problem, Jack? I'm here now. We all do shit that in hindsight we might have done differently. I was tied up with Outreach. They had a hold on me. Sometimes you have to do what you have to do. It's deeper than that. There are things going on that you need to know about."

"I don't care about that," said Jack quietly. "I haven't got time to worry about that now. Well, I do, but that's not the point."

"What is the point then?"

"You hurt Billie."

The silence that came in response was lengthy, punctuated only by the creaks of the building around them. Finally Dog spoke.

"But—"

"Not a word," said Jack, whirling to face him. "Not a fucking word."

Dog looked away, whatever he was about to say dying in his mouth.

"Yeah," Jack said, and turned his attention back to watching the street.

The minutes dragged on, the anger still working inside him, until Jack adjudged it was time. He had one last thought before heading out and crossed to the bag Dog had kicked into the corner. He reached in, pulled out one of the spare guns, and, after inspecting it, shoved it into the back of his belt.

"Right, let's do it."

He didn't even check that Dog was following. Keeping the rifle held close to the side of his body, he stepped out onto the street, looked first one way, then the other, and then crossed and started walking up to the shuttle stop. They would change at Mid-Central, then catch the New-bound shuttle right up to near Twelfth.

As he walked, he admired Billie's handiwork, the words, the images, crawling over buildings and up above on the ceiling panels, sliding along the street. They were still stuttering, intermittent down here, but you couldn't ignore them. Hell, why did you need graffiti when you had this? The ultimate urban protest. There, in public, writ large, was the litany of Outreach's sins.

As they waited for the shuttle, they did so in silence, Dog wisely keeping his mouth shut, rocking slightly on his heels. Jack glanced at him once or twice, but Dog didn't—or at least pretended that he didn't—notice. As the shuttle whirred to a stop, it became evident that Billie's infection had spread even to the vehicles themselves. Jack wondered how the Locality's cleaning routines were going to cope with that. It served them right.

He stepped into the shuttle, clutching one of the handrails, and moved slightly aside to allow Dog to pass. The rifle made it a little difficult even to consider sitting. He just hoped that they weren't going to have many fellow passengers on the way up. They should be okay as far as Mid-Central, but from there, the problems were likely to start. When they changed, Jack would have to find a corner where he could shield the weapon from other passengers, or even use McCreedy to block the accidental press by a fellow traveler against the hard, unmistakable shape.

As it was, the journey proceeded without incident. They got off at the Fourteenth Street stop, and wandered slowly up to the corner of Twelfth, Jack conscious of their scruffy appearance and their lack of "fit" in the district. Dog looked like Dog, and that was bad enough, but Jack was rumpled and disheveled, in need of a good shower. Living on the run just wasn't the best for personal hygiene.

Daman was already waiting for them by the time they reached the spot. He stood there calmly, leaning against a wall, scanning the people passing by. Jack felt anything but calm.

"Hey," he said.

Daman nodded.

"Billie and Alice?"

Daman gestured with his head. "Around the corner with the others." He tracked someone walking past and heading down the street leading to the Outreach headquarters. "There is something going on," he said.

"Well, yeah," said Jack. "Look around you."

Daman appeared annoyed. "No, I don't mean that."

Jack reached inside his perception, but there were no alarm bells going off. "Okay," he said. "So, are we going to stand around here discussing?"

Daman shook his head and pushed himself off the wall. "Now is as good a time as any, I suppose," he said.

Twenty-seven

The building soared above them, reaching like a metallic finger toward the text-filled ceiling panels scrolling words in a blanket that blocked out the sky. Off in the distance, the clear ceiling panels were the only ones untouched by Billie's programming and Jack felt a certain satisfaction at that. As they rounded the corner, Billie was patting her pocket, constantly checking that she had the small piece of Locality structure that would act as the key to get them into Outreach's inner sanctum. Jack's coat concealed the rifle held close against his leg. Dog's weapon was hidden behind his jacket. He glanced at the other two members of Daman's crew who had joined them, but their own weaponry was well concealed too. Jack felt the effects of adrenaline in his mouth, robbing the moisture, and in the pounding in his chest. As they moved down the street closer to the building, a subtle noise increased, first what sounded like a low rumble and then more of a buzz. What the hell?

It soon became apparent what was causing the disturbance. As their group moved into the plaza where Outreach's offices sat, there were people, first in ones and twos, and then more, walking quickly or simply strolling toward a gathering throng clustered outside the front of the Outreach Industries corporate headquarters. Jack looked at Daman, then at Dog, the unspoken question apparent. What were they going to do now? This was a problem. Despite the fact that this was exactly what they wanted to happen, it was now working against them. The Locality's residents had been reading and viewing everything that was appearing on buildings, streets, and walls, the catalog of Outreach's misdemeanors, and they were not happy. In their hundreds, they were not happy.

"Shit," said Jack, pulling back against a wall at one corner of the square. "What now?"

"Good question," said Dog, also dropping back. The others clustered around Jack, looking at him apparently for answers.

Jack scanned the crowd. For now, it was reasonably peaceful, but the rumble of voices spoke of a potential for something else. The assembled citizens were staying back from the front doors at the moment, but Jack didn't know how long it would be before the crowd wanted to express its displeasure closer to the source. A crowd was something hard to predict, something with a mind of its own. Jack considered.

A pair of security guards stood nervously at the top of the stairs on either side of the wide double doors, surveying the mass of people assembled in front of them. Jack bet that they were assessing their options too. The Locality wasn't a place where social violence was a normal happening and they'd be unused to this sort of potential confrontation.

"We might be able to use this," said Jack. "But we aren't going anywhere unless the crowd does something. Those guards aren't likely to let anyone through the front doors now."

"Is there another way in?" asked Dog.

Alice pulled out her handipad and tapped a couple of pages before finding what she was looking for. "There's a rear entrance and one to the side. There's also the parking facility underneath."

Jack thought about that for a moment, imagining what

the Locality's lower levels must look like. The underbelly of the beast. The parking area would be maybe one floor, two at most. There'd definitely be a way in there, and with the crowd keeping the guards otherwise occupied . . .

"Can I see?" he said.

Alice angled her handipad so it was in view. He'd been right in his assumptions. The plan showed two levels of parking and two separate access points to the floors above. He leaned across her and tapped the display. The darkened area at the center of the building was not directly above those access points, so they'd have to work their way through the floors and corridors anyway. Coming up from below might give them a better chance than coming in from the front. He glanced up from Alice's handipad and looked at the crowd. They were definitely becoming more restless, more agitated, which could work to their advantage.

"So?" said Dog.

"We take the back," said Jack. "Come up from the parking area. They're going to be more concerned about what's going on out front at the moment. With any luck, their attention isn't going to be focused on what's happening underneath."

"What about the automatic routines?" said Billie.

"Um, yeah," said Jack. "Don't know."

"If there's a point at the outside," said Billie, "I can get in and introduce a shadow before we go in. I think I remember how. I haven't done it for a while, though."

Jack frowned. When had she . . . ? And then he realized. It must have been during her time with Pinpin Dan.

"Okay, let's see what they've got back there."

One more quick glance at the guards, then at the crowd, and Jack decided it was time to move. If the crowd became too restless, Outreach might lock down the building entirely, and they didn't want that. He had to rely on his luck keeping the timing of events working in their favor.

Damn. Too obvious, Stein. He stopped in his tracks.

"Daman, you go with a couple of the others around the other side. We'll meet at the back." He stepped closer to Billie and put his arm around her shoulders. "Come on. You come with me. Alice, Dog, you follow a couple of minutes after. Stay here and hang back for a little while. Alice, you'd better give Billie the handipad."

Alice handed over the device and Billie slipped it into her back pocket. Daman nodded and headed off with his boys toward the other side of the square, skirting the rear of the crowd. Jack waited a couple of seconds, then continued in his direction, holding Billie close to him.

"You okay?" he asked her.

"Uh-huh."

"And Dog?"

She shrugged beneath his arm.

"Okay."

It would do for now. Jack tried to adopt as casual a demeanor as possible, just wandering past the gathering in front of the building, interested but not involved. He hoped it was enough. He steered Billie along the outside edge of the square, and then back out of sight. They passed a few people drifting in from the opposite direction, but they were subjected to little more than passing glances. In the Locality, people mostly tended to mind their own business.

They reached the rear of the block—the Outreach offices occupied one entire city square on the grid—and turned the corner. Daman and his two companions were already near the entrance to the parking space, standing near the ramp leading down. An unmarked white vehicle emerged, turned to the right, and headed off up the street. If the occupants had paid any attention to Daman, they'd shown no sign. Okay. Jack felt his breathing ease. He quickened his pace. He would have to be wary of other vehicles coming in or out, but he didn't imagine there could be too many, unless Outreach decided they had to send out to bolster the security presence. Alice and Dog were just rounding the far corner when Jack and Billie caught up to Daman. The entrance was positioned closer to the other end of the building to the direction that Dog and Alice had come.

While they waited for Dog and Alice, Daman sent one of his kids down the ramp to scout out what lay ahead of them. The boy returned a couple of minutes later, just as Dog and Alice joined them.

"There's not much down there. A few transports. It's open. There's a barrier, but it's open too."

Daman nodded and looked to Jack.

For a place that survived on the things that went on below the surface, it was a strange contrast how easily Outreach took things for granted. Outreach had become complacent with its own sense of power.

"Okay, let's do it," Jack said. "Did you see any kind of control panel or anything down there?" he asked the boy, receiving a shake of the head in response. "Okay, we'll have to take it as it comes. Billie, have you got the plans?"

Billie showed him the handipad. He traced the area with one finger, getting his bearings. The nearest access point to the upper levels was clear across the other side of the building. There was bound to be surveillance capability down there, but he had to count on the factor of complacency, that Outreach would feel impregnable in this, their home. Locality citizens just didn't mess with Outreach. He handed the device back to Alice.

Removing his arm from Billie's shoulders, Jack strode down the ramp.

The parking area was just as the boy had said. Two or three solitary white vehicles sat parked in bays. The marks of their comings and goings were still evident on the floor, despite the building's self-cleaning routines. Maybe Outreach thought it just wasn't worth the effort. He scanned for traps, leading the way, probing ahead with his inner senses, but nothing was triggering his alarms. He walked quickly across the open space, looking left and right, his hand resting against the rifle underneath his coat, ready to drag it out and up if it was needed. So far, nothing had shown him that it would be.

"Damn," he said as they reached the point marked on the schematics. The way up was an elevator. He should have thought about that. He wasn't going to put the seven of them into an enclosed elevator where they could be boxed in. That was way too easy.

"Alice," he said in a low voice. "Let me see again."

Once more, she pushed her handipad forward.

"Hmm, okay. We need to try over this way. Dog, you keep an eye out for company."

McCreedy gave him a mock salute and Jack narrowed his eyes, but contained his reaction. Just one time, McCreedy would be a little too smart too easily. Not now, though. Jack needed him.

Making sure of the direction he was facing, Jack strode off across the floor to the opposite corner . . . and ended up facing a blank wall. He frowned, reaching out a hand and beckoning Alice forward once more. Somewhere here, there was supposed to be a staircase. No, not somewhere here— exactly here.

He put his hand flat against the wall, but there was nothing.

"Here, Jack," said Billie, reaching for Alice's handipad and pushing him out of the way. She tapped a couple of sequences into the device, then held it up, pointing at the wall. The wall slid back, revealing a stairwell behind. "There," she said, the old smug look on her face.

"Yeah, okay," Jack said, and stepped through the newly formed doorway. "Which floor?"

"Fourth," said Alice.

"Billie, can you shut that behind us?"

She nodded, waiting till the last of them was through the door, and did just that.

"Okay," said Jack, pulling out the rifle. He checked its settings, then headed up the stairs. There was no going back now.

Jack took the steps cautiously, one by one, listening and feeling at the same time. A vague hum came from the walls around them, but apart from the sound of their footsteps and their breathing, there was no other sound. So far, so good. Behind him, the others had their weapons out too. It was strange, but the only one of them who looked natural with a gun in his hand was Dog McCreedy. Jack shouldn't really have been surprised.

One by one, they ascended the floors, stopping at each landing, listening and checking for any sign that they'd been discovered. When they reached the fourth, Jack held up one hand, looking down at the small group on the stairs below him.

"Dog, up here," he said quietly. Dog eased past Daman and one of the boys, and joined Jack near the door—a conventional door this time. Jack had a quick thought. It could be alarmed. There was no way to tell from here. Taking a deep breath, he reached forward and eased it open a couple of inches. Nothing. He slowly let the air out from his lungs. Opening it just a fraction wider, he moved his face closer to the space and scanned the corridor beyond. For the moment, it appeared empty. He pulled it closed again. He gestured for the handipad and checked the direction. Whatever it was they were after lay down the corridor to the right, and then, if the map was correct, to the right again.

Jack signaled with his hands. He and Dog would take the lead, followed by Billie and Alice; then Daman and his two would bring up the rear. All of them nodded their understanding, and Jack turned back to the door. Once more, he opened it a fraction, testing with every sense available to him, and then he stepped through.

The corridor was long and wide, carpeted in blue, with regularly spaced panels illuminating its length, several doors breaking the even walls. Jack looked in both directions and then stepped back to allow the others to pass. He walked quickly down to where the corridor branched, and kept his weapon at the ready. No one seemed to be around. He passed empty offices on either side. Perhaps everyone was at the front of the building watching the demonstration. Maybe his luck was holding after all. Either that, or they were being set up.

Another empty corridor, and then a blank wall. Jack had expected nothing else. Daman was down at the other end of the passageway, his boys pressed against either side, keeping back out of sight, standing guard. Jack pulled Billie forward, then gestured once more for the handipad. He pointed to where he thought they were, giving Billie a questioning look. She frowned at the handipad, then looked back up the corridor, as if matching it to the schematics in her mind's eye. She chewed her bottom lip, frowned again, and then finally nodded. Jack lifted the rifle so that he held it perpendicular to the floor, waiting while she dug in her pocket and pulled out the small silvery square that she'd programmed for just this moment. Carefully, she lifted it and placed it flat against the wall at head height, held it there for a moment, and then stepped back.

The metallic square stayed, apparently affixed to the wall, and then gradually, as they watched, began to lose definition, the color fading into the background texture of the wall till there was nothing to show that it had been there the instant before. Jack's heart was hammering, and he kept glancing back down the corridor to where Daman and the boys stood. Dog was watching the proceedings with apparent disinterest. Nothing.

Jack frowned at Billie.

Still nothing.

She held up one hand and frowned back, urging him to have patience.

Then there, a slight discoloration in the wall's surface, gradually spreading. A hole appeared, square, the same size as the piece that Billie had placed there, and then it grew, the wall folding back on itself in sections.

"Yes," breathed Billie.

She'd done it. Jack ducked his head through the space in the wall. The folding back had stopped, leaving a rectangular shape large enough for one person to step through.

Behind the wall lay another short corridor and then a conventional doorway. Yes, this looked like what they were after. He motioned to Dog to step through. Weapon raised, Dog lifted his foot over what remained of the wall at the base and followed it with his other. He was down at the other door in an instant.

With a quick check to make sure everything was still

clear, Jack stepped through in turn. He joined Dog at the
door and then waved Alice and Billie to follow.

"Okay," he whispered. "More than likely there are people
in there. Keep low, just in case."

In the meantime, Daman had backed down the corridor
on the other side and had positioned himself just behind the
rectangular doorway Billie's programmed device had fash-
ioned. He nodded to Jack, indicating he was ready too.

Jack gave Dog a single nod. Dog pushed the door open
and entered, Jack closely behind. Another corridor and another door at the end. Halfway down this corridor was another door.

"Dog, wait," said Jack beneath his breath.

Dog turned to look.

Jack pointed to himself, then in front of Dog. It made
more sense for Jack to go first, carrying the rifle. That way
he'd have room to fire if he needed to and Dog could shoot
over Jack's shoulder. Dog nodded his understanding and
stood back to let Jack pass. That put him right next to Billie.
He looked at her, his gaze lingering. She returned the look
and a sudden mix of emotions flitted across her face.

"Jesus, you two. No. Particularly not now," hissed Jack.

Billie turned away again, instead turning her attention to
Jack. He gave her what he hoped passed for a half smile.
Though she bit her lip and sucked in her breath, she gave
him a short nod and closed her eyes and then opened them
again quickly.

Jack stepped closer to the next door and listened. A slight
hum, almost below the threshold of his hearing, was the only
thing that came to him. Okay. Nothing for it.

Jack pushed the door and stepped through, swinging the
rifle down to bear on whatever lay before him.

"Um, hello," said a voice. Jack swung to face it. A round-faced man with thinning hair, dressed casually, seated behind a desk and leaning back in a chair, was looking at him as if trying to parse the scene and make sense of it. One side of his shirt hung out of his jeans, and he pushed at it ineffectually as if he thought he should make some sort of effort. A bunch of pens stuck out from his top pocket. "Are you sure you're in the right place?" he said.

"Yeah, I think so," said Jack. He gave the room a quick scan. A few desks sat at various points around the room, uncluttered. There seemed to be no one else there. "Don't think about doing anything stupid," said Jack.

The man chuckled. "I'm not very good at stupid, actually," he said, letting his chair tilt forward again. "So, what can I do for you?"

This wasn't what Jack had been expecting at all.

Twenty-eight

The man stood, this time making a better effort at tucking in his shirt. Jack tracked him with the rifle, leaving no doubt about the seriousness of his intent. He glanced back over his shoulder at Dog, standing in the doorway, flicking his hair out of his eyes with a toss of his head, short nasty gun held at an upright angle.

"Where are the others?" said Jack.

The man stopped paying attention to his shirt and looked up. "I don't know. There was something going on out front. I guess they went to look."

Luck again, Stein.

He motioned to Dog to let Alice and Billie into the room. He stepped to one side and Billie walked into the room first, holding her pocket and looking around at the facilities. Alice appeared a pace behind and then Dog moved back into position, guarding the doorway, alternating between watching the corridor behind the door and keeping an eye on the room in which Jack now stood.

"What do you want?" said the Outreach guy, starting to look concerned.

"We need access to your systems," said Billie.

The man scratched the back of his neck and grimaced. "I'm not sure I can really do that."

Billie walked over to him. "They're your systems, right?"

"Well, yes."

"You have access?"

He nodded.

"Well, access them."

He looked at Billie, at Jack and at the rifle; then, his lips pursed, he leaned over the desk that he had been occupying a few moments before. He glanced over at Jack once more, and placed his hand on the surface. A wall in front of the desk immediately bled into life and color, links and symbols indicating various areas taking shape.

"And really, I mean it. Don't think about doing anything stupid," said Jack.

The guy looked over at him and half rolled his eyes.

"What's your name?" said Billie, moving over to stand beside him at the desk.

"Lovell. Philip Lovell," he said without looking up.

Something wasn't quite right about the scene, but Jack couldn't pin it down. Then it hit him. When they'd walked in, the guy, Lovell, was alone, but the system was shut down. If he worked here, shouldn't he have been doing just that, working with the system?

"Billie, wait a second," said Jack.

She looked up at him questioningly.

"How come the system wasn't on, Lovell?" he said.

Lovell hesitated.

"Well?"

"I was doing something else," he said.

"Like what?"

"Composing. The screens distract me."

Jack frowned. "Huh?"

Lovell sighed. "I write poetry, if you must know. I take the opportunity when I'm here alone to use the quiet spaces to compose. I'm supposed to be monitoring things, but the system will alert me anyway if I'm supposed to do anything."

Jack could live with that, however unlikely it seemed under the circumstances, and however unlikely it might seem that the overly padded tech guy in front of him was a secret poet.

"So what about all this other stuff happening in the Locality? You know, the words, the vids, etc. Doesn't that concern you?"

Lovell suddenly got an enthusiastic look on his face. "Oh yeah," he said. "I love it. Normally everything's straightforward. The Locality looks after itself. That's a nice little problem. We haven't found a solution to it yet."

Jack motioned for Billie to continue. They didn't have time for chatting, and Lovell seemed to be in the mood to do just that. It didn't surprise him that, locked away here in the heart of Outreach, this guy might look for a chance to have some conversation. And he did seem to be a talker.

"What are you going to do?" Lovell asked Billie.

Billie gave him a little grin. "Watch," she said.

She reached into her pocket and pulled out another small square, then placed it carefully on the desk. Lovell bent closer and peered at it.

"Don't touch," said Billie. "Get me into your file network. I need the access routines. Have you any search algorithms set up?"

Lovell nodded and manipulated the desk surface with his fingertips, looking at the screen, but seeming to have difficulty dragging his attention away from the thing Billie had placed on the desk.

The wall display changed, other links folding out and expanding among the other images on the screen.

"No," said Billie. "Where's the search?"

"Here," said Lovell, tapping on the desk.

"Too much for voice," said Billie. "I don't want it on the system. Can you set up manual?"

Lovell nodded. He tapped at another couple of points and an alphabetical display appeared on the desk surface. "There."

Billie signaled her understanding. She typed the name of Dog's ship and watched the screen. After a couple of seconds, she shook her head. "Alice, I need the handipad," she called.

Alice walked quickly over and handed her the device. Billie thumbed it on, tapped out a couple of steps, and then held it out, pointing at the desk. A small black box appeared in the center of the wall display and Billie nodded. She reached to the desk again and tapped another couple of sequences. On-screen, the box unfolded, opening out like some sort of square black flower, shedding angular petals that drifted away to all parts of the screen. They melted into the display, as if they were never there. The next moment, sequences of images flashed past, changing the screen display, flicking rapidly through the partitions of the Outreach system.

"Nice," said Lovell appreciatively.

"Oh, you wait," said Billie, again giving him a little grin.

Somehow, there had been an instant connection between them.

Jack was starting to become nervous. All this was still taking too long. He glanced at Dog, who checked the corridor, still holding his position, then looked back at Jack and gave him a confirming nod.

Even though he couldn't trust McCreedy, despite everything that had happened, Jack felt some relief that Dog was here. The ease of communication, the way they understood each other's signals, was all working in his favor. He turned back to watch what Billie was up to. It looked like this Lovell guy wasn't going to be any trouble. He was watching what she was doing too, fascinated.

Poetry. Who would have thought it?

"There," said Billie. She peered at the wallscreen, concentrating. "Yeah, that's the stuff."

A muffled shout came from the corridor and Jack whirled. Shit, they had company. There was the sound of a shot, and then return fire.

"Billie," said Jack.

"Give me a couple of minutes," she said.

Dog was crouched by the door now, his weapon held out, pointing through the doorway.

"Dog?"

"Okay," he said, not turning. "Secure for now. Can't see anything, but Daman seems to be holding them off."

"Okay," said Jack. "Keep position. Yell if you need help."

"Billie?"

"Yeah, Jack. Shut up and let me do it."

He resisted the urge to stride over and hurry her along. There was nothing he could do. Alice was standing by helplessly, looking from Billie to Jack and then to Dog in the doorway. What the hell had Jack gotten her into now? He couldn't think about that now, though. He stepped over to the doorway, peering past Dog, but just as McCreedy had said, there wasn't anything there to see yet. The sound of weapons fire came from that direction, and a flash or two, followed by darkness. There was no line of sight to Daman from this position. He turned back into the room to check what Billie was doing.

"Got it," she said.

She reached over and tapped the small piece she had left

on top of the desk, once, twice, in three different positions. The square lost definition, bleeding across the surface and then disappearing into the top of the desk itself.

"Now what?" said Lovell.

"Wait," said Billie.

The technician seemed completely unconcerned by the fact that this would probably lose him his position with Outreach. The sound of the ongoing battle outside appeared to have totally bypassed his awareness.

Jack stepped closer. Both Lovell and Billie were standing watching the place where moments before, the small square had lain.

A dark ripple, pulsing, appeared in the desk surface, just the same way it had done back at Daman's building when Billie had shown him before. The pulsing lines increased in intensity, then drew together in a central point, and spread out, like ripples in a pool.

Jack knew precisely what was going to happen next. A small mound swelled on the desk surface. The ripples slowed. The dark protuberance blossomed, then opened at the very top, drawing back like lips opening on a darkened mouth. Jack glanced over at Dog, and he nodded back. Still the sound of the exchange of fire drifted up the corridor and through the door. There was a cry, and another shout—Jack couldn't tell whose voice.

Silver legs pushed up within the hole, straddling the edges, and then another set. They levered a body free, a body that sat rocking, balanced precariously on the edge of the mound, and then the surface irregularity faded away, merging back into the surface of the desk, leaving it smooth as if it had never been disturbed.

The silver spider sat rocking slightly on the surface.

"What's that?" said Lovell, still unfazed by the noises coming from the corridor.

"It's a bug," said Billie. "It contains information coded into its body. It can transfer the information by contact with programmable structures."

"Huh," said Lovell with an interested tone. "Okay, but what can it do? There's only one of them."

Again, Billie grinned. "Right now. But not for long. We've got to wait for the routines to kick in and filter through the systems. That's just the first one."

Noises were coming down the corridor, closer. Dog had shifted his position, shielding most of his body by the door. He took aim and fired. There was a loud zipping sound, almost like a rip in the air, and a red flash. The smell of ionization drew strong.

"Shit," said Dog. "Jack, they're through."

Jack quickly took the couple of steps needed to get him to the doorway on the opposite side of Dog. He ducked his head around the doorway, catching a brief view of Daman, staggering down the corridor toward them, clutching at his shoulder, his face screwed up in pain. A bright flash seared through the air and impacted on the wall just above his head. One arm hung down, the gun held loosely in his fingers, threatening to drop to the floor. He staggered forward another few steps, but then lurched, his shoulders thrown back as something hit him from behind. He cried out. Somehow, he managed to stumble into the room, falling, a deep groan escaping his lips, his face contorted with the pain.

Alice rushed over, leaning down beside him.

Jack couldn't watch; he had to keep his attention on the corridor.

"Lovell," he called back over his shoulder. "Is there another way out of here?"

"Um, yeah. It's back over that way."

Jack allowed himself a glance to see. It was diagonally across the room. Lovell seemed transfixed by the sight of Daman's fallen form. Jack turned his attention back to the corridor. They could seal the door, but it wouldn't allow them much breathing space. He had to worry about Alice and Billie too.

"Billie, you done?" he called.

"Nearly," said Billie. "Not yet."

A shape appeared at the other end of the corridor and Dog fired. The shadow ducked out of sight.

Think, Jack. Shut the door; get everyone across the room to the other side. Daman was down. They couldn't take him with them. Another shadowed shape appeared, and this time Jack fired. A returning shot burned down the corridor, hitting the wall high up, then another closer. Jack ducked back. The shooters were getting their range. Dog let loose with another shot.

Daman was really down. Alice could do little more than offer comfort at this stage, and this close to the door, she was at risk.

"Alice," he said. "You need to get away from the door."

She looked at him. "Jack, but—"

"Just do it." He swung around the doorframe for another shot. Returning fire seared a track in the wall just above his head and zipped past and into the room. Alice crouched and scurried back across to where Billie and Lovell were still standing.

"Billie," he said. "Go and check the other way out."

"Not yet," she said.

"What the . . . ?" Jack pushed himself to his feet and swung into the room. "Hold here, Dog," he said.

He was over at the desk in a couple of strides. "Billie, we can't afford this—"

Billie had her hand up.

Jack looked down at the bug. It had stopped its rocking. It looked like a motionless piece of metal sculpture. Billie was frowning.

"It shouldn't be doing that," she said.

"Shit," Jack said, and reached forward with a finger to prod at the thing.

"Jack!" said Billie, but it was too late.

And suddenly, Jack wasn't there.

"Not now!" yelled Jack. "Not! Now!"

His voice echoed from bare walls and a ceiling far above. The room was empty. It had never been empty before. It was full of nothing but shadows. He looked down at his hands. The rifle was gone. On the back of his right hand was a wound, trickling blood. Now, how had that gotten there? He frowned. It was minor compared with the anger and frustration boiling within.

"Not now. Do you hear me?" His own voice came back to him. "I have to be back there."

Jack closed his eyes and tried to will himself back, away from this place, back to where he was supposed to be. He had deserted them.

"Where are you?" he shouted to the darkness. "Show yourselves."

Nothing came back but echoes.

This was the dream room on the alien planet. The Silvers were supposed to be here.

He looked around, some sense of rationality coming to his thoughts. What if this wasn't their doing? What if this was simply his own ability kicking in, shaping what he was seeing? He clenched his teeth and willed. Again, nothing.

Jesus, Stein. You own this. Do it.

Twenty-nine

A nd he was back.
   "Jack!" said Billie.

Jack blinked, trying to reorient himself. One moment he'd been standing in a shadowed empty room, and the next he was here, almost as if he hadn't moved. He looked down at his hand. The end of his finger still touched the body of the silver bug sitting on the desk in front of them.

"Jack?" asked Alice. "What just happened?"

How could he explain? He didn't really understand himself.

The sound of a shot came from the doorway.

"Come on," said Dog. "I'm not going to be able to hold them for much longer."

Real awareness came back to him then, knowledge of where he was and the gravity of their situation.

"Now, Jack Stein," came a voice in his head.

"What?" he said. This shouldn't be happening.

"Now." The single word echoed through his mind, washing against his awareness of his surrounds, and breaking in a foam of mental reverberations.

He looked down at his hand, still held out, the finger outstretched.

"Jack?" came Billie's voice again.

He couldn't turn to look at her. There was something flowing through him, coursing through his nerves, holding him where he was. A pale energy washed out around him. He could almost see it. Then the bug turned, rocking again, tilting slightly back and forth on its spindly silver legs. The front legs rose, the back ones lowered, and the body angled, higher toward Jack and lower at the rear. It jumped.

For the barest instant, it rested on the back of his outstretched hand, and then it bore down, plunging something into his skin.

Jack felt a sharp pain and immediately shook the thing from him, clattering it against the wall. It scuttled away beneath some furniture and out of sight.

"Shit," said Jack, looking down at his hand. "What the fuck was that?"

A small trickle of blood trailed from the wound.

Again Dog urged him to get a move on, pausing between shots. Dog was right. He couldn't afford to worry about this now. He left the desk, shaking his hand, trying to thrust the discomfort of the wound from him, pushing past Lovell toward the corner of the room that the technician had indicated.

As he reached the door, Dog was backing into the room.

"Can't hold them, Jack," he said.

Jack spun, and tested the door. It held fast, refusing to open.

Dammit. "Lovell, how do I get this open?"

"The place must be locked down," he said. "I can't do anything."

There was no locking mechanism visible for Jack to shoot out. The door was probably sealed all the way around. He growled, swung back to the room.

Dog stood pressed against one wall, his hands up, gun held loosely in one of them. In the next moment, he dropped the weapon and it clattered to the floor. Jack trained his rifle on the open doorway. Dog shook his head.

Jack scanned the room, looking for options. Billie, Alice, and Lovell still stood by the desk, watching the doorway now, a clear target. He was out of direct sight of the entrance, but he would have the chance to take out only one or two before he was outgunned. Meanwhile it would put the others at risk. Whatever Dog was seeing, it was enough to make him disarm. Jack waited, rifle held at the ready.

An Outreach guy stepped through the doorway, pushing the figure of Matthias before him with one hand, bunched in the fabric of the boy's clothes up near his neck. There was a gun pressed tightly to the back of Matthias's head. The man wore a pale uniform and a don't-mess-with-me look on his face. He pushed Matthias fully into the room, glancing around and taking in the scene. He was quickly followed by another in a similar uniform, who stepped in, swinging his weapon to point at Jack. He gestured and Jack lowered the rifle even farther, pointing it down at the floor.

"No," said the man. "Drop it."

He turned his own weapon to point at Alice, at the same time moving to one side of the doorway.

Shit. Jack swallowed and dropped the rifle.

Another uniform followed, and then a familiar figure, dressed in a dark suit and dispassionately surveying the scene.

"Hello, Jack," said Thorpe. "We've missed you." He turned to look at Dog. "And Mr. McCreedy too. How interesting."

Dog sneered.

Billie was looking at Jack, waiting for something. He didn't know what.

Thorpe stepped farther into the room. "I'm disappointed, Jack. You've caused us quite a bit of trouble."

Jack snorted. "Cut the clichéd dialogue, Thorpe. It's not very original."

"I don't know what you mean."

"Anyone would think they gave lessons in corporate bad guy."

Thorpe frowned, not bothering to respond to the remark. "You." He gestured to Lovell. "Out now."

Lovell ducked his head and scurried past the uniformed security men, slipping quickly out the door. Thorpe waited until he was out of the room, and then turned back to scan each of them. His gaze lingered only for an instant on Daman's still, quiet form on the floor, the clothes stained dark where he'd been hit; then he faced Jack again.

"Look at what you've cost, Jack. I hope you're happy. It didn't have to be like this."

Jack pursed his lips, knowing that in part, what Thorpe was saying was true, but he wasn't going to give him the satisfaction of acknowledging it.

"I presume that the little trick with the Locality's programming is your doing too, or one of your friends'."

Jack said nothing. He was going to give Thorpe and Outreach exactly that—nothing.

"Fine," said Thorpe, his voice all business now. "Enough. McCreedy we can use," he said. "Stein stays in one piece. Get rid of the other three."

Matthias put up a brief struggle in his captor's grip. The uniform grunted and cuffed the kid with his weapon. Matthias cried out but stopped struggling, one hand going up to hold his head where the guard had hit him.

"*Enough* yourself, Thorpe," said Jack, taking a step forward. "Let them go."

"I'm afraid not," said Thorpe, turning back to look at him. "We'll have a lot less trouble in future—you have to admit that much, Jack. Particularly with that one out of the way." He glanced down at Daman.

What happened next seemed to Jack like it occurred in slow motion.

From beneath one of the desks, the bug scuttled across the floor, one leg hanging at a strange angle. The nearest guard watched it, his eyes going wide.

"What the hell?" he said, backing out of its way, training his weapon to track it across the floor. The other guard turned to look and at the same moment, Matthias took his opportunity. He pulled his head to one side and kicked back, hard. The guard holding him cried out, reaching for the source of the pain. The instant after he yelled, a quiet voice came from the floor.

"Hello, Thorpe," said Daman weakly.

Andrew Thorpe didn't get a chance to respond. The fresh hole in the center of his forehead seemed to interfere with his ability to control himself, and he collapsed to the side, looking slightly surprised.

The third guard spun and shot back at Daman, but Daman had already collapsed back to the floor, the gun falling from limp fingers. Jack seized the chance, whipping the spare gun from behind his back, and dropped the first guard in a single shot. Dog crouched, scooped up his own weapon, and took out the guard that had held Matthias. In the next instant, Jack was launching himself across the intervening space as the remaining guard raised his weapon in Billie's direction. Dog leaped across the distance, firing just as the guard squeezed the trigger. The shot caught Dog in the arm, and he grunted, falling to the floor. Jack turned his weapon on the guard who had fired, but it was too late. Dog's shot had caught him in the chest, and he was back against the wall, unmoving, weapon next to him. Matthias dropped to his knees beside Daman, but it was too late there as well. Grief washed over the kid's face, then was gone. He stood again, holding the weapon that Daman had dropped.

"They got Grigor too," he said.

Shit, what a mess.

Billie and Alice stood by the desk, Alice looking pale and wide-eyed, Billie just taking in the scene, her expression blank. Dog staggered to his feet, clutching at his arm.

"What now?" she said.

"They're going to come in this way," said Dog, pointing at the door with his gun. He quickly scanned the room. "Everyone over there."

There was a bank of files or machines or something—Jack couldn't tell which—but there was a shielded place behind them. Billie, Alice, and Matthias did as Dog asked and moved to that spot. Dog dug something out of his pocket and stepped rapidly over to where Jack was standing.

"You too, Jack," Dog said to him.

"You okay?" asked Jack.

"Yeah, I'll live," Dog replied. He glanced back at Billie. She was staring at him over the top of the bank of equipment, her expression unreadable. Jack wondered briefly how much currency taking a shot for her had garnered.

Jack scooped up the rifle from the floor and moved over to join the others.

"Okay, babies," said Dog. "Do your stuff."

He did something at a couple of points on the sealed door, then dashed back to join them.

"Down," he said.

A mere second later and there was the noise and compression of an explosion. The smell of chemicals mingled with the wash of cauterized blood within the room.

Dog poked his head above the intervening barrier. "Yeah," he said. "Come on."

Jack stood up too. Dog's explosive charges had done their work. There was now a ragged hole, revealing the passageway beyond.

Dog led the way.

"Do we know where we're going?" asked Jack.

"Good point," said Alice, reaching for the handipad. It wouldn't be long before more Outreach guards were down on top of them. She quickly tapped up the schematics, and then turned the handipad this way and that until she'd oriented herself to the map.

"Okay," she said. "Down this passage, then right at the end. There's another corridor. We follow it all the way to the very end, and then just to the right, there's a way down."

Dog nodded, and set off through the newly opened doorway at a jog, seemingly having forgotten his wounded arm. Jack waited for the others to pass through, and brought up the rear, giving the heart of Outreach's system one more look, his gaze lingering on Thorpe's fallen form for an instant, before he too stepped through. The last thing he saw was Daman's body, spread-eagled on the floor. He grimaced and turned away, moving quickly up the passageway. The shattered doorway was already starting to grow back. If they were lucky, it might have resealed by the time the pursuit had reached them. They needed all the luck they could get right now.

"Wait," said Jack. He caught up with Dog. "You got those other charges."

Dog dug into his pocket, and handed them over. Jack inspected them briefly, then sprinted back down the corridor and, stepping through the ragged hole, placed them carefully on either side of the desk. He set them for fifteen minutes. Sure, there was a risk there, but after all that had happened, the number of innocents that lived within Outreach's walls were fewer. Anything that would slow pursuit was worth it.

He had to squeeze back through the hole. Outreach's repair capacity seemed to be faster than that of most places, but that didn't surprise him. Only the best for Warburg and his team. Alice waited for him at the corridor's end, looking worried. As he joined her, she relaxed visibly.

"Are we okay, Jack?" she said.

"I don't know," he said. "Let's get out of here first and then worry about that."

Dog, Billie, and Matthias were already halfway up the next corridor, and he and Alice had to hurry to catch up. Together, they moved to the next corner, Matthias leading, checking quickly with a darting look around the edge of the wall, weapon held at the ready.

"It's clear," he said.

Dog stepped into the corridor first, Matthias close behind. Dog was grimacing now. The initial adrenaline rush had worn off and the wound was starting to trouble him.

"Dog, hang back," said Jack. "I'll take the lead."

Dog nodded and let Jack pass. This door was different, an internal fire escape, not that it was likely that anything in the Locality would catch fire. Old hangovers from the past took a while to fade. He opened the door, checked the stairs behind, and waved everyone forward.

"It's clear. Let's get the hell out of here."

Four floors don't take long down a fire escape when you're in a hurry and in no more than a minute they were at the ground. He felt rather than heard the explosion at the center of Outreach's operation. The charges had done their

work. Jack smiled with a sense of grim satisfaction. The
door at the bottom opened out onto the street at the side of
the building, and they slipped through it, trying not be
observed.

Dog's arm was a problem. It was bound to attract attention. Jack frowned at it.

Billie caught the look, pulled off her jacket, and handed
it to Dog. He winced as he stripped off his own and dropped
it to the ground. Billie's was a little tight, but it covered the
damage for now.

Dog looked wistfully at his own jacket, lying bundled
and damaged on the ground. The Locality's programming
would take care of it in short order, absorbing it with the re-
cycling routines.

"Okay," said Jack, "we should separate. Meet back in Old
and then we can work out what we do next."

"The same place?" asked Alice.

Jack nodded.

He glanced up. The face of William Warburg stared down
at them like a baleful moon again. They weren't done yet.

"Dog, Billie, Matthias, you go together. I'm going with
Alice."

Billie gave Jack a short meaningful look, then sighed.
She took Dog's good arm and started leading him up the
street. Matthias, appearing slightly lost, joined them on the
other side. Jack hung back until they were a good distance
ahead, then, allowing Alice to take his arm, headed toward
the front square as well. Noise was coming from the building's front, voices, chanting.

As they rounded the corner, Jack saw why. The crowd
had grown, and there were still people joining the group.
They were chanting now.

"Out! Out! Outreach out!"

Jack heard the words and felt a sense of satisfaction burgeoning. That would keep them busy for a while. Let's see how good Outreach and Warburg were at getting out of this one. Jack suspected they'd have some work to do.

The crowd was through the front of the building and into the front lobby. There was action there, movement amid the angry shouts. For too long, the Locality's populace had kept what they felt suppressed, had been lulled into the comfort of their own belief. Now the truth was breaking free.

A group of uniformed security was forcing its way through the masses, clustered around a figure. Even from this distance, Jack recognized the man. The face was the same as the face that stared down at them from the ceiling panels above. Warburg. Jack smiled with a sense of grim accomplishment as the crowd pressed tighter and a look of panic started to grow on Warburg's face. And then Jack could see no more. The crush of people hid them from view.

He and Alice slipped through the back of the crowd, hearing the voices swell and grow around them. Vague echoes came from the walls and from the ceiling far above, and worked inside him, spicing the satisfaction he was feeling.

The words followed them all the way out of the square, and right up the length of Twelfth.

Next stop the shuttle to Mid-Central, and then all the way down to Old. And then . . . he didn't know. He was playing this a step at a time.

Together, Alice and he stood at the shuttle stop, trying to look like a couple out for the day. People had other things to be more interested in anyway.

The back of his hand stung, and he looked down. He'd forgotten completely about the bug. He lifted his hand to look more closely at the small wound. He didn't get it. And what had happened to the bug anyway? He flexed his fingers, but really, it was little more than a scratch. He dropped his hand again, dismissing it.

"Um, Jack," said Alice.

"Hmmm?" he said, looking at her. She was staring up at the ceiling. He followed her gaze.

"Oh, shit," he said.

William Warburg's giant face had been replaced by another. Slowly turning, giving first a front and then a side view, a far-too-familiar face was high above them. First one way and then the other, like a glaring announcement, hung the head of Jack Stein.

"Oh, shit," he said again, ducking his face into her shoulder.

Thirty

The shuttle was with them in only a couple of minutes. All the time, Jack kept his face averted from passersby, feeling the old pounding back in his chest. He was a fugitive and his face was plastered all over the Locality in plain sight. The image they had was an outdated one, one taken before the jumps. He looked younger now and perhaps that could work to his advantage. As the shuttle doors hissed open, Alice urged him forward.

"Come on, Jack," she said quietly. "Let's get you out of here."

He was conscious too of the rifle still held under his coat, hampering his easy movement. It was short enough, but still it was awkward. They stepped onto the shuttle together and moved across to the other side. There were already other passengers on board and Jack avoided looking at them. His picture had just recently appeared, though, and they might not have seen it yet.

"Is anyone looking?" he said quietly.

"No, we're fine," she said.

Jack risked a glance around the compartment, and then buried his face again in her hair. Such public displays of affection weren't too usual, but people were more likely to avert their eyes than to stare. That would work too.

"Tell me when we're getting close to Mid-Central," he said quietly, feeling Alice nod in response.

One by one, the other passengers got off, but there were still a couple left by the time Alice indicated they were approaching their destination. Jack grimaced inside. There was no way he could get rid of the rifle yet. He felt comfortable that they had enough security with the other, smaller gun tucked into his waistband.

The shuttle whirred into the platform and eased to a stop. Jack held back until the other passengers had alighted, then quickly ducked to the back and slid the rifle under one of the seats right at the rear. What if a kid found it? No, dammit, he couldn't worry about that now.

"Okay," he said. "Let's go." He pulled his collar up and kept his head down as they walked together briskly across the platforms. There was no Old-bound shuttle in sight.

His hand was starting to throb now. He looked down at it. The area around the small mark was red and inflamed. He shook the hand and shoved it in his pocket.

"You okay, Jack?"

"Yeah, yeah, fine," he said.

He didn't know what the damned bug had done to him, but it didn't look like it was good. He remembered stories about spiders, about the different effects the venom might have. Spiders. The things reminded him of spiders. Maybe it had poisoned him. He pulled his hand out of his pocket and inspected it again. How could he tell?

Stupid, Stein. It was the damned Silvers. They had caused it.

"You can't defeat them." That's what they'd said. Well, he couldn't defeat his inevitable linkage to the Silvers and Outreach either.

Alice was stroking his arm. "The shuttle's here," she said. He looked into her face, noting the concern in her eyes, and despite everything, he felt himself smile.

"Thanks," he said.

"For what?"

"Just thanks."

No one else was on the platform and Jack felt himself relax a little. Having Alice with him eased the darkness threatening to take over his thoughts. He just couldn't afford to slip into the blackness now.

They boarded the Old-bound shuttle and found a seat, huddling close together. Jack kept his head down, the nervousness rising again every time they slowed into the next stop. His was bouncing one leg up and down, and Alice reached out to place one hand on top of his thigh, stilling the motion.

"It's okay, Jack. We'll be there soon."

He appreciated the words, but it didn't quell the feeling. He couldn't see how they were going to get out of this now. He didn't care about his face being out there. How long would it be before Alice's face, or Billie's, would be up there too? They didn't have a choice. They had to get out of the Locality and away. What about the kid, Matthias? What was going to happen to him? McCreedy could look after himself, and frankly, Jack couldn't care less about Dog.

They were nearly there. The shuttle pulled into its stop and they stepped out, checking up and down the street, not that Jack expected to see anyone this far down in Old.

The others were already there when they walked into the building they'd been using as a base. Dog's black bag was still over in the corner, looking like it hadn't been disturbed. He was sitting nearby, nursing his arm, Billie crouched not far away. Jack noted that and put it away. Matthias was just inside the door, weapon held in his lap, a faraway look in his eyes.

Jack moved to the opposite side of the room and lowered

himself, his back against the wall. Alice sat down beside him, crossing her legs.

"What now?" said Dog.

"I don't know," said Jack. And he really didn't.

He looked over at the kid, Matthias, and thought about the options. Dog, Billie, Alice—they were all a part of this now. Matthias was there just because of Daman. The kid was still staring at the floor in front of him, occasionally glancing out of the doorway and checking the street.

"Matthias," said Jack. "I'm grateful for everything you've done, and I'm sorry about Daman and Grigor. We couldn't have done it without you guys."

Matthias looked up at him, waiting.

"I think you should go now," Jack continued. "You should go and find your friends, keep low for a while, keep out of sight. I don't think they'll be looking for you. You'd be better off on your own. Outreach is going to have other things to worry about for a while."

Matthias held his gaze for a couple of seconds and then nodded. No words, no arguments. He got to his feet, looked at the others in the room in turn, and then shoved the gun away and out of sight and slipped out the door. Jack stared at the empty doorway for a few moments after he'd gone, and then looked across at Billie. She bit her lower lip, closed her eyes briefly, and then gave a quick nod too.

Alice got up and crossed to the door, peering out and then up.

"They've still got your face up there, Jack. They're asking for any information about your whereabouts."

"Can we trust the kid?" said Dog.

"I don't think we have a choice," said Jack. "We have to find some way to get out of here. Let Outreach concentrate on its own problems for a while."

"And how are we supposed to do that now?" said Dog.

He had a point.

"I've got an idea," said Billie.

Jack gave her a questioning glance.

"Well, this stuff with the doors, the program square. I don't know if it will work, but we might be able to use it on the walls."

"Which walls?"

"The ones to the outside."

Jack looked at her, considering. "And then?"

"I don't know," she said. "But if we did that, we could get out without having to go up to New."

"And I've still got the ship," said Dog. "Unless Outreach have taken that as well."

Alice turned back in the doorway. "It could work, Jack," she said. "We could go up to my apartment to do it. Or use the library if we're careful. I could get some patches for Dog too, for his arm. We're going to need some food as well."

Jack hadn't thought about food, but the mention now made him aware of the empty feeling in his stomach. He could do with some coffee too, but somehow he suspected that was right out.

"Okay, yeah," he said. "It's worth a try."

Billie got to her feet eagerly.

"Here, take this," said Dog, wincing as he handed across his weapon. Billie shook her head.

"Come on," said Dog. "You never know." Then, "Fine," as she made no move to take it.

Alice crossed to where Jack was sitting and crouched beside him. "It's our best chance, Jack," she said, reading the hesitation in him. "We'll be fine, and we'll be back as soon as we can. You need to stay here and out of sight."

"Yeah," he said, and sighed. He reached out and took her hand. "You be careful."

"We will," she said, and stood.

Billie came over to join her, looking down at Jack with an expression of concern on her face. He met her eyes, not having to say anything, and gave her a little nod.

"Okay," said Billie, taking Alice's arm, and then they were out the door.

Jack went back to staring at the floor, the thoughts about what they were going to do next working through his head.

"Listen, Jack," said Dog from across the room.

Jack lifted a hand without looking up. "I don't want to hear it, McCreedy," he said. "Just don't talk, okay?"

"Fine," said Dog again.

Around them, the building groaned with the pain of its decline. A small chunk of something fell to the ground outside and a trickle of dust floated down from somewhere above. Jack leaned his head back and closed his eyes, reconciled to the wait, seeing Billie and Alice wandering up to Mid in his mind's eye, hoping they were going to be all right. He knew Billie could look after herself, but he wasn't sure yet about Alice. He had a lot to answer for concerning what he'd done to her life and what he was putting her through. Somehow, though, he thought she was probably making the choice herself.

Dog was tapping on the ground with the base of his gun, moving it from side to side in a rhythmic pattern. Jack opened his eyes, frowning as Dog became aware of the gaze and also looked up. Dog gave a heavy sigh and placed the gun in his lap. Jack held the gaze for a second, and then closed his eyes again.

Somewhere in the back of his head, something sparked. Jack frowned again, without opening his eyes. Not again.

He didn't need the Silvers playing with him now. He just wanted to be left alone for a little while. But no, this was different. It was a bright, hard presence, a small flame in the darkness of his mental landscape.

Jack concentrated. There was something there all right. It was reminiscent of the awareness generated by the Silvers during the episode at the Outreach building, but different, almost familiar. Jack sought it, trying to give it shape. There was something he had to do. Jack focused his concentration, channeling his awareness into locating the source. A bright spark, there, pulling him toward it. He concentrated harder. The brightness was distant; he could feel that.

"Jack," said Dog.

"Shut up, McCreedy," he said without opening his eyes.

He regained his concentration, shattered by Dog's interruption, and pulled the strands together again. Where was it? There. It took form again and he went after it, sending out tendrils of his awareness. He knew it now: There was a physical presence behind the spark, but more important, there was a mind.

Jack sent his awareness out, soaring beyond the Locality, over fields and mountains, across rivers and oceans. It was a long way away, a very long way. There, beneath him, lay a pearl of brightness and he swept down toward it.

A woman sat at a table, her hands clasped in front of her. It was a small cottage. Jack moved in even closer still. She had dark hair, slightly graying, but a smooth open face, now gazing up. She looked questioningly, gave the slightest frown. And then she spoke.

"Who are you?" she said. "Where are you?"

Shit. His awareness retracted across the spaces in a rush. Jack opened his eyes. He was back in the room, the building noises around him, Dog on the opposite side of the room looking at him curiously. She had seen him, touched him. She had known he was there. Now, that was something new.

Jack's hand was throbbing, and he looked down at it.

Was it something that the bug had . . . ? No, it couldn't be. He flexed his fingers.

Who had she been? He closed his eyes, feeling for her presence. There, in the very back of his awareness, sat the spark, undeniably present now, but strangely, it didn't feel unusual. It was as if it had always been there, but he had simply never seen it. Not that he'd become aware of it—it was just there. As he looked, he became aware of other presences, not as bright, not as clearly defined, but they were there all the same. Okay, why had he never noticed that before? And why now? Surely, he had better things to worry about for the moment. Outside, an entire city was seeing his face and ready to track him down.

Outside. Out. Out. Outreach out. The words of the chant rolled through his head. If only he thought they'd have any effect. And anyway, Outreach was only part of the problem.

Thirty-one

"Jack," said Dog again.

"Dammit, McCreedy, what is it?"

"I don't care," said Dog, wincing as he shifted position. "You *have* to listen to me."

Jack didn't respond, just looked at him.

"Okay," said Dog, hesitating before continuing. "I did what I did for a reason, Jack."

"Yeah, I know that," Jack said, and snorted.

"No, you don't get it," said Dog. "This thing's big. We've been watching Outreach for a while. We've been watching the SOU too, and others. It's just unfortunate that you got caught up in it the way you did."

"We? Who's we?"

Dog bit his lip and nodded slowly. "You've been to the orbital."

"Yeah, so?"

"Think about it. Think about the people you met. Steve, the others. Why do you think I have the sort of access I do? I told you a bit of a story about *Amaranth*, about how I was connected to Outreach, but I had to. The ship, the contacts, everything, all that's part of the orbital and the people you met and others like them. We're a space-based community, Jack, have been for a couple of decades now. The orbital, others like us around other worlds, and we're all inter-connected. We live by our own rules, but Outreach, others, they're all dependent on us, and the others like us. We exist outside of their rules, regulations, and their direct control. Because of their dependency on us, corporations like Outreach and the others have financed our growth and existence. They couldn't shut us down even if they wanted to anymore. There are too many competing interests."

Jack frowned. "I don't—"

Dog shook his head, cutting him off. "I don't expect you to. Not right away. We've been interested in what's been going on with you, Outreach, and the others for a little while. It's no coincidence that we met in that bar back on Utrecht. The guy who runs the bar, remember him? He's one of ours. We have connections to others too, people who are of a sympathetic frame of mind. Hervé Antille is one of those. Sometimes they're aware of us, sometimes they're not. Hervé is one of those who is not—at least not directly. But there are lots like him."

Jack stared across at Dog. Was he suddenly supposed to believe that Dog was some sort of idealist, working for the common good? No, he didn't buy it.

"What makes you think I'd believe any of this, McCreedy?" he said.

Dog gave a little shake of his head. "You don't have to, Jack. That'll come in time. You'll see. All that matters now is that you have to know that I'm on your side. We're working for the same thing. I don't care if you think I'm doing it for the payoff or because of what I'm going to get out of it personally. That's not important right now. All that matters is that you know we have to work together to see this through. It's too big. Don't forget, I've been there *with* you. I've seen."

Any further talk was cut short by the sound of running feet that had Dog reaching for his gun. He took aim at the doorway with his good hand, and Jack quickly pushed himself up from the wall, crouching where he had been, his own gun in his hand.

Alice came in first, quickly followed by Billie, and Jack felt himself relax. They looked out of breath, but Billie was grinning.

"You okay?" asked Jack, standing and crossing to place his hand on Alice's shoulder. She smiled at him.

"Yes," she said. "One close moment, but we're fine."

She was carrying a small bag on one shoulder and she slipped it off and walked to where Dog sat.

"Here," she said, pulling out a couple of patches and handing them to him. He wasted no time affixing them to his neck and smoothing them in place.

"Thanks," he said.

"I've brought some things to eat," she said. "We can have them now, or we can wait. What do you think, Jack?"

He was more worried about what Billie had managed to achieve.

"So, did you do it?" he said to her.

Billie dug into her pocket and pulled out a square of material. "Maybe. I think so. We will have to try it."

Jack nodded. "Okay. Eat now. We might need it. I'm not sure how long it will take us to get to where we're going."

"And where is that?" asked Alice, rummaging in the bag and starting to hand out food.

"Dog's ship," said Jack. "Have you got your handipad, Alice?"

She passed it over and he thumbed it on, calling up the Locality map. They were far down Old, and the outer walls were as distant as in any other point at the Locality's length, but there was a route that would lead them there in about fifteen minutes. Either the device that Billie had crafted would work, or it wouldn't. They could figure out their options then. For the moment, he had decided, he was going to keep the information about the woman and the cottage to himself. They had enough to worry about. He slipped the gun into his waistband and accepted the roll that Alice offered, taking a bite and chewing as he thought, staring across at Dog, considering what he'd said, not even aware of whatever the roll was spread with.

The streets were empty as they reached the intersection and took a right. One long, narrow street led down to the Locality's perimeter, coming hard up against the iridescent outer walls. Jack could see the enclosing barrier right at the very end; it was clearly there, visible to all, but when you lived here, it became a part of day-to-day life, sitting in the back of the consciousness, there but unseen, rather than something you noticed every time you passed by.

It felt weird walking on the empty street, with his own image staring down at him, the nervousness of threatened discovery working in his chest. Jack reached back, checking the gun one more time. Billie was walking beside Dog, and Jack wondered at that. Alice was close by his own side. He guessed it was natural, this pairing, and would look a little less suspicious, but still, he had to wonder what was going on in Billie's head.

They drew closer to the outer wall, and as they neared, Jack could see that there was something different happening in its surface. Barely perceptible veins of darkness pulsed through the surface, tracing random lines beneath the shining skin. The beat was regular, like a heart. Intermittently, a cluster of those veins drew together, forming a darker spot like a blemish beneath the skin, barely visible, and then they faded, to resume the regular pulsing.

"See," said Billie. "It's working." She sounded pleased with herself.

Jack acknowledged it. They would have to wait and judge how well it was working and what effect it might have. It still didn't solve the problem about what they were going to do with the rest of the populated worlds in the system. This was just one world, after all, but he kept that thought to himself.

As they reached the edge of the district, they had to search for a way through to the wall. All along the street, powdery buildings sat side by side, blocking access. Jack stood in the middle of the street, looking first one way, then the other. After a moment, he risked a look upward. His face was still there, emblazoned across the ceiling panels, and, though flickering from here, clearly recognizable. He grimaced and turned his attention back to seeking a way through.

It was Dog who found it. "Over there," he said, pointing.

A narrow alley ran down the side of one of the buildings, almost too small to allow passage. They moved toward it, looking down its length at the chunks of building material and pools of dust that half blocked the way.

"I guess this is it," said Jack. There wasn't much choice.

Jack led the way, clambering over the obstacles and trying to make sure of his footing along the treacherous path. He held out one hand, helping Alice over a large chunk of masonry. Billie lent assistance to Dog, whose movement was impeded by his wounded arm. Then they were at the very end, standing together in the shadows of the surrounding buildings and of the outer wall itself. Down here, up close, the wall shed a slight golden glow, illuminating their faces in the darkness with a yellow, sickly light. The even sheen was marred by the blackened pulses that ran in throbbing traceries beneath the surface. It reminded Jack of something alive, like an egg sac or something, and he was put in mind of spiders once again. He swallowed. Not a nice thought.

"Billie?" he said, eager to get this done.

She dug around in her pocket and pulled out the small flat square she'd programmed to act as a key, and hesitantly reached out and placed it against the wall. The material adhered to the wall, sticking in place, and she stepped back. For a couple of seconds, nothing happened. Billie was holding her breath, watching the spot intently.

"Come on," she said between closed teeth.

Then it happened. An area around the square grew dark, and the darkness seeped into the square itself, fading the shape into the wall's surface. In the next moment, a small square hole opened up, and then a piece of the wall folded back onto itself and then another, and another, merging into its surroundings as if it had never been there. As the hole opened, light flooded through the gap, revealing grass and landscape beyond. A rocky escarpment sat off in the distance, and Jack recognized it. He had stood at the top of that place years ago, side by side with a much younger Billie, watching the Locality below, almost as their final act before they had left for Yorkstone.

"Quickly," said Billie. "I don't know how long it will last."

She stepped through, Alice close behind, and then Dog. Jack was the last to leave, negotiating the short drop to the ground, and taking one last lingering look up the alleyway to the Locality's heart beyond.

"Yeah. Fuck you, Outreach," he said as he dropped to the ground.

They needed to get out of here and quickly, but something stopped him. The pulse within the walls was visible here on the outside too. As he watched, one of the sections drew together, then puckered, and twin silvery legs pushed out of the space. It was one of Billie's bugs. It squeezed out of the hole, and tumbled to land, barely missing Jack's shoulder as it fell.

"Shit," said Jack, stepping back out of its way.

For a moment, the bug lay on its back, four spindly legs kicking in the air, and then it righted itself, rocking on the spot for a moment more before taking off across the ground, skittering across the grass and away. Higher up the wall, another dark patch was forming. Billie's programming was working all right. Jack swallowed as he watched another bug start to detach itself from the wall. This one dropped too, landing on its legs after skidding down the wall's outer surface, then charged away across the open landscape in a different direction.

Jack tracked it. Eventually the bugs would reach other places, other cities, and eventually, they'd infect them with the information dragged from Outreach's heart. If it worked—if—then Outreach would have nowhere to hide. People were going to know what went on in the guts of Outreach's corruption. They wouldn't be able to ignore it anymore. He glanced back up at the wall. The hole that they'd come through was already starting to close, sealing the Locality and its residents away. Had he and the others done enough? He didn't know.

"Which way?" said Dog.

Jack looked at him blankly, his thoughts in other places.

"We need to get to my shuttle."

Jack shook his head, coming back to the immediate. Of course they did. He reached for Alice's handipad and sought the map of the Locality's current bearing. The spaceport was to the east. It would be a long trek, but if nothing went wrong, they'd be there in about four hours. He slipped the handipad away and indicated their direction.

With any luck, Outreach would still be looking for them inside, but they had better get out of the immediate vicinity in case one of the Locality's monitoring routines picked them up and alerted whoever was watching.

Jack headed off after Dog, Alice by his side. They walked quickly, but he knew they couldn't keep the pace up for too long. They'd have to take stops, find water. It was a long way to the spaceport. Once there, they'd have the problem of getting to Dog's flier without being challenged.

Jack's hand was throbbing again, and he lifted it to inspect at the small wound as they walked. Alice leaned across to look also and she frowned.

"That doesn't appear too healthy, Jack. You need to cover it."

He grimaced. "Yeah, but I don't know if it will do any good." Again, he flexed the hand.

A bug shot past them, its tiny legs propelling it through the grass. Jack watched it disappear.

"I think the damned thing poisoned me," he said.

"That doesn't sound right," said Alice. "Why did it do that anyway?"

"I don't know. It was almost as if I did it. When we were there, something weird happened. One minute I was there and then the next I was gone, away, with the Silvers. It was like time stopped and then they set me this task to find them."

"I'm not sure I understand."

"Well, I was there in the dream room, back on the alien homeworld, but this time it was empty. None of the Silvers were there. Then they spoke to me and told me to find them.

So, that's what I did. They were out somewhere, away from their city. It was as if they had gathered there simply to test me. The other thing was, I suddenly realized how few of them there really are."

Alice gently gripped the top of his arm. "So what do you think that was for?"

Jack pursed his lips. "I'm not sure. As soon as I got back, that's when the thing bit me. But it happened immediately. One moment I had the urge to reach out and touch the thing, and the next I was gone, and then I was back and it bit me. It was as if I hadn't been gone at all."

"Have you been feeling anything else? Dizzy? Sick?"

He shook his head. "No, but something else is happening. I'm not sure what it is yet. I need to work on it, work out what it means."

"And you think it's connected?"

"Uh-huh. I'm sure it is. I just don't know how yet."

She blinked, processing that, but didn't press him further.

"We can patch it," she said, reaching back for her bag.

"No," said Jack. "I'd rather let it run its course."

Alice looked doubtful, giving him a little frown, but she seemed prepared to acquiesce for the moment.

Up ahead, Billie and Dog were talking. Jack couldn't make out what they were saying and he wasn't sure he was comfortable about this turn of events. Maybe they were making plans about what they were going to do next. Maybe he was telling her what he'd divulged a few hours before. Jack still wasn't sure that he bought it, but there were things about it, like the sequences of coincidence, that lent it a credence that he couldn't ignore.

Jack looked back over his shoulder at the Locality's bulk rearing up behind them. As he watched, at the front tip, a flier took off and streaked away across the sky. He wondered if it was Outreach. They were managing to put some distance between themselves and the city, but he wouldn't be happy until they'd put a lot more distance behind them.

Somewhere in the back of his head, a small, steady spark burned, tickling his awareness. He tried to turn his attention away from it.

"Alice, I'm sorry for this," he said.

"For what?" she said.

"For dragging you into it."

She stopped. "It's not all about you, you know, Jack," she said. "Some of us have our own minds."

"No, I didn't mean—"

She cut him off. "Listen, I chose to be here with you. I chose to do what we're doing. Me, Jack. Not you. You'd better understand that now."

He didn't know what to say.

"Remember," she said. "I chose to be here *with you*."

He nodded, feeling slightly chastened. He had underestimated her, perhaps, too bound up in his own thoughts.

"Come on," he said. "We need to move."

"You going to shut up now, you stupid man?" she said.

"Uh-huh," he said.

They hiked the next section in silence, Jack thinking about what she'd said. Strangely, the thought didn't make him feel uncomfortable at all.

Still, somewhere deep within his awareness, the spark continued to burn.

Thirty-two

They were tired and sweaty by the time they reached the low hill that allowed them to look down on the spaceport. They stood for a few minutes, watching the comings and goings, checking for unusual activity. Dog pointed out his shuttle, and it seemed untouched from this distance. Jack stood with his hands on his knees, breathing deeply, considering their next steps.

"If we can get down there without being noticed, we should be okay for a while," he said.

"And then what?" said Dog.

"And then once we're on the *Amaranth*, we can think about our options. That is, if she's still there."

Dog narrowed his eyes and flicked a stray strand of hair away from his face. "She'll be there," he said.

"But didn't you say Outreach had already gotten to her?" asked Billie.

"Yeah," he answered, and sighed. "But that was remote. I don't think they would have done anything else to her. No point. I have a few countermeasures of my own built in. No, I think she'll be okay."

Jack stood upright and looked back down the hill. "Well, we can only hope so," he said.

Taking a deep breath, he started to walk down toward the spaceport.

They made the shuttle without being challenged. Dog let

them in, and together, they bundled into the small craft. Dog
started checking the controls, flipping through the sequences,
all business. He stripped off Billie's jacket and dropped it unceremoniously on the floor beside him. The burn across his
arm was plainly visible.

"Okay, strap in," he said. They all reached for their har-
nesses.

Dog dispensed with contacting control, and as the querying voices chattered through the shuttle's systems demand-
ing confirmation and authority, he shut off the sound.

"Fuck 'em," he said. "We're out of here."

As the shuttle lurched off the ground and swept skyward,
Jack closed his eyes, and then opened them again. With his
eyes closed, his awareness of that lightly burning presence
and the clusters of stars around it became too real.

The shuttle soared higher and higher and Jack looked out
at the spaceport receding behind them, and there, off in the
distance, the shining bulk of the Locality. Somehow he be-
lieved, he hoped, this was the last time he'd be seeing it. He
was leaving again, but this time, he thought, this time it was
for good. He was unlikely to be welcome there ever again.
He thought it would be a long time before the Locality itself
became somewhere it would be comfortable to live. Outreach's days were numbered now. If the population was no
longer prepared to let themselves be manipulated, to silently
accept and ignore what was going on around them, then the
mechanisms of control were gone.

He turned away from the picture and closed his eyes
again, but not before looking at Alice's face and thinking
about how lucky he was, in some small and immediate
ways, perhaps, but lucky all the same. Lucky Stein. Well,
maybe this time.

The ever-present spark was still there. Now was as good a time as any. He reached out and touched.

Again, he was flying with his consciousness, out across the planet, across oceans and continents, sweeping down toward a small cottage. The dark-haired woman was there again, sitting at a simple rustic table.

She looked up, directly at him.

"You're here," she said. "I thought I'd lost you." Her words appeared inside his head as well as outside.

He was hovering just below the small ceiling.

"Who are you?" he said.

"I am Elena."

"Why am I here?"

"I don't know," she said. "Are you alive?"

"Yeah," said Jack. "I'm Jack. Jack Stein."

"If you're alive, where are you?"

"Right now?" he said. "I'm on a shuttle heading up toward a ship in orbit."

She frowned. "A ship? Are you human?"

"Yeah. I think so."

Elena nodded. "I was aware of you before, but only dimly, like the others. You suddenly grew stronger. I was able to sense you more clearly."

"Can you see me?" asked Jack.

"No. Not directly. But I am aware of your presence."

"I don't know why I'm here," said Jack. "I have an idea, but I'm not sure yet."

Elena held her gaze for a time and then looked away. "Tell me when you are ready," she said. "Come back then."

Jack had a momentary thought. "Can you come to me?"

"No," she said. "I'm afraid I don't have that ability. I can merely feel that you are here. I can feel your mind."

Jack opened his eyes. Alice was watching him.

As soon as he'd opened his eyes, his awareness had swept back in, severing the contact in a rush.

"What's happening, Jack?" Alice asked him.

He shook his head. "I don't know yet. I can't talk about it. I'll let you know when I can."

Who the hell was this Elena, and why was he being drawn to her? He couldn't explain the contact, the sudden connection. He had known this Elena was aware of him in just the same way that he had known the Black had been aware of him with its cold, savage intelligence in the dream-state.

They breached the atmosphere and Dog guided the ship up and out, tracking the *Amaranth*. The familiar shape grew in front of them, becoming larger by the moment.

"There she is," said Dog unnecessarily.

There was something comforting about the shape, despite the fact that it was still a ship, and Jack was never going to stop hating the damned things. He reached out and took Alice's hand.

He'd realized as soon as they'd left the surface that he'd forgotten something significant. Now that they'd left the Locality, they'd lost access to the Outreach systems and the information they contained. Outreach still had the edge and the omission meant that Jack had to come up with some other way to spread the information to level the field. It was weird, though, he thought—the paradox contained in his intention to give people like the SOU exactly what they wanted. Perhaps Jack could get what they needed from somewhere else—from Antille, maybe.

Dog docked with the *Amaranth* and, as soon as they'd settled, unstrapped himself and headed for the lock. Billie released her own harness, and reached down for her jacket. As she lifted it, something fell from the top pocket and clattered on the floor. Jack frowned down at it. A small ovoid shape sat there, rocking slightly, one leg splayed and askew. It was the bug from the facility. What the hell?

"Oh yeah," said Billie. "I forgot. I grabbed it before we got out of there." She reached down and picked up the bug, slipping it back into the top pocket of her jacket.

Jack grinned involuntarily. They had what they needed after all. Saved by an afterthought. Funny how things worked. With that single bug, they'd be able to spread the information virus, spread it out beyond a single world. Maybe one world at a time, but perhaps it would be enough and along the way, they could augment it with other information, things about what really went on in the various worlds.

On board the ship, together, they headed for the bridge, Dog checking as he walked and patting the passageway walls.

"She looks like she's in one piece. I'll check the rest of her from the bridge."

Alice, Dog, and Billie stepped inside, but Jack hung back in the doorway. He looked at them one by one.

"I have to do something," he said. "I'll be with you in a couple of minutes."

Billie looked at him, concerned.

"No, it's okay," he said.

He left them there and headed back down the passageway to the cabin he'd used last time they'd traveled on the *Amaranth*. He was exhausted, but he had to do this. There was no longer any choice.

He shut the cabin door and lay down on the bunk, closing his eyes and stilling his breathing. With an effort, he calmed his thoughts, letting them drift.

The bright spark grew brighter, but now there was more than one. A small cluster of light hovered in the depths of his awareness. He focused on the most intense of the group, reaching out.

Elena was before him again. This time, she was sitting on a chair, and she looked up from something she was reading.

"Hello, Elena," he said.

"Hello, Jack. Have you seen what's happening?"

"Yes," he said. "There are more, aren't there?"

Elena nodded.

"How?" said Jack.

She took a few moments before answering. "I spoke with a couple of them. It's like an infection. They were bitten by something. I didn't understand at first. They were talking about some sort of silver insect."

"A bug?"

"Yes, that's right."

Jack understood then. The bugs carried more than the Outreach stuff, much more. This was what had been happening to him. He was changing, becoming more aware. It was the same with the others. Billie's bugs were spreading more than mere information. They contained the means for Jack and others like him to communicate together, to be truly aware of one another, and maybe more. How much more remained to be seen.

"They'd always been partially aware," Elena continued. "But after that, their awareness grew. This is the first time I've actually been able to talk to them in any meaningful way."

Jack thought about it. "I have to go, Elena. I have to do something."

Elena signaled her understanding with a raised hand.

Jack knew exactly what he had to do. He shifted his focus, changing his concentration to bear on the Silvers, building an image of them in his mind.

Elena was gone. He was back on the alien homeworld, back in the dream room.

"Jack Stein." The voice swelled and died in his head.

"Why?" said Jack. "Why are you doing this?"

"You have seen them," said the Silvers, their voices massed inside his head.

"Yeah, so? I still don't get it."

"You cannot defeat them," they said.

Jack frowned and the next words burst from him, hurled at the alien forms. "Then why the hell are we doing this?"

"You cannot defeat them."

Jack growled his frustration. "Tell me!" he yelled.

"You cannot defeat them alone," they said.

Jack shut his mouth. Alone? He wasn't alone. Not anymore. There was Elena; there were others. He could feel them even now.

He felt the sparks in the depths of his awareness and felt their strength. He reached out and touched them, caressing them with his senses and drawing from them. He wasn't alone. They wouldn't defeat the Blacks alone. He knew now, knew what he was doing.

"We're okay," said Jack to the Silvers. "We will be ready, together."

Somehow, the Silvers had known. Deep within, they had known the key to humanity's awakening. They just simply hadn't had the means to tell him properly. Their thought processes were too different.

He opened his eyes, severing the connection, and swung his legs off the bunk. He didn't need the Silvers anymore. They had things to do, all of them, Jack, Elena, the others. Jack didn't know quite how they were going to deal with the impending threat, but he thought they now had the means. Perhaps there was a way, when the Blacks finally came. Just

as he had withdrawn from that solitary presence back in
the darkness, perhaps they all would have the means. They
wouldn't stop the threat with weapons or with technology.
They would stop it with their minds, somehow, some way,
enmeshed together. It would take work, preparation, but somehow, they would be ready.

Filled with understanding, Jack left the cabin and walked
up the passage to the bridge, the realization working within
him. As he entered, Alice looked up at him questioningly.
Jack smiled at her. Dog and Billie were huddled in the front,
running through some sequence on the controls.

Billie turned to look at him; then Dog, noticing her gaze,
also turned.

"What now, Jack?" he said.

"Time to go," said Jack. "We've got a lot to do."

"Go? Where? Do you know?" said Dog.

"Yeah, back to Utrecht," said Jack. "To the orbital, and
then . . . and then we'll see."

He looked at Dog meaningfully and Dog nodded slowly
in response.

There was uncertainty there, but Jack knew one thing for
sure. The Blacks might be coming, the Silvers might have
done what they could, and there might not be anything more
they could do. Now it was up to Jack, Billie, Dog, and Alice.
Whatever they did, they wouldn't be doing it alone. None of
them would ever be alone again. Somehow, Outreach Industries didn't figure in that particular equation. Sure, they'd
have to keep an eye on Outreach and the SOU and others
like them, but there was a bigger task at hand.

Jack moved across the bridge to sit next to Alice, and
leaning forward, he took her hand in his own. She gave him
an uncertain half smile.

"I'll explain on the way," he said quietly. "I'll explain it all."

He turned to Dog. "And in the meantime, I think you've got some explaining to do as well, Dog McCreedy."

Dog nodded in response. For once in his life, he actually looked serious.

Jack came back to his thoughts. The one thing he knew for sure was that Jack Stein psychic investigator was no more. He had a bigger job now—a much bigger job—and with it came a much greater responsibility. One by one, he looked at their faces—Dog's, Alice's, Billie's—and he knew. Now he'd be sharing that responsibility. They all would be, together.

JAY CASELBERG

Meet Jack Stein,
Psychic Investigator.

Wyrmhole

0-451-45949-0

Jack's specialty: Drawing clues from dreams and
psychic impressions. His assignment: A mining crew
has mysteriously disappeared. And Jack has to sniff
them out...in his dreams.

Metal Sky

0-451-45999-7

Two years after the events of *Wyrmhole*, Jack is
tracking down a missing artifact—a metal tablet. But
Jack's investigation is about to lead him into the
clutches of a shadowy political organization that knows
the tablets secrets—and will kill to keep them.

The Star Tablet

0-451-46060-X

Jack's sixteen year-old ward Billie has vanished
somewhere in the metropolis of Balance City. His
search for her brings him to the attention of a corrupt
millionaire, the fanatical Sons of Utrecht, and an alien
conspiracy that may alter the future of humanity.

**Available wherever books are sold or at
penguin.com**

Classic Science Fiction & Fantasy
from
ROC

2001: A SPACE ODYSSEY by Arthur C. Clarke
Based on the screenplay written with Stanley Kubrick, this
novel represents a milestone in the genre.
"The greatest science fiction novel of all time." —*Time*

0-451-45799-4

ROBOT VISIONS by Isaac Asimov
Here are 36 magnificent stories and essays about Asimov's
most beloved creations—Robots. This collection includes
some of his best known and best loved robot stories.

0-451-45064-7

THE FOREST HOUSE by Marion Zimmer Bradley
The stunning prequel to *The Mists of Avalon*, this is
the story of Druidic priestesses who guard their ancient
rites from the encroaching might of Imperial Rome.

0-451-45424-3

BORED OF THE RINGS by The Harvard Lampoon
This hilarious spoof lambastes all the favorite
characters from Tolkien's fantasy trilogy. An instant
cult classic, this is a must read for anyone who has ever
wished to wander the green hills of the shire—and after
almost sixty years in print, it has become a classic itself.

0-451-45261-5

Available wherever books are sold or at
penguin.com

Penguin Group (USA) Online

What will you be reading tomorrow?

Tom Clancy, Patricia Cornwell, W.E.B. Griffin,
Nora Roberts, William Gibson, Robin Cook,
Brian Jacques, Catherine Coulter, Stephen King,
Dean Koontz, Ken Follett, Clive Cussler,
Eric Jerome Dickey, John Sandford,
Terry McMillan, Sue Monk Kidd, Amy Tan,
John Berendt...

You'll find them all at
penguin.com

*Read excerpts and newsletters,
find tour schedules and reading group guides,
and enter contests.*

Subscribe to Penguin Group (USA) newsletters
and get an exclusive inside look
at exciting new titles and the authors you love
long before everyone else does.

PENGUIN GROUP (USA)
us.penguingroup.com